Douglas, Colin

Bleeders come
first

J954   8.95

BLEEDERS COME FIRST

Colin Douglas

BLEEDERS COME FIRST

TAPLINGER PUBLISHING COMPANY

NEW YORK

First published in the United States in 1979 by
TAPLINGER PUBLISHING CO., INC.
New York, New York

Copyright © 1979 by Colin Douglas
Printed in the U.S.A.

Library of Congress Cataloging in Publication Data

Douglas, Colin, 1945-
  Bleeders come first.

  I. Title.
PZ4.D7343BL   1979   [PR6054.0825]   823'.9'14   79-64156
ISBN 0-8008-0816-9

9 8 7 6 5 4 3 2 1

BLEEDERS COME FIRST

ONE

Ahead, traffic was slowing. Red lights brightened as cars braked and formed into a long orderly slowing line. Campbell braked too. Jean looked across to him.

'Will it be all right?' he asked.

'Should be. Unless this takes ages.' She nodded at the traffic ahead. 'Jim's expecting me back . . . And food's organised for half past seven.'

'That sounds terribly married.'

'I am, David.' She put her hand on his. He looked round, to see her smiling at him. 'Well, fairly married. What do you think this is?'

They had slowed to what seemed like a walking pace but was still twenty miles an hour. There was no clue in the darkness as to why things were being held up, only the double line of red lights curving up the hill ahead. Jean took her hand away.

'Road-works probably,' said Campbell.

'Maybe an accident.'

'Maybe.'

'D'you think we should nip up the outside and look?'

Everyone else in the now stationary queue of some dozens of cars was behaving in the Ministry of Transport approved fashion. Campbell wondered if Jean's eagerness to find out what was happening in front had more to do with getting back to her husband.

'There were about half a dozen chaps in my year in medical school who seemed to be in it so they could charge through life rushing into things shouting ''Let me through, I'm a doctor''.'

'But we are doctors,' said Jean. 'And you're not like that. And there probably *has* been an accident. There weren't any road-works here on the way out.'

She put her hand on Campbell's again. He signalled right, turned out and headed up towards the front of the line.

There had been an accident. An old maroon Thames trader, its front stove in, was sitting at an awkward angle a few feet behind a parked lorry, whose tailboard was projecting well on to the road and showed signs of impact. A smaller lorry, old and half-laden with scrap metal, was being used in an attempt to pull the driver's door from the maroon van. Campbell parked and got out, leaving his headlights on so

5

that, with the lights of the first car in the queue, they lit the two lorries and the van.

The smaller lorry revved and strained. The rope joining it to the door of the maroon van was frayed and knotted. It took the strain and parted. One end lashed back and drummed the door. An onlooker cursed. The driver of the smaller lorry got out. He was thin and dirty and dressed in oily dungarees, and appeared to come from that stratum of Scottish society where scrap merchants shaded off imperceptibly into tinkerhood.

'Bastard rope,' he remarked to Campbell. 'That's twice. Wish't I had a wire yin. That'd fix the bastard.'

'Is there someone in there?' asked Campbell, to maintain the conversation and to quell a tiny suspicion that this possible tinker's motives were less than honourable.

'Just yin. A darkie. Black.'

'Oh?'

'Been trying' to get the bastard oot for aboot twenty minutes.'

'Is he all right?' said Campbell. 'I'd better have a look at him.'

'He's greetin', so he's breathin',' said the man. 'You a doctor or somethin'?'

The driver of the van was slumped low in his seat, his head just level with the bottom of the window, which had disappeared. The windscreen in front of him was cracked and opaque, but still held. The steering wheel was not where Campbell expected it, but lower, firm against the man's chest. The victim was a middle-aged Indian, sallow and obviously in pain. His eyes were open and he was breathing rapidly in shallow grunting sighs. He looked up at Campbell when he saw him.

'Bastard lorry. Nae lights.' He spoke with both a strong Indian and a strong Glasgow accent. Only the words were English. 'If nae insurance too, I'll kill him. But driver no there.'

'Are you all right?'

'Ah canny get oot.'

'Apart from that?'

'Ma chest's sair.'

'Any pain anywhere else?'

'Ma chest's terrible. Worse when the tinker pu' ma airms tae get me oot.'

'We'll do our best,' said Campbell.

'No' by the airms,' said the man, obviously distressed.

'Anywhere else hurt?'

'Foot.'

'Which foot?'

6

The man's face clouded with the effort of sorting out his various pains. Campbell counted his respiratory rate. It was about thirty to the minute. Probably a crushed chest.

'Right,' said the man. 'Ma right foot.'

'OK. Anywhere else?' Campbell reached into the cab through the window space in the driver's door, and took the man's wrist. He shrieked, 'Dinnae pu' me.'

'I'm trying to take your pulse.' It was rapid too. Between the chest injury and whatever had happened to his right foot, the man might have lost a fair amount of blood. 'Were you knocked out? Unconscious?'

'No' verry much,' said the man. 'A wee wee while.'

'Sore when you breathe?'

'Terrible.'

'Where?'

'Front. Side. Everywhere.'

The man was conscious, alert and breathing. There was evidence of a serious chest injury, blood loss and a possible limb fracture too. But the main problem was none of these. He was stuck in a tiny space in the reduced cab, crammed in by door, seat and steering wheel. To give himself time to think Campbell embarked upon the very limited clinical examination permitted by circumstances. He told the man to move his head, which he did without obvious pain or difficulty. Then he removed the man's skullcap and ran his hands over his scalp and neck. There was no blood or tenderness or deformity to suggest injury there. The man had no facial injuries and his pupils were equal. Campbell told him to move his arms, which he did. Then he ran his hands over the man's arms and shoulders and collarbones. Again no fracture. Leaning right over into the cab, he slid his arms under the driver's shabby black jacket to feel his chest, starting at the sides. Behind him, he could hear the scrap merchant's voice announcing, 'Stand back, please. The doctor's makin' an examination of the victim.' Very gently, Campbell sprung the man's ribs, pressing the chest from the sides as though it were a precious antique accordion, as fragile as an eggshell. The man screamed obscenely for a fraction of a second then stopped because that hurt too, and as he did so Campbell felt between his spread, waiting hands the ugly moist crunch of broken ribs.

'Sorry . . . Trying to help.'

'Shouldnae yell. Daein' yer best.'

'Move your legs.'

'Canny.'

Campbell leaned even further into the cab. The van smelled of soaps

7

and various penetrating and exotic perfumes. The patient smelled of curry. He was jammed in too tight to let Campbell's hands round to feel his backbone. Before further attempts to move him, it would be nice to know it wasn't broken. Campbell remembered the man had said his foot hurt, which meant he could feel it, which meant in turn that he had not transected his spinal cord. In itself that did not mean he did not have a spinal injury which might do very badly if roughly handled, but it was a small reassurance. Campbell slid his hands further down and squeezed him again, to check for a fractured pelvis. The bones were firm. The man did not scream.

'Move your legs?'

'I canny.'

'Try.'

Beneath the steering wheel, the man's thighs moved slightly.

'Sore when you do that?'

'Jist right foot.'

'Not in your thighs?'

'Naw.'

To further check for fractures, Campbell pressed the man's thighs downwards, reaching under the steering column to do so. Nothing gave, and the Indian was not distressed. His right foot was in darkness far under the dashboard. Campbell tried to reach down towards it, to feel what was going on and in doing so almost lost his footing on the running board. The man said, 'Doctor, I need a pee.'

'Good,' said Campbell. It was more evidence that the spinal cord was still intact.

When he straightened up and turned round there was a respectful semicircle of spectators standing in the pool of light made by the first two cars' headlights. The scrap-merchant was standing at one end and Jean at the other. Campbell spoke to her. 'It might be an idea to get an ambulance organised. And the fire brigade. And the police I suppose.'

Jean smiled and said, 'I asked a chap in a car to go off and find a phone and organise all that.'

'Wouldn't the fire brigade and the ambulance be enough?' said the scrap merchant. Far ahead of the scene of the accident, there was a wailing noise, and the brief recurrent blue flash of an emergency vehicle. The scrap merchant looked around then braced himself. 'Mibbe we'd jist better get on wi' it.'

'Well,' said Campbell, 'we've tried the door and had no luck . . . I'll have another look.' He said that because the semi-circle of people, including Jean, was looking at him in search, perhaps, of some leadership for their efforts, or even just a focus of their collective

8

goodwill towards the man trapped in the cab. Campbell got up and leaned into the window space again to have another look at the steering wheel. The lower half was buried in the Indian's clothing. The steering column, though bent downwards, was firm even when Campbell pulled on it with as much force as he could exert. It moved just enough to cause the trapped driver another spasm of pain.

The door, jammed in its buckled frame, was as solid as if it had been welded there. This new look at things suggested that, of the various components of the van which confined the driver, the most shiftable might prove to be the seat itself. Car seats, Campbell knew, and presumably van seats, even in very elderly vans, usually ran on rails. If the seat could be moved backwards, pressure could be taken off the man's chest, and there would be access to find out what was causing the pain in his as yet unseen right foot, and the chances of getting him out alive would greatly improve.

A more detailed examination of this new possibility was not very encouraging. From the general state of the cab it would be dangerous to assume that, even if the catch on the front of the seat could be released, it would move freely on its rails. And a less hypothetical objection was already there to see: the back of the van was packed solid with cardboard boxes. Campbell thought of the people behind him. There were four or five fairly fit-looking men. Unloading the van would improve access to the back of the driver's seat, and at least give them a chance of hauling it back, and as an immediate move it had the merit of requiring neither expert manpower nor special equipment.

'What's in the boxes?' Campbell asked the Indian.

'All sorts of things. Soap. Fancy Goods. Oriental toiletries. Many clothes. Nice stockings.' He seemed to have momentarily forgotten his predicament and reverted automatically to his presumed role of trader in miscellaneous oriental wares.

'Might be easier to get you out if we shift some of the stuff there.'

The man looked anxious. 'You got to? You mean open the back?'

'I'm afraid so,' said Campbell.

'OK, boss.' The man smiled.

Suddenly there was a mighty splintering crash right next to Campbell's ear. He and the driver were showered with fragments of perspex. Another similar crash followed and cool air filled the cab. Though Campbell was scared out of his wits the Indian had hardly reacted. Campbell looked round to see a shiny brown boot waving where the windscreen had been, and the legs of a man standing on the bonnet and evidently trying to improve access to the victim in this direct but rather abrupt fashion.

9

'Come down oot o' that, you,' said a voice. It was the scrap-merchant's. The legs disappeared. Campbell looked more closely at the driver. He was paler than before, and his eyes were half closed. 'Wake up,' ordered Campbell. 'Come on. Wake up.' The man's eyes opened a little. 'OK. Still here,' he whispered. 'Good,' said Campbell. 'We'll get started.' The smell from the back of the van was stronger than previously. To the various casbah odours of patchouli, or whatever comprised oriental toiletries, a new harsher component was added. Recognising it, Campbell caught his breath. Petrol, whether from a leaking tank or spilled cans in the back, added a new nasty twist to the problem already labelled in his mind as the Extrication of Abdul.

Not fried Abdul, please, thought Campbell. Just the way he is: breathing, speaking Glasgow Pakistani and quite a nice pale brown colour. No holocausts. No nasty screaming deaths. Just a reasonably orderly step-by-step delivery of driver from squashed cab, with no needless drama. And why weren't the professionals here already?

The number of spectators had increased, and the first of the professionals had arrived. An ambulance stood ten yards away, its blue light still flashing. The crew, two men in neat uniforms, were getting the story from the man in oily dungarees, who looked scruffier than ever beside them.

'Here's the doc,' said the dirty man. The ambulance men nodded, and one went off to look at the trapped driver.

'A crushed chest, I think. And he's stuck. I thought we might start by getting the things out of the back.'

At this the little knot of spectators, having been standing around, disposed in the manner of race-goers awaiting the 'off' at a dull provincial meeting, changed in an instant. Simply having overheard Campbell's remark to the ambulance man, they became an unstoppable force of volunteers. The man who had kicked the windscreen in (his highly polished brown leather boots, having been so close, were immediately recognisable to Campbell), took a last drag at a cigarette, and threw it down, stamping it into the ground. Campbell remembered the petrol, and followed the little band round to the back of the van. Already the doors were open and three men were inside, throwing the cardboard boxes out on to the road and the verge.

'We'll soon have this little lot out of here, doc,' said a man who had perhaps been watching a lot of television recently, as a box crashed at Campbell's feet, spilling a cascade of costume jewellery.

'Perhaps just one in the back of the van, and the rest carrying stuff to the side,' said Campbell in a voice that surprised him by its

10

authority. If there was going to be a fry-up it would be less unpleasant if it was only a small one. Two of the men in the back got out, and left the enthusiast heaving away in its recesses, grunting encouragements to himself, and moving the boxes just as fast as the three had done together.

'His pulse is a hundred and forty and he looks pretty ill.'

Campbell turned round. It was Jean, very close and using the voice she used talking in bed. Her fingers wound round Campbell's. 'You're being very efficient. I don't know what's happened to the police and the firemen. My motorist must have found a phone because the ambulance got here all right.'

Feeling very steely-jawed Campbell said 'Good' then asked what the man's respiration rate was. Jean said 'Thirty-two' as though she had been expecting to be asked that, then added, 'He's got a crushed chest.' She squeezed his hand and went off, leaving him standing alone, watching the men empty the van, and worrying about the petrol. He remembered something else.

'Jean.'

She came back.

'There's a lot of petrol about . . . Could you stop people smoking?'

'Yessir.'

'Thanks.'

Campbell watched Jean move away and round the little groups of onlookers, now numbering in total perhaps twenty. She was slim and graceful and calm. He could imagine her tone in the errand: unemphatic but authoritative and not without a certain appropriate sex appeal, the standard mixture used by people like air-hostesses to control everything from amorous drunkenness to mass panic. If Jean hadn't been a doctor, that was something else she could have done to perfection. In response a few men stubbed out cigarettes.

The man who had been hurling boxes out of the back of the van emerged from its depths, bustling and breathless, and yelled to Campbell, 'Ready when you are, doc.'

The inside of the van was dark, and musky from the goods just unloaded. The smell of petrol lingered unmistakably but no more strongly than before. Campbell knelt with the eager little man at his side, trying to find the catch securing the driver's seat. It wasn't easy. The passenger seat was still laden with cardboard boxes, and both doors still jammed. Though indirect, the approach from the back of the van was the best available. Eventually, reaching under the driver's seat, between the runners, he found the catch. It was stiff but not unmovable. In the near darkness, curled up in the back of the van,

11

with his right arm far under the driver's seat, Campbell found himself wondering about the petrol again, not that it helped. The catch clicked sideways and he straightened up to kneel behind the driver, who was still breathing, and sometimes grunting.

'Gently now.'

'Right, doc,' said the little man, wrenching the seat smartly backwards a full six inches. The driver screamed in a panicky interrupted crescendo then was quiet again.

'Steady on. Wait here,' said Campbell. 'Hold the seat where it is and I'll go and see if the ambulancemen have got anything to knock him out while we shift him.'

Campbell got out and went round to the front, where the ambulance men were standing waiting for their patient.

'Do you carry anything for pain?'

'Only the gas — an Entonox cylinder — Need it?'

'No morphine or anything like that?'?

'No. It's not issued. Just the gas.'

The other man went across to the ambulance and came back with a wooden box like a baby's coffin, opened it and brought out a blue and white cylinder, fitted with a wide rubber hose and a black face mask.

'That's it. Just hold it on his face, turn that and press it. A few deep breaths before you do anything nasty to him.'

'Thanks.'

Another flashing blue light drew closer, and a fire tender pulled up behind the ambulance. Firemen, about half a dozen of them, poured out as it stopped and one, wearing a white helmet, joined Campbell and the ambulance driver in their impromptu conference. The two uniformed men had a conversation so elliptical that it might have been in code then turned to Campbell.

'Can we take the doors off without ruining him?' asked the fireman. Campbell nodded.

'And it might be better if you did the gassing. Seeing his chest's bad.' The ambulance man handed Campbell the box. The head fireman said a few things in code to the nearest two firemen, who ran over to the tender and came back with crowbars almost as big as themselves and set about the driver's door. The metal creaked and strained and the door popped out, while Campbell sat on the bonnet, first explaining to the Indian what was happening, then, when the man in the back made ready to move the seat again, holding the mask over his face. Very gently this time, the little man moved the driver's seat fractionally backwards, freeing the Indian completely from the vice formed by seat and steering wheel. The Indian took a couple of bigger breaths then leant forward, supported by the wheel, not crushed by it as he had been for however long.

'That's enough,' said Campbell, as the man in the back prepared himself for another heave. There was still the problem of unseen right foot.

The firemen, having dealt so neatly with the offside door, turned their attentions to the nearside. In even less time it too was open, and the boxes from the passenger seat joined the jumble of other boxes on the verge.

It was very impressive, this half-amateur, half-professional effort which had stripped the van of its load in five or ten minutes, leaving only the driver sagging in his seat. But could he yet be moved? Firemen rigged lights on the lorry in front, and on free-standing tripod things, with an air of calm efficiency that was in itself most reassuring. The previous aura of chaos and uncertainty was dissipated, and though grave problems remained, there was a feeling that, whatever happened now, the man had been given a fair chance of being brought out alive.

When Campbell knelt to look at the man's feet there was clear liquid dripping from the floor of the cab unto the running board. I sparkled in the light and ran on to the tarmac to form a dark puddle, trailing away under the vehicle. Rather gingerly, Campbell leant into the cab to inspect the damage, the smell of the liquid, when he recognised it, was familiar but surprising. It was not petrol but pee. Campbell remembered the driver's earlier complaint. In the circumstances, a little urinary incontinence was nothing among friends, so to speak, provided it was not accompanied by any other signs of spinal damage.

'How's your foot?'

'Bloody painful.' He pronounced the word to rhyme with 'moody'.

No wonder. The man's right foot was jammed between the accelerator and brake pedals with the ankle at an unnatural right angle, pointing inwards. Campbell ran his hand over it. There was a jagged splinter of bone spiking through the sock. When Campbell withdrew his hand there was blood on it.

'We'll soon move you, and we'll try to make it hurt as little as possible. You'll have the gas again. So for most bits you won't feel anything.'

The man almost smiled. The head fireman joined Campbell and, pretending to ignore the driver's sodden trousers and the puddle in the cab, made his assessment. Moments later another fireman appeared with a huge pair of foreceps, perhaps from the armoury of some Brobdingnagian dentist. Seeing them the Indian flinched.

'Maybe some gas,' said Campbell.

'Let me know when he's ready,' said the fireman.

'We're going to bend the pedals to save your foot,' said Campbell, in what he hoped was the least terrifying way of assuring the Indian that no mutilation was about to take place. 'But it might hurt a bit. So we'll use the gas.'

Ashen now, his respiration shallower than ever, the driver submitted for a second time to the black rubber mask. His eyes closed.

'You could try it now,' said Campbell.

The coarse unconscious parody of anaesthetist and surgeon continued as the fireman, nuzzling among the pedals with his giant pincers, glanced nervously at Campbell and the patient's face. With a sort of ponderous delicacy, he peeled back the metal stalk of the accelerator pedal and freed the trapped ankle, which flopped slackly and bled not a little on its release. Campbell and the fireman grinned self-consciously at each other as the patient woke again, this time slowly. When he was conscious Campbell had a quick look at his legs, and very gently felt his spine, from the neck downwards, running his fingers over each little bone, checking the alignment and prodding gently in search of evidence of a fracture which might still at this late stage move if badly handled and leave the man irreversibly paralysed. When he was as sure as he could be that all was well he said to the fireman and the ambulanceman, 'We could gas him a little more, and get him out.'

'Three this side, one of mine in the van on the other side. Risk of petrol fire,' said the head fireman.

'Gassing him through the windscreen again, doc?' said the ambulanceman.

'Fine.'

Almost lightheartedly they set to work. One of the ambulance men asked the Indian his name and, when the reply was obscure and faint, said, 'Never mind, Jimmy. We'll just call you Jimmy.' Everyone laughed, even, wanly and painfully, the injured driver. A whiff of gas, a few remarks in the 'Steady with your end till I've got the weight' genre, reminiscent of furniture removal men, and the victim was laid on a stretcher, so neat and straight, apart from his foot, that Campbell wanted to hug these cheerful and efficient firemen and ambulance men or at least slap their backs and say 'A grand job, men' or something congratulatory if less redolent of comic military patronage.

And there was the samaritan in oily dungarees, whose initial arm-pulling efforts had been only marginally less inappropriate than the oil and wine-pouring first-aid of his biblical prototype, but whose later contributions to crowd control had been really helpful. Where was he? Campbell looked round just in time to see his lorry rattling off into the night, as a third flashing blue light arrived on the scene. A police car, sleek and white, disgorged three constables and a sergeant. Campbell, who, to his surprise, seemed to be regarded by all concerned as the host of this peculiar party, received the sergeant's apologies for lateness with grave tolerance, while the stretcher was being loaded into the ambulance.

Feeling suddenly elated at the success of the mission so far — the driver was free, and nobody had been burned to death in a petrol fire — Campbell was tempted to issue some vague invitation to the police to sort out the traffic, or stuff all those boxes of oriental toiletries back in the van, or something, but a presbyterian solemnity, reinforced by the size of the sergeant, prevailed, and instead they agreed that the police would split, two constables to stay and restore order, the others with the car to provide a fast escort to the Casualty Department of the Institute. Campbell was to travel in the ambulance with the victim.

'Ye'll know the Institute's Casualty Department,' said the sergeant.

'I work there, as it happens,' Campbell admitted.

The sergeant was only momentarily taken aback. 'This'll be what you call a night off, I suppose,' he said, grinning fiercely. 'We'd better be getting on. What about your car?'

Jean appeared from nowhere holding the car keys and said, 'That'll be all right,' and smiled lovingly at Campbell.

'Oh. Your wife,' said the sergeant.

'Yes,' said Campbell, feeling there was neither point nor relevance in depriving a police sergeant in a hurry of an assumption with which he seemed perfectly happy. Jean looked as if butter would not melt in her warmest orifice. The sergeant looked at Campbell again. 'You'd better hold tight. We could do seventy or eighty if your man can stand it.'

'He seems one of the tough kind.'

'Fine.'

Jean whispered, 'I'll leave the car at your flat, and drop the keys through your letterbox, . . . husband. And I'll ring you later from home. Don't worry about Jim. I'll think of something.'

The ambulance driver had started his engine. The back door was open and as Campbell stepped in a crackling roar erupted from the direction of the maroon van. He turned round to see it engulfed by leaping yellow and orange flames.

'All aboard,' said the ambulance man in the back. 'Mind the doors now.'

The door slammed and the ambulance took off, its rear end crouching down as the back wheels skidded and then gripped. They surged into

15

the night. Campbell leaned over his patient, who now looked remarkably
well.

'You all right . . . Jimmy?' The man smiled. 'But you know your
van's away? A petrol fire.'

The man smiled again, and then, as though he had spent a moment
wondering how much it would hurt, let out a tiny painful laugh.

It was odd to be sitting in an ambulance hurtling towards one's place
of work on one's night off, Campbell reflected as they followed the
wailing police car into town. He could picture the scene in the department. The ambulance driver would have radioed in direct, to the
squawking crash box in Sister's room, and whoever was on, the sister
or the nurse in charge, would acknowledge the call and inform the
duty casualty officer.

A lot of crash box cases turned out to be of less than expected
seriousness. There had been a farmer brought in by heroic efforts
through storm and snow-drift who turned out to be suffering from
moderately severe piles. And quite a few came in too late: a cold
drowned man, not far from decay, sprang to mind. The Indian was the
genuine article, ill but saveable. He would need a quick transfusion, a
chest X-ray, a thoracic surgery opinion and perhaps emergency
surgery that night to fix the unstable segment of his chest. A few days
thereafter on a ventilator, having artificial respiration, might perk him
up quite a bit.

The ankle injury looked nasty but didn't matter much: it posed no
threat to life, as the chest injury did, and the man would walk again,
eventually, when the fracture had been cleaned and pinned and closed
and suitably encased in plaster, though he would probably limp for the
rest of his days.

With any luck Sister would be off duty. She was known to dislike
Indians, which was bad enough, but in addition she had an aversion to
seriously injured patients which in a more rational world would have
disqualified her from holding her present job. When it was blood and
guts in the resuscitation room she was to be found tidying up the
things on the desk in the orthopod's office at the other end of the
department, or fussing over the nurses' off-duty rota in her own, or
simply, when things were really bad, hiding in the loo.

The duty casualty officer this evening was Bones, who, by contrast
with Sister, positively revelled in the gorier aspects of the job. He saw
himself as a thoracic surgeon in the making, or rather as one chosen by
God to be a thoracic surgeon and meantime compelled to pass time in
menial roles decreed by lesser authorities as necessary preliminaries to

his true and divinely ordained vocation. He could be relied upon to get the man sorted out in double quick time, getting an intra-venous line up, and flashing over the victim in a form of clinical examination he referred to as 'my battle surgery routine' and, by the overbearing pressure of his surgical enthusiasm, bully the X-ray girls into producing quicker and better pictures than they managed for anyone else.

On the outskirts of town it became clear that the police, though late entrants to the drama, were making up for this by a contribution of considerable efficiency: at every major intersection a panda car was waiting and all the lights were at green. The speed of the little two-vehicle convoy barely dropped at all from the first dash along the dual carriageway until almost the centre of Edinburgh. It was all very exhilarating, especially now that it looked very much as if the extricated Abdul or Jimmy was going to make it to the department.

They sped along Princes Street and turned right up the Mound towards the Institute. On the hill the ambulance began to show its age a little, and the police car loitered for them before picking up speed on the long straight of George IV Bridge then slewing round a complex series of one-way streets and down the little hill to the Institute's Casualty Department.

Bones was waiting under the canopy outside. He was clearly taking the crash box call at its face value. Campbell waited in the ambulance as the crew manoeuvred the stretcher with the patient down the steps to the rear. The leading ambulance man stopped and said something to Bones who in reply gesticulated impatiently towards the resuscitation room.

Campbell followed them. The Indian was transferred to a trolley and whisked into the big room which served as an assessment and treatment area for seriously ill patients coming into Casualty. It was fitted out with all the various appurtenances of high-drama medicine: infusion sets permanently at the ready; an electrocardiograph and monitor to observe and record the rhythm of the heart in extremis; a vast array of emergency drugs; a fridge filled with blood and plasma; a series of green-wrapped trays each containing sets of surgical instruments, and a simple anaesthetic machine. At a pinch the resuscitation room could be used as an operating theatre but few patients of whom hopes of survival were seriously entertained were so ill as to be unfit for a brief trolley ride to more auspicious surgical surroundings after their circulation and respiration had been patched up in this front line outpost of hospital medicine.

Bones was in his element. Campbell watched him slide a cannula into a vein, take off blood for cross-matching and set up an infusion with plasma substitute. He was doing his hand-waving, out-of-my-way, put-up-with-me-I'm-a-brilliant-surgeon thing. Campbell moved from the door and went into the resuscitation room and stood on the opposite side of the patient from his colleague. A staff nurse recognised him and smiled. Bones leant over, listening with his stethoscope to the man's bared midriff. His bald spot was pink with concentration.

'He was stuck in his van for about half an hour. Maybe more,' said Campbell.

Without looking up Bones said, 'Whyntcha go sit in the visitors' waiting room, huh?' He quite often talked American when he was doing his surgical-genius-in-a-hurry thing. The staff nurse winked at Campbell.

'He's got a chest.'

'I said whyntcha go sit . . . Oh.' He looked up, still listening with his stethoscope then said, 'Oh, it's you. Sorry, Campbell. I thought it was some ghoulish accident freak and ambulance chaser.'

'You could say that. We found him out at Westburn. His van went up in flames just after we got him out.'

'A chest, is he?'

'Yes. A good crunchy one. I could really feel his ribs.' The Indian moaned. Campbell said 'Sorry'.

'I'd better have a look, I hadn't come to that bit yet. And a chest X-ray, I suppose.'

'I'd like to see it. Oh, and he's got an ankle.'

'I found that.'

'Good. Look, I'll poke off and let you get on with it. I'm going round the back to have a well-earned coffee.'

'You'll be lucky. That stupid bitch has locked up all the milk.'

The staff nurse was looking the other way in a semblance of loyally not listening to criticism of her superior.

'Sister?'

'Yeah. Only stupid bitch I know round here. But drop me the word if you find any more. We could introduce them.'

'I'll leave you to it. See you later.'

'Pint at ten?' asked Bones, still listening intently to the man's belly.

'Fine.'

'Gawd. He's pissed himself.'

Campbell walked round to the room at the back of the department which functioned as doctor's rest room, library, conference room, coffee room and lounge. The bad news about Sister's latest move in the Milk War was unsettling but not unexpected. Officially the doctors had no entitlement to free milk on the NHS, but it was available to them almost universally. Odd bottles left over from patients' supplies came their way and had done for as long as anyone could remember. Recently, under a brave new organisational purge, some desk-bound Cromwell had sniffed out this misappropriation of public provisions, and had set about ending it. His efforts were genially disregarded throughout the hospital, except, so far as anyone knew, in the Casualty Department, where a little notice had appeared on the door of the kitchen fridge, in Sister's incurably primary school handwriting, reading 'Milk. Attention is drawn to the fact that doctors are not entitled to milk from NHS sources. (Signed) J. MacInnes, Sister in Charge.'

The doctors in the department had ignored this and, since the fridge did not lock, used the forbidden store exactly as they had done in the past. How had she contrived to put the milk in a place of safety? The drugs fridge was a possibility: it was lockable and the keys went from sister to sister (or staff nurse in charge) with the vast clinking bunch of keys which symbolised nursing responsibility for the department. Perhaps she'd just chucked all the insulins and so on into an ordinary cupboard, to deteriorate at room temperature, to conserve her precious stocks of milk. Such behaviour, alas, was not entirely beyond her.

Campbell was still exercising his mind with this problem when he reached the coffee room. A man was standing looking at the little shelf of superannuated textbooks that comprised the library. He was about Campbell's own height, of medium build and neatly dressed in a dark suit. His neck was deeply tanned and his glossy black hair trimmed short. He turned round. Another Indian. This one was a tidy, professional-looking man of thirty-five or so. Was he some relative of the man from the road traffic accident? It was not unknown for next of kin, in search of the relatives waiting room that Bones had just so warmly recommended to Campbell, to find their way round to this inner sanctum of medical idleness. Campbell regarded him quizzically.

The man walked across the room. He was holding a cup of black coffee in one hand. He held out the other towards Campbell.

'Dr Campbell, I presume.' They shook hands.

'Yes.' How did he know that? Campbell had no recollection of ever having seen the man before and had no reason to expect to be recognised by him. The Indian smiled broadly. He was perhaps older than thirty-five. There were crowded little lines round the corners of his eyes, and flecks of silver at his temples. As he came closer Campbell had noted a clinical sign unusual in under-forties. The man had a thin white line extending round the lower border of the iris in

19

both eyes: the arcus senilis, a minor curiosity consisting of fatty material deposited in the front of the eye, common in old age but sufficiently rare in people of this man's apparent age to be noticeable.

'You are puzzled that I know your name?' The Indian was smiling more broadly.

'No . . . I've just brought someone into the department . . . who's probably from India . . . I thought you might be a relative.' He realised right away how foolish that sounded.

The Indian smiled again and spread a tolerant pink palm. 'It's a big continent. Or should I say sub-continent. And very crowded. But we are all God's children.'

Campbell felt a double disadvantage, first that the man knew his name and secondly that he clearly considered him a half-wit. There was an awkward silence which the Indian broke by saying, 'Will you have some coffee?'

That did nothing to put Campbell at his ease. To be offered coffee on his own ground by a total stranger only added to his disorientation. But it was coffee that he had come round here for, and it didn't matter much who made it.

'The kettle is only just boiling. I'm afraid there appears to be no milk. So we are having it, as you say, black. It is no matter, for in my own country coffee is routinely served thus. Even in the best families. Perhaps I should say particularly in the best families.' He put down his own cup and switched on the kettle, which boiled almost right away, and made Campbell a cup of instant coffee. 'Sugar? No. I will remember, since we will be working together.'

'Thank you.'

'You are now wondering how I know your name. Pardon me. I am Dr Subhadar. Hakeem Subhadar.'

'Indian?'

'Not strictly, no. It is true I am from the Indian sub-continent, and in saying that I may have misled you into thinking I am a citizen of the Republic of India, but that is not the case. I am from Pakistan. From Karachi, actually.'

He gave his town of origin as if it were something deserving of minor congratulation, about which he strove to be modest.

'I see.'

'And you still must be wondering how . . . The coffee is to your satisfaction? Apart perhaps from the unavoidable absence of milk, no? You must still be wondering how I know the name of my future colleague before I had set eyes on you.'

All this perverse mystification was beginning to get through to

Campbell. And the colleague business was almost as obscure as the unreciprocated prescience of his name. 'Yes,' he admitted. 'I am.'

'Aha,' said the new colleague, grinning like a magician at a children's party and elevating his free index finger next to his face. 'It is not oriental necromancy but western electronics. I have discovered in my short time in the department that this device' — he pointed to the intercom system on the wall beside them — 'can be used to keep awareness of the goings on of the department. I heard there was a crash box emergency case coming in so listened with interest as I was having my coffee to the process of clinical assessment in the resuscitation room.' He lowered his head and drawled in a fair imitation of Bones, 'Gee, he's really crooked this ankle,' and 'Whyntcha go sit in the visitors' waiting room, huh?'

He smiled again. 'It is easy. See.' He pressed a button on the intercom and they listened. Bones' voice came over, first indistinct then saying, 'Hope the thoracic guy on tonight can cope with a flail chest,' followed by 'Tough on Campbell to be out somewhere quiet with Mrs Thing that we're not supposed to know about and then this happening to break up the party.' The staff nurse laughed in the background. The Indian looked at Campbell and switched off the intercom.

'So you rescued a compatriot, or perhaps we should say a fellow-subcontinental of mine?'

'Yes. Some sort of trader.'

'Really?'

'Yes. Oriental toiletries.'

'Our culture has contributed much to the trading life of your little country. Your great little country. These people work very hard. Even the Indians.'

Campbell must have looked puzzled. The man went on, 'I think the more you go into it the more you will find the energies concentrated among the Pakistanis. Over here and over there. In the south there are little black Dravidians of no culture and no consequence, whereas we are an energetic and organised people. Take my scholarship for example . . .'

Campbell was sitting wondering if Jean would have reached his flat with the car yet. He struck a pose of polite interest while Dr Subhadar expounded on the wisdom and munificence of the scheme which had brought him to Edinburgh to further his surgical training. After a time Bones wandered in to the coffee room. There was blood on his white coat. He was looking pleased with himself.

'Yes, thanks, Hak, I'll have some coffee too. You two introduced

21

yourselves? David Campbell. Hak . . ., I've forgotten your surname.'
'Subhadar. And my first name is Hakeem.'
'You don't have Christian names out there, do you?' remarked
Bones airily. Dr Subhadar glanced at Campbell in a manner designed to
affirm their joint superiority over this troglodyte. 'Nice case, Campbell.
I only hope that thoracic registrar knows about wiring these things.
And the ankle should do reasonably well. Oh, I meant to tell you. You
missed a fractured toe on the left.'
'I wasn't looking for one,' said Campbell. 'I was trying to get him
out of his van before it fried us all.'
'Oooh, brave,' said Bones. 'No sugar, thanks, Hak . . . I think he'll
pull through.' Bones was the only person in the department who used
that time-worn phrase seriously.
'And what was our possibly Indian patient's name?' Dr Subhadar
enquired.
'Mr Salah Karim of fifteen hundred and forty-three Dumbarton
Road West, Glasgow.'
'A good Ismaili name. So perhaps he is my kinsman after all.'
'You're starting work here, Dr Subhadar?' Campbell asked,
anxious to get things straightened out as quickly as possible.
'This very night. And please call me Hakeem.'
'Of course. The locum for Dr Woodruff.'
'Locum meantime. I would like to think that if I give satisfaction a
substantive post awaits. And please call me Hakeem. It is the better of
my names.'
'Oh?'
'It means . . . something between ''expert'' and ''wise man''.
There is no exact English equivalent. The Swahili word ''Foondi'' is
nearest, and that cannot be translated either.'
'Of course not.'
'I say my better name because my other name means simply
''sergeant major''.'
'Your dad must have been hopeful for you,' said Bones through a
mouthful of biscuit crumbs. 'My son the very wise sergeant major.'
Dr Subhadar smiled delightedly. 'Many people tease me about this.
From when I was a small boy. May I call you David?'
'Sure . . . It's tough, you starting with night duty. But we're pleased
to see you. It would have been tight with no locum. The registrars
were going to cover nights between them.'
'Under protest,' mumbled Bones through his gypsy cream.
'It will be a pleasure to help. I found your superior, the surgeon in
charge, Mr Gillon, a gentleman of the old school. He was most polite

22

and encouraging.'

Campbell recalled some remarks made by Mr Gillon on the subject of 'our colleagues from the new commonwealth' at his own interview, and concluded that J.G. must have been very stuck for locums but characteristically suave in the face of adversity.

'Done much Casualty?'

'None at home. There I did only housejobs, with the professorial units in our major teaching hospital. But since coming here for surgical training I have done more than the minimum required by your Royal College here in Edinburgh as practical experience for fellowship.' Which was a tedious way of saying 'more than six months'.

'Whereabouts?'

'Glasgow. Interesting work with Rangers and Celtic injuries.' They all laughed.

'You're a bit early for night duty.'

'I thought it best to come and familiarise myself with the working of the department, find out where everything is and make acquaintance with my new colleagues. I am sorry to take up your time.'

'No trouble,' said Bones. 'It's quiet. Usually is when I'm on duty. And Campbell here enjoys coming in on his evenings off . . . I thought you said you were going out for a drink somewhere.'

'I have been.'

'With her?'

Campbell had had too many of that sort of conversation with Bones, who not only worked in the same department but lived in the same flat. The game was to try to make Campbell say something about Jean which might lead to a more detailed discussion of her marital status and her husband's health.

'We went out to a nice pub near Bavelaw. The Cot Inn. You should go sometime.' The counter-game was to try to head Bones off into a tempting non-Jean area of conversation.

'Was hardly out of it when I worked at Bavelaw. Wasn't she the same?'

Jean had worked at Bavelaw too, for six months in surgery, just after Bones had left. She didn't drink much, but to point that out would have been to lose the game. Instead Campbell adjourned it. He wanted to get back to the flat for her phone call. He looked at his watch.

'I haven't eaten yet. I'm going back to the flat.'

'You must be hungry after all that bravery. You can finish the gazpacho in the fridge, if you want. It was an experiment. I made too much.'

'Thanks.'

'It didn't really work.'

'Thanks anyway.' Bones' cooking experiments usually didn't work.

'Pint at ten?'

'Fine.'

'See you then. Goodbye, Hakeem. Have a quiet night.'

'Believe me I would rather be having a pint with you. But perhaps some other time.'

Campbell walked back across the park to his flat. The car was parked outside, more neatly than was usual when he had been driving it himself. The keys were on the floor just inside the front door, wrapped in a page torn from a give-away drug company memo pad. The crumpled piece of paper informed Campbell that Vanoval vanquished vaginitis and that Jean thought he was marvellous. He put the keys in his pocket and went into the kitchen.

Evidence of Bones' experiment was everywhere. The sink was full of dishes and utensils, and an assortment of fragmented vegetables covered the table. When he was on the late day duty, from two till ten, Bones frequently cooked himself an adventurous lunch before work. This one, to judge from the pot, had been unsuccessful. A layer of viscid black, like melted Oxo cube, but stinking of garlic, covered its base. Before opening the fridge, Campbell tried to remember what gazpacho was supposed to be like.

The phone rang and Campbell answered it. It was Jean.

'David, you were terrific.'

'Mmm?'

'At the car crash. You were super. You really were. Just sorting things out like that.'

'Thanks for helping. You were really good. You did all the important things. Getting the ambulance and all that.'

'Didn't the police take ages . . .? David, you're changing the subject. You really were marvellous. Getting people to do sensible things and looking after the poor chap and getting him out. And remembering about stopping people setting the whole thing on fire. I was impressed, really impressed.'

'It just sort of happened. I didn't mean to take the thing over. It just happened. Are you all right?'

'You mean about Jim? Yes. He just came here and ate . . . and then went back to the lab. He left me a nice note.'

'Is he all right?'

'Yes.'

24

Nowadays the answer was usually yes. It had not always been so. A week after Jean and Campbell had started their long-delayed affair, her husband had developed a headache. It had got worse, and a strange, wasting illness, with nausea, lassitude, fever and eventually an alarming series of fits, had followed. Campbell, diagnosing a brain tumour, had supported Jean manfully through these difficult times, and in turn had been impressed by her resilience. When, at operation only a few weeks previously, an apparently benign cyst was found and removed, their relationship had changed subtly. But Jim still had occasional headaches.

'Really all right?'

'Yes. Really . . . Well enough to want to work.'

'No problems.'

'No. No problems . . . Are you all right?'

'Yes.'

'I thought you might feel sort of . . . let down. You know. Flat. After all that business.'

'It seemed more important at the time than it does now. Once we got him into the department he was just another slightly squashed bod. Bones is on. He took it very much in his stride. Just another routine drama and only a bit of arm-waving. It's funny. Come to think of it, most of the bad traffic stuff, all those chests and femurs and things, must have been through something like that before we ever see them inside the sacred portals. Never thought of it before. Now I know why sometimes the ambulance drivers look a bit pleased with themselves.'

'You should be pleased with yourself.'

'I suppose I am a bit.'

'I'm pleased with you.'

'That's nice.'

'David.'

'What?'

'We haven't . . . seen each other properly, have we?'

'Mm. No.'

There was a longish pause. Campbell, in his feeble way, was trying to stop all this, and so, in her peculiarly opaque and convoluted fashion, was Jean. It wasn't easy.

'It isn't easy.'

'No.'

'But I'd like to see you properly.'

'Will it be all right?'

'Jim's doing a frog. He said till about ten.'

That fitted in quite neatly with meeting Bones in the pub.

25

'Is he?'

'He's trying to catch up after being off. I want to come round.'

'Fine. Lovely.'

'Five minutes?'

'I'll be here.'

In less than five minutes Jean was round at Campbell's flat. She had changed, into trousers and a big blue Marks and Sparks pullover. She wasn't wearing a bra. They kissed at the door.

'You smell nice,' said Campbell.

'I had a quick bath, and changed.'

'I meant to have a shower but haven't yet.'

'You still smell a bit of petrol.' She hugged him. 'You were super.'

'You keep saying that.'

Still, sometimes, Jean behaved as she had done at the beginning, when her enthusiasm had often outrun Campbell's, and become positively indiscreet. But for most of the time now she appeared to be following some sort of policy of trying to be faithful to Jim now that he was getting better, and sometimes she simply appeared to exemplify one of Rochefoucauld's more cynical maxims, the one about women whose best efforts at fidelity to their husbands amounted only to making their lovers feel uneasy. And yet aberrations, amounting almost to gay abandon, of the sort which now appeared to be shaping up, still occurred just frequently enough to be unsettling. She mouthed his neck.

'A drink?' said Campbell.

'A quick one.' She slid her hands under his waistband at the back. Campbell found himself responding with caution at first, because sometimes this sort of thing happened, and stopped short of bed, and left him feeling angry with himself and furious with Jean, but she kept mouthing his neck and kissing his ear wetly, until it became absurd to be standing in he hallway. They broke off and walked quickly, just holding hands, into Campbell's bedroom.

'What about your drink?'

'Later,' said Jean, taking off her pullover. Her nipples were eager and erect.

'I'll get it now for later. And one for me now.'

'Sorry. Am I rushing you?' she said, sitting on his bed taking her shoes off.

'I could do with a drink as well. It must be delayed shock.' Campbell went into the kitchen and made two large gin and tonics. One of the more permanent effects of their affair was that Jean sometimes had a

26

proper drink now. When he went back into his bedroom her clothes were neatly folded on the chair and she was in bed, with the downie up to her chin.

'I'm cold.'

'I thought you'd started without me.'

'David, don't be awful.'

He took a large gulp of gin and tonic, undressed and got into bed. They made love efficiently and affectionately. When they lay warm and sticky together Campbell found himself half asleep and loving her very much. She sensed that and got up at quarter to ten and went away, leaving him plenty of time to get dressed and go back across to the pub opposite the Institute to get drunk with Bones. On the way through the park he remembered he still hadn't had anything to eat.

Next morning Campbell went into work with a hangover, leaving Bones to sleep his off before his late day duty at two. Dr Subhadar was sitting with his feet up in the room at the back of the department. He was reading the *Telegraph*. He looked up when Campbell came in and shook his head.

'Ah, these industrial unrests,' he said sadly. 'Holding the country up to ransom. A strike of key workers in its sixteenth week.' From his intonation Campbell wondered if he thought the key workers concerned were something to do with locksmiths and allied trades. Perhaps they were. He shook his head again. 'I do not know what is happening.'

'Quiet night?'

'Not too bad. A strange man in the middle of night with spots he had had for months. Interesting. Looked like dermatitis herpetiformis.'

Most people, dermatologists included, lost interest in dermatology at about five o'clock each evening. It was verging on the saintly for a casualty officer to spend time on a skin problem in the middle of the night, especially when it had been rotting along for months. And what was dermatitis herpetiformis anyway? Campbell made a mental note to go and look it up.

'What did you do?'

'I thought it would be presumptuous of me to start him on the appropriate chemotherapy, which, as you know, is Dapsone. So instead I wrote to the GP suggesting an urgent skins outpatient appointment. And of course not omitting to mention my views as to the diagnosis.'

That, from a trainee surgeon, was impressive. The new colleague appeared to know the ropes, and the books too.

'Anything much else?'

'Only routine things. A fractured femur of course. A dear old thing of ninety-three who tripped over the corner of the bedroom carpet at half past eleven, snapped her hip and was in theatre having it nailed up again by half past four. She is doing well this morning. I rang the ward.'

More points, thought Campbell. 'So you've settled in?'

'I think so. And I made my small contribution towards the solution of the current milk crisis.' He smiled his magician's smile and waited for Campbell's admiring question. Campbell made it in dumb show, which seemed to suit Dr Subhadar well enough. He continued, 'I prevailed upon the policeman who brings the morning rolls into the department for the staff nurses to extend his journey as far as a diary. He is a most interesting fellow. He is thinking of emigrating to Rhodesia. There are two pints in that cupboard there and I have the key. It should see you through the day.'

'Thanks very much. Anything lying about the department?'

'Perhaps you would like to take a walk through with me before I go off.'

'Fine.'

'I refrained from calling the night X-ray girl so near her time for going off, so one or two patients await X-rays. Nothing serious. The patients are here and there in the department, according to their injuries, waiting for the day staff to come on. They are documented as far as ''awaiting X-ray'' and I trust you will be able to read my handwriting. Shall we go?'

They went out of the coffee room and along the corridor to the room on the right, Minor Trauma, where patients who could walk waited and were called one by one across to little cubicles to be assessed. Usually it had the sullen, overcrowded, idle atmosphere of a labour exchange in a major centre of unemployment. People with not very much wrong with them sat around with little to occupy their minds except trying to work out who was next and who else was still to be seen before them. As it was still before nine o'clock there were very few people waiting. A man in dusty white overalls came in and sat down, looking carefully round to note his place in the order of things. The established clientele, a vast lady with a sprained ankle, a workman with a cut thumb and a girl with a pad of white gauze over her right eye sat peacefully as a cleaning lady swirled a clattering electric floor-polisher round their feet. Dr Subhadar raised his voice above its sound. 'The lady is awaiting the X-ray of the ankle, and I am afraid I have not seen the rest. They are awaiting assessment.'

'I'll see them,' said Campbell expansively. It was still three minutes before nine o'clock, when responsibility officially changed hands.

'And there are one or two still in trolley room.'

They walked along the main corridor of the department to the other assessment area, where stretcher cases were seen. It was a big room, with spaces for twenty or so patients. Each space could be curtained off independently. Now all but a few of the curtains were drawn back and looped over their rails. Only four spaces were screened. At the far end was a desk with stationery racks and a telephone and around it shelves loaded with clinical equipment and blood-letting things. On the desk sat a staff nurse swinging her legs. She smiled at Campbell.

'Enjoy your evening off, Dr Campbell?'

'It was all right.' Campbell tried to remember if this staff nurse was the one who had been in the resuscitation room with Bones last night.

'The ambulance driver said you did rather well.'

'Oh. That. It was interesting.'

'Lots of willing helpers?'

She had been in the department last night but not in the resuscitation room. Her enquiry, had it come from Bones, or even from the other staff nurse, might have been construed as a veiled barb about Jean. But probably not from this one. She was big and blonde, a pleasant well-adjusted girl who rarely slept with doctors. He remembered she was called Maureen.

'There were enough people around. Have you heard how the chap's doing?'

'Oh, he's in Respiratory Intensive Care. All right, I think.'

'I took the liberty of going up there about four this morning when the department was quiet,' said Dr Subhadar. 'The thoracic surgeons considered no operation necessary but thought he needed a period on a ventilator, to stabilise the flail segment of chest you correctly diagnosed at the time of the accident, David, and he also went to the orthopods for some attention to his ankle. They are pleased with him, though of course he still requires respiratory support.'

'You saw him?'

'Yes. As the staff nurse says, he is in the capable hands of the Respiratory Unit. On a Cape ventilator and doing well.'

'That's nice. Have they found his next of kin and all that?'

'Yes.' Subhadar smiled. 'Ismaili people are close within the family. His cousin and uncle were through from Glasgow by midnight. As I mentioned at the time, I suspected that he was of the same way of life as I, so it was a pleasure to be able to help them.'

'Oh,' said the staff nurse, who with all her virtues was a bit stupid, and was clearly failing to follow the subtleties of the oriental

29

mind. Not that Campbell would have known an Ismaili if one had leapt fully-armed from his porridge that morning.

'These relatives were simple trading people from Glasgow,' said Hakeem by way of explanation, 'and I was happy to explain things to them in terms they understood. Of course they were very concerned with their kinsman, seeing him on the machine, as indeed I was myself, but I think I managed to put their minds at rest.'

'Good,' said Campbell. 'I hope he does well. Now, what have we got in here?'

'Oh, nothing too problematical . . . There . . .' — he indicated one set of curtains — 'is a lady with right upper abdominal pain, a fever and almost certainly a hot gall-bag. The medical registrar will see her in due course. There . . .' — he nodded further up the row — 'is an early appendix, unless I am mistaken. He is awaiting a surgical opinion, or perhaps I should say a further surgical opinion and of course an operation. There is another elderly lady with a fractured neck of femur. She will have an X-ray to confirm, then orthopaedic management. And this gentleman will go home as soon as he has slept off what was making him ill.'

This last case got Campbell's immediate sympathy. 'Well, thank you very much, Dr Subhadar. Everything seems to have been sorted out.'

'No problems at all. It was a quiet night, but I think I can say I am playing myself in satisfactorily.' He smiled, handed over a little key and went away, leaving Campbell with the staff nurse.

'What's the key for?' Maureen looked quite pretty. Her hair was interestingly, non-uniformly blonde. For some reason which escaped him, Campbell knew she was not naturally so, but it still looked very nice. She had a non-regulation blue ribbon, similar to the one officially trimming the edge of her staff-nurses's hat, tying her hair back in a nice bouncy bunch which, again in contravention of the regulations, touched her collar. 'What's the key for?' she said again.

'Oh. The milk problem. Phase three.'

'Sister?'

'fraid so.'

'It's the rules,' said Maureen not in her own voice but in a thin wheedling West Highland whine not at all unlike Sister's. Campbell laughed, and so did she.

'Doctor Campbell,' said a similar, disembodied voice from above the desk, 'There are three patients waiting in Minor Trauma.'

Campbell turned round and spoke to the intercom. 'Thank you, Sister.' Maureen looked at it as if it had been eavesdropping, as indeed it might have been. Then she looked at Campbell as though she wanted to say something fairly pungent but was beginning to think the better of it. The light was still on under the loudspeaker.

'Doctor Campbell,' the disembodied Highland whine incanted. Campbell stood silent. 'Doctor Campbell, are you there?' He turned round to the machine again and addressed it closely and politely, 'Good morning, Sister.'

'Doctor Campbell,' said the voice again, 'there are three patients waiting in Minor Trauma.'

'Thank you, Sister.' The light went out. Maureen mouthed a moderately rude word and Campbell laughed. The light came on again.

'Doctor Campbell, are you coming through to see them?'

'Thank you, Sister. What time is it, please?'

There was a short pause. 'Almost nine o'clock.' A certain tetchiness had crept into her voice.

'Thank you, Sister.' After a further short pause, the light went out. Both Campbell and Sister knew that the day staff did not make any particular point of seeing non-urgent cases in Minor Trauma before the official handover time of nine o'clock, but such ritual exchanges were an established part of the routine of the department. A polite, disembodied clash like that would probably count as a draw, and she would find something else to whine about soon. Campbell reflected on the dismissive, even insulting potential of the words 'thank you'. Maureen sat swinging her legs again.

'Ah well. I suppose I'd better go and get a white coat on and start playing doctors.'

Maureen smiled. 'If Mr Hadden isn't around I'll let you know when the X-rays on Mrs Matthews come through.'

'Who?'

'Mrs Matthews. The old lady with the femur.'

'Oh. Thanks.'

Campbell went round to the room at the back of the department again. It was empty. Hakeem's jacket had gone and been replaced by his white coat. Someone had put two bottles of milk beside the kettle; that was four, counting Hakeem's two in the locked cupboard. Campbell took off his jacket and hung it up, and put on his white coat, which was heavy with clinical responsibility in the form of stethoscope, tendon hammer and ophthalmoscope. The pockets had also accumulated such junk as a free drug company diary, a giveaway slide-rulish thing to help make sense of electrocardiagraph tracings, a packet of peppermints and about six tourniquets. These little rubber straps, with velcro fastenings, were used a dozen times a day in taking blood from patients. They were a source of great trouble in the department, since there were never quite enough, and Sister was as parsimonious in her accounting of them as she was in the matter of the milk. Campbell, who was always under the impression that he'd just lost one, was in the habit of picking them up if they happened to be lying about, which sometimes caused inconvenience to his colleagues, but permitted agreeable displays of largesse from time to time.

The name badge on his left lapel described him as 'Dr David Campbell, Senior House Officer, Casualty Department.' Mr Gillon, the surgeon in charge, made a great thing of name badges. Each new member of his medical staff was greeted personally by him and handed an appropriately engraved white plastic rectangle. In idle retrospect it even seemed as if he had pinned it onto the proud breasts of Bones and Campbell when they had joined, in the manner of a warrior and leader of men passing on to his subordinates some token of the responsibilities they had just accepted and of the privilege of serving under him. He hadn't done that, but it would not have been out of character if he had. White-coated, labelled, and by now only a little hung over, Campbell walked forth to face whatever the day might bring.

By the time he had to go round to Minor Trauma again the queue had grown to six. The staff nurse on duty there, a leathery dug-out of a married part-timer, had them organised in a row in the examination cubicles. She bade Campbell good morning and nodded to the first patient in the row, the fat lady with a sprained ankle. She was florid of face as though permanently angry, and wore a fur coat. Her right shoe was off and she was bare legged. There was a painful looking lump on the outside of the ankle. Campbell picked up the yellow sheet clipped to the curtain rail along the front of the cubicle.

'Don't talk to me about weight,' she snapped.

'Hmm?'

'Don't talk to me about weight. I hardly eat a thing. And what's more I know plenty of fat doctors.'

Campbell read Hakeem's notes. 'Forced inversion injury of right ankle at 0730 this a.m. while coming downstairs. Walking since. Pain plus plus. On examination. Tender swelling over right lateral malleolus. Ankle stable. No bony deformity. Prob. ligamentous injury. X-ray, PA and lateral right ankle awaited. H.S.'

'I see.'

'I could tell you a thing or two about doctors,' said the lady, tightening her hold on a large brown plastic handbag.

'It's your ankle, isn't it?'

32

'They never listen to a word you say.'

'Sore?'

'And their diet sheets never did me the least bit of good.'

Perhaps she'd eaten them, thought Campbell, kneeling down to examine her ankle. There was no bony deformity, just the tender swelling on the outside of the ankle, as described in Hakeem's notes. He took the foot and gently moved it through a full range of movements. 'All right?'

'They didn't do a blind bit of good.'

'I'll just have a look at your X-rays.' The large brown envelope containing them also hung from the curtain rail. 'Excuse me.' He took the films out and went over to the viewing box. The films were of good quality, and showed in detail the fine structure of the bones round the ankle. The likeliest candidate for a fracture in her case, and even then only a remote possibility to be excluded for medico-legal safety, was the lower end of the fibula, the narrow bone on the outside of the leg, widening to form the lateral malleolus of the ankle. The little white lines within the bone were intact, and its outline clearly seen and continuous. Campbell checked the name on the corner of the film and went back to the patient.

'The bones are fine, Mrs Munro . . .'

'I've always been big-boned. We were a big-boned family.'

'. . . but you appear to have strained the little ligament on the outside of your ankle. We'll give you something for the pain, and a supportive bandage and it'll be all right in a few days if you rest it.'

'D'you think my weight's excessive, doctor?'

'Well, certainly, if you go over on your ankle . . .'

She glared at him contemptuously. 'That's all you ever talk about, you doctors.' Campbell scribbled a prescription. The staff nurse was already advancing with a large roll of blue line elastic bandage. Campbell smiled and said, 'Good morning, Mrs Munro.' The patient nodded curtly and stuck out her foot for the staff nurse.

The next patient was less of a social effort. He was a stocky workman of about sixty, dressed in worn dungarees and an old tweed jacket. His left hand was swathed in gauze swabs and clean white departmental bandaging, through which blood was beginning to seep.

'How did this happen?'

The man smiled. 'Sheer damned carelessness. That, and not looking. A chisel. It slipped because it wisnae sharp enough.'

'Can I see it?' They unwrapped his hand and dumped the dressings in a plastic bin.

'Look at that,' said the man. 'And I've been at the job for about forty years.'

There was an irregular gash running from the wrist to the joint of the thumb on its palmar aspect. Campbell dabbed at it with a fresh swab, trying to clear the blood and see how deep the damage went. At first glance it was superficial.

'Clean chisel?'

'Clean enough. Just blunt.'

'Bend your thumb.'

'Oh, that's all right.'

'Good. Touch it across to your pinkie.' The man did so. 'Good. Bend just the end bit. Fine straighten it.' There was no evidence of tendon or muscle damage. 'Now, tell me if the feeling's normal round the cut. Campbell ran a corner of the swab up each side of the gash. 'That feel OK?'

'A bit dull on that side. There.' He pointed to the inside edge. 'Sort of numb.' Campbell went along the line of the cut with the swab and they mapped out the numb patch, where the division of a superficial branch of a cutaneous nerve had produced a little area of anaesthesia.

'Don't worry. It'll come back. Takes a while, though. Can you feel the end of your thumb OK?'

'Fine.'

'Nothing in the cut?'

'Don't think so, son.'

'Chisel didn't break or anything?'

'No. Just needs sharpening.'

'Fine. Well, if you wait while I see the rest of this lot, I'll stitch it up in the next room in about fifteen or twenty minutes.' Campbell scribbled a note including a sketch of the cut and a cross-hatched area indicating the numb patch. Full, accurate and immediate clinical notes, Mr Gillon was fond of saying, were the key to enjoyable survival as a casualty officer. The nurse applied another temporary dressing and marched the man out of Minor Trauma and leftwards into a single room with a simple operating table and a lamp and a trolley of suturing materials. There he would wait until Campbell could cobble up his hand.

You didn't have to be Sherlock Holmes or the eminent Edinburgh physician upon whom he was said to have been modelled to work out that the next patient was a baker. He wore white overalls and was covered in flour. There was an ancient leather finger cot on his right index finger. Campbell took it off. It did not smell nice. The finger revealed, when stripped of an equally offensive essay in bandaging, was an unlovely sight, blueish and purple at its tip with a half-detached nail evidently floating on pus, and shading of in a series of dusky reds towards its base.

'How long have you had this?'

'Been coming on for about three days. In addition to being embarrassed by the state of the dressing, the man looked guilty.

'Been working?'

'Yes. Couldn't afford to not work.'

'Seen your own doctor?'

'No '

'What were you working on?'

'Everything. Pastries. Rolls. Pies. Meringues. Everything.'

The baker knew, as Campbell knew, that that was irresponsible. A good-going septic finger, dripping staphylococci and their toxins into a series of cream puffs, meringues, meat pies, vanilla slabs, jam tarts, etc., could give an awful lot of people the heaving nasty vomits.

'I tried, doc.'

'What?'

'Tae see my own doctor.'

'Who's that?'

He named one of the lazier members of one of the city's larger group practices.

'Honest. I really tried to see him. Rang in yesterday and the day before to get an appointment. The nearest thing was the day after tomorrow. And the lassie wasnae very nice about it. I wasnae bothered about it being sore, but I thought I was coming up for losing the finger, so I just came in here.'

'Glad you did. All you'll lose is the nail. The rest should be all right. You probably shouldn't have been working.'

'No,' said the man, rather shame-facedly. 'But I tried tae keep it covered up.'

'It'll get better quicker if we get the nail off. Shouldn't bother you. It's half way off already. Nurse McCraw . . .'

'Dirty turret?' The staff nurse was standing loosely to attention at Campbell's left elbow.

'Yes, please. I'll do it after the laceration.' Campbell started on a note, wondering how far and how fast this man's meringues might have travelled, and to what effect.

'Dr Campbell. Resuscitation room please.' It was Maureen on the intercom. He put down his clipboard and walked through to the resuscitation room. He hardly ever ran in the firm's time. 'Walk quickly, don't run. The department is not large, and often crowded. And most things are not so bad as they seem at first.' The thoughts of surgeon Gillon came readily to mind, and usually offered sound advice.

On arriving in the resuscitation room Campbell wondered if he should have run there after all. A young man in a shabby office suit lay on a trolley. Maureen had tipped it so that his head was lower than his feet. He was lying half over on his side, with a trickle of thin vomit running from his mouth. He was pale, sweaty and scarcely breathing. Maureen was trying to get his jacket off. Campbell helped her. The man was unconscious and completely limp. Maureen pulled across a drip stand with a bottle of saline at the ready and wrapped a sphygmomanometer cuff round the man's bared arm to take his blood pressure. Campbell reached for an intravenous cannula to get an IV line up straight away because that was what Maureen, by her actions, had indicated, and she was an experienced Casualty nurse. While she took the blood pressure, he looked more closely at the man's face. He was deathly pale and cold. His eyes were closed and when Campbell pulled back the lids his pupils were large. He pulled out his pocket torch and shone it in each eye. Both pupils reacted, but not as quickly as they might have done. He sniffed the man's breath for some clue as to the cause of his unconsciousness. The smell of drink, or the acetone on the breath of an under-treated diabetic would have given them something to work on. He smelled only of vomit. There were various other possibilities. A catastrophic internal haemorrhage could look like this: the pallor, sweating and unconsciousness might mean he had bled half his circulating volume into his stomach and intestines. But there was no blood in his vomit. And you always had to think of drugs. Though the state of the pupils virtually ruled out the opiates, there were plenty of others.

'Any story at all?'

'None. Found collapsed. George Street.'

'What's his BP?'

'Sixty over something. And pulse a hundred and twenty.'

Campbell broke open the plastic container and unsheathed an IV cannula. Maureen held the man's arm. His veins were flat and hard to find. She used the sphygmomanometer cuff as a tourniquet and a thin bluish vein began to fill out just below the man's elbow. She stroked it gently with her open hand and it filled out a little more. Very carefully Campbell laid the cannula along it and advanced it into the skin. The man was too flat to react at all. The vein slithered away from under the tip of his cannula, and Campbell cursed, withdrew it a little and pushed deeper. Blood welled back into the clear plastic hilt. He turned to ask Maureen for a twenty ml. syringe, and she handed him one. He drew off blood for laboratory tests and cross-matching, uncoupled the syringe, handed it back to Maureen then fitted on to the cannula the lead from the bottle of saline, and taped the whole lot firmly down to the man's arm with strips of Elastoplast that magically appeared on the ends of Maureen's fingers.

Salty water into a vein would not save this man's life. It would only give them access to his circulation and a few minutes to think. Then they could either treat him for something that they knew was wrong, or just keep his circulating volume up by slinging in fluids in the form of plasma, or plasma substitute, or, if it became apparent that the man had lost blood, some of the 'Direst emergency only' universal donor blood from the resuscitation room fridge.

Campbell went on with his examination. He listened to the chest. The man's heart was racing, but its sounds were normal. His respiration rate was slow, and he wasn't shifting much air, but the breath sounds were normal too. His belly was soft and quiet, which was against a big bleed. Campbell worked systematically down the patient, coming eventually to his feet. When he took off the man's shoes they smelt foul. With the little spike on the handle of his tendon hammer Campbell scratched the man's sole through his sock. The big toe rose, sinister and majestic, instead of curling downwards as it should have done. The other foot was the same. Whatever was wrong with the patient, that was a bad sign. Campbell went back up to the head. The man's breathing was shallower than ever.

'What are these, David?'

'What?'

'These.' Maureen had rolled up the man's shirt sleeve to take his blood pressure. Over the biceps the skin was abnormal in patches. Little shallow pits, not obviously infected or punctured, but caused apparently by some wasting of the subcutaneous tissue, covered the front and side of the man's upper arm.

'Drugs?'

'Doesn't look much like it. Not infected.'

'Not over veins either.'

'So not drugs . . . Christ.'

'What?'

'I forget what it's called, but diabetics get it. From insulin.'

'Hell, yes. And he's not ketotic.'

'No. No ketones on his breath. So . . .'

'Let's give him some sugar. And test that blood. And if it isn't that it won't do him any harm. Whatever he's got.'

Maureen took down a big glass vial of concentrated glucose for injection, grasped its top through a fold of her apron and snapped it open. Campbell drew up the solution into a syringe and stuck the needle through the rubber cuff in the IV-giving set. Maureen closed the valve on the line above. Campbell pushed the stuff in as fast as it would go.

Nothing happened. Maureen reached up for a brown bottle marked Dextrostix, and took out a little cardboard strip. She squeezed a drop of the patient's blood from the first syringe on to it and glanced at the watch pinned to the top of her apron. Campbell started to take the man's pulse again and to his surprise his hand was brushed away.

'He's coming up.'

'Good.'

'Great stuff the sugary water.' The man heaved a huge stertorous sigh and then another, then slowly reached out to claw the air in front of him. He coughed and then vomited again. Campbell held the man's head low to keep the vomit out of his airway. Maureen was rinsing the cardboard strip under a tap. She looked at it then showed it to Campbell.

'That's it,' she said. 'A diabetic with his blood sugar in his boots.'

Having vomited the man lay still again, and his respiration slowed down once more to occasional shallow sighs.

'Hell. He's going off again. Let's give him some more.'

Maureen snatched another vial of fifty percent glucose and expertly decapitated it.

'Have we got five hundreds of ten percent dextrose?'

'I think so. Somewhere. Shoot that in and I'll have a look.'

She gave him a quick encouraging smile. She had worked in Casualty for a long time, at least since Campbell had been a houseman, and was probably much less exerted by this sort of thing than he was. She turned to a cupboard, opened it and pulled out a bottle and proceeded to rip off the foil outer top, and transfer it to the giving set in place of the original bottle of saline.

'That should perk him up.'

With the second shot of fifty percent glucose the man's breathing got better for longer, and he became much more lively. He waved his arms about and Campbell grabbed the one with the drip up and held it firmly to protect their access to his circulation, through which they were probably saving his life. The other arm flailed first wildly in the air, then against the trolley and finally gripped the lapel of Campbell's white coat and dragged it firmly downwards. It was all most inelegant, but interesting.

Someone appeared at the door of the resuscitation room. It was the staff nurse from Minor Trauma. She looked in on the scene, in which the man was now thrashing about, with Campbell and Maureen trying to immobilise him and protect the IV line, which had taken on a life of its own, lashing around between the wildly swinging bottle and the man's arm. She was not impressed. 'Oh, him,' she said. 'A regular. Diabetic. Gets his insulins mixed up. Broke a porter's nose last week. Will you be long?'

'Depends on him,' said Campbell, with what he privately considered to be remarkable restraint.

'Doctor Campbell,' A whining spectral voice came from the resuscitation room intercom. As the patient's blood sugar came up his conscious level had improved a little and his struggles subsided to mere playful drunken wrestling. 'Doctor Campbell.' Campbell and Maureen, still entangled with the patient, both looked round at the intercom and laughed out loud. Its light went off abruptly. The man on the trolley got slowly pinker. His pulse became slower and stronger and his breathing returned to normal. His struggling ceased and he seemed eventually to be merely sleeping. Campbell felt rather pleased with himself for the second time in twenty-four hours, though he would have been happier without staff nurse McCraw's intervention. Having seen such miracles many times, Maureen was less elated. 'Come on, wake up,' she commanded and the man did so, yawning and saying sleepily, 'Time I was at my work.' His eyes widened with disbelief when he saw the drip stand, the lights above and Maureen and Campbell. 'Oh, not again.'

'I hear you're making a habit of this,' said Maureen, smiling. 'How much insulin are you on?'

'Forty of one and twenty-four of the other.'

'Do you know which is which?'

'I'm beginning to wonder.'

'What's your name,' said Campbell in his official voice.

'Duncan,' said the man. 'Basil Duncan . . . I've been in before.'

'Whose looking after your diabetes?'

'The Institute. You know. Diabetic Out-patients.'

'Do you know which doctor?'

'No, to tell you the truth . . . I haven't been in it long.' He made it sound like a club.

'Do you take forty of the insulin with the green and pink label? Or the all-green labelled stuff?' Maureen was trying to sort things out.

Campbell was impressed by her grasp of the practicalities of diabetes.

'I can't remember,' said the man. 'In fact I'm thinking of starting again.'

'How d'you feel now?'

'Pretty rough.'

'I'm not surprised,' said Maureen. 'You nearly killed yourself.'

'I really think I ought to get all this straightened out again. You know. Which is which and all that. And get to my work.'

'Well, we'll see,' said Campbell. 'I want one of the specialists from DOPD to come up and have a look at you. And you'd better have something by mouth as well.'

'I always carry sugar lumps. They told me about that.'

'Did you take any this morning, when all this started?'

The man felt in his trouser pockets and looked round for his jacket. 'No, as a matter of fact. I must have come out without them this morning.'

'Oh, well. They might want to have a general look at you and maybe a chat, so if you don't mind waiting across in the trolley room . . .'

'And I'll get you something to drink,' said Maureen.

'Doctor Campbell, are you busy,' whined the intercom.

Apart from the avulsion of a fingernail, the suture of a laceration of thumb, and the assessment of an as yet unknown assortment of pathology in Minor Trauma, Campbell had nothing whatsoever to do. And this poor chap, whose approach to the treatment of his diabetes was reminiscent of Russian roulette, was just about out of trouble. A clerkess appeared with his notes from the last such episode. Campbell began to write.

'Doctor Campbell, are you busy?'

'Less so now, thank you, Sister.'

'There are two policemen waiting to see you in the back room, Doctor Campbell.'

When he had first joined the department some six weeks previously, Campbell had been quite taken aback by the multiplicity of contacts with the forces of law and order that his new post entailed. Every time a policeman had approached him in the first week he had thought panicky consecutive thoughts about his driving licence, his parking permit, his insurance, the last time he'd been grossly drunk and the states of health of various of his more frail relatives, usually in that order. Now policemen were no more alarming than postmen. This summons was at least an excuse for going round the back and perhaps even fitting in a quick coffee if circumstances were conducive.

40

There was a sergeant, and a constable who was trying to read the polysyllabic titles of the predominantly orthopaedic textbooks that formed the department library. Campbell invited them to sit down. They did so, taking their hats off at the same time, in perfect unison, as though executing a drill movement. The sergeant said, 'You are Dr David Campbell,' and the constable brought out a notebook. Campbell agreed that he was and they got down to more serious business. They asked him his qualifications, his age and his address, and confirmed that he was employed as a Senior House Officer in the Casualty Department of the Royal Charitable Institute for the Care of the Indigent Sick, Edinburgh. The sergeant seemed to relish the sonorities of names and titles. The constable scribbled furiously. After 'Edinburgh' he closed his notebook. They both stood up and put on their hats.

'Thank you, Doctor Campbell. Just checking.'

'Oh. Anything in particular.'

The sergeant smiled indulgently at Campbell's idle curiosity. 'Witnesses. You know. Names and addresses.'

'I see.' Campbell wondered which of the endless procession of drunk drivers, beaten wives, road traffic victims, sudden deaths and criminal injuries this pair were investigating, but was too polite to ask. The sergeant saw he was not satisfied.

'I believe you stopped at a road traffic accident. Off duty, according to my colleague who attended the incident.'

'Oh yes. Last night.'

'At Westburn in West Lothian,' said the sergeant in a manner which suggested he suspected Campbell of zigzagging across Scotland in his spare time, collecting RTAs. 'There may be proceedings arising. In which case we'll be back.'

'I'll be glad to help if I can.'

The policemen left silently, the sergeant taking the lead. Campbell was standing wondering if a quick coffee would spruce him up for a couple of rounds of minor surgery when Hadden came in.

'Hullo, lad. Or should I say hullo hullo hullo? In trouble again?'

'Don't think so. A squashed Paki last night. Routine stuff. A lorry parked without lights.'

'You were off.'

'I know. I just stopped for an RTA.'

'Making coffee?'

'Just about to have a quick one. Got some stuff waiting from Minor Trauma.'

'Oh, don't worry. I had a look through that end while you were in resus. Tweaked off a fingernail and did some embroidery on someone's thenar eminence.'

'Thanks very much.'

'Dirty sod, that baker. Put you right off your angel cake.'

'That's what I thought.'

'Signed him off for a few days and sentenced him to a buttockful of penicillin, to be injected forthwith. And that thumb wasn't as bad as it looked.'

Campbell filled the kettle. 'What about the rest? A girl with an eye and a few other bods Sister seemed quite agitato about?'

'I suppose if you really worked at it you could get to like Minor Trauma. But I couldn't. Department of Triviatric Medicine. I sort of swept through them and tidied them up. A couple waiting for X-rays. So we'll have a coffee. What do you make of our colleague from the furthest corner of Empire?'

'Hakeem? OK. Seems to know his stuff, but wants you to know about it. Dermatitis bloody herpetiformis.'

'With Latin like that, my boy, you could be a bishop or a dermatologist. How is he on surgery?'

'How would I know? But he does go on a bit about his surgical training scholarship.'

'J.G. said he was a bit on the old side.'

'Looks about thirty-five. Maybe more.'

'Has he passed the wee test?'

'He didn't say. But I think he would have if he had. Seems to have been here a long time.'

'His references looked a bit tired, according to J.G. "Distinguished but dog-eared. Always a little suspicious," he said.'

'He's done a bit of battle surgery in Glasgow.'

'Good. He's on for Friday here.'

Hadden was a couple of years ahead of Campbell, and also an Edinburgh graduate. They had worked together for Alester Ravelston Orr when Campbell had been doing his pre-registration surgery and Hadden had been registrar 'at the court of the Mad Mullah of Morningside', in his own phrase. They had kept up acquaintance since, mainly in pubs, and now that Campbell had escaped from the inane posturings of a six month brush with medical research, they found themselves working together in one department again. From Campbell's point of view it was very satisfactory: Hadden knew a lot of surgery, and was good company.

'Milk?'

42

'Oh. I thought she'd locked it all away in the frozen recesses of her bosom, or somewhere like that.'

'Hakeem got some in. And someone else dropped in with a couple of pints this morning.'

'A glut, even. Have you seen her this morning?'

'No. But heard her a lot. It's beginning to get through to me. "Doctor Campbell. There's thirty-six haemophiliacs from a plane crash waiting in trolleys . . . I thought you'd like to know . . . Doctor Campbell . . . Doctor Campbell . . ."'

Having thus mocked Sister, Campbell found himself looking nervously round at the intercom. Hadden was looking at it too. He put down his coffee and got up, walked over to it, pressed the button marked 'Sister's Office', and, putting his mouth close to it, lowed softly into it, making a peaceful pastoral sound of bovine contentment, redolent of lush meadows and summer evenings. A sharp little shriek came back from the intercom in reply. He switched it off and returned smiling to his coffee.

'If she comes to you complaining of auditory hallucinations . . .'

'I'll tell her to drink more milk.'

'What a bitch. Thank God the rest are all right. Who's on in trolleys?'

'Maureen. The blonde.'

'Oh, Maureen. I can remember her when she was a brunette. Nice girl.'

'Yes. Good nurse too. Doesn't mind ill people and knows what to do and all that. What's . . . she up to . . . these days?'

'Don't really know. I'm trying to remember who she went blonde for. I think it was some bloke in my year.'

'She was blonde when I was a houseman,' said Campbell, aware that to talk thus was to concede the passage of the years, and worse. All rampant medical bores made free use of the phrase 'when I was a houseman'. 'In fact a chap in my year drifted off from a Residency party with her. Mac. The chap who died. She practically reformed him. He went out with her for weeks. And they had an amazing party. A flat of Casualty staff nurses.' Campbell drank his coffee and remembered being in the bathroom at that party, very drunk, and finding the secret of Maureen's blondeness, which had seemed enormously depressing at the time.

'Can't help you there,' said Hadden. 'No idea what the scene is. Thinking of living dangerously?'

'Not really. Just wondered.'

43

'Thought you might be. Now that Jim's decided to stay alive after all. Nice girl Maureen. Sensible. Well, dense but sensible.' Hadden stretched himself and sighed. 'Roll on death or December. I don't mind which. Casualty's lost its charm. Where's the Dormouse?'

'Don't know. Haven't seen him.' Dr McDiarmid was Hadden's opposite number and Hadden made much of his undoubted inertia.

'Probably dozing over the fracture clinic. "Next patient . . . zzzzzz . . .", or having tea in Sister's office. "Please don't stuff me in the teapot again, Sister. I promise never to put a furry little paw near your precious milk as long as I live . . . Eeeek!" Or maybe he's just still in bed. With his pyjama collar turned up, dreaming of being a great surgeon.'

Another of Dr McDiarmid's more mockable characteristics was his habit of wearing the collar of his white coat turned up. It was a mysterious mannerism, practised by certain surgeons in the Institute, and by their followers, as a sort of caste mark. Hadden warmed to his topic. 'D'you think he'll wear the collar of his charcoal pinstripe up when he goes along to satisfy the examiners orally in the wee test at the college. It's probably like funny handshakes. Ten marks extra if you're lucky, or twenty marks off it you meet the wrong chap.' Hadden turned up the collar of his white coat and pretended to wake from a profound sleep. 'What? Everyone gone hime? Exam over already? Bless my tail and whiskers. Wish they'd wakened me.'

Dr McDiarmid had not had much luck so far with the primary FRCS examination, which was administered by the Royal College of Surgeons to test knowledge of the basic sciences — anatomy, physiology, pathology, etc. — as a preliminary to the exam in surgery for the fellowship. It was unlikely that he'd actually slept through any of his three or four attempts so far, but probable that his lethargic attitude to most things was reflected in his preparation for what Hadden called 'the wee test'.

'Is he trying it again this time? Or having a complete rest?'

'I think he's having another go. It's quite soon. Next week I think. It's the only way. Grind the buggers down. You thinking of doing it?'

'Not next week or ever,' said Campbell. His surgical ambitions went no further than Casualty, which he regarded as good non-committal experience. ("Ideal for the chap who doesn't know what he wants to end up in", Mr Gillon had said at the interview). The higher reaches of surgery offered no delights to Campbell, and the thought of learning anatomy again was abhorrent. 'No chance. I might try the rest of the Physician's wee test. In a year or two.' Campbell, much to his surprise, had passed the first part of the exam for membership of the Royal College of Physicians, first time.

'Yes,' mused Hadden. 'They're in a much nicer part of Edinburgh. Down there between the BBC and the Corporation Transport Lost Property Office.'

Hadden's college, and he was a fully fledged fellow of the Royal College of Surgeons, filled an undistinguished space on a down-market shopping street, between a greengrocer and a mountebank herbalist. Another reason for being a physician. Campbell finished his coffee and got up. 'Ah well. Back to the suffering millions, I suppose.'

'I suppose so,' said Hadden. 'Do you want to do trolleys for a while? It's more physicianly. I wouldn't mind resting my brain in triviatrics for the rest of the morning.'

'Fine. Thanks.' Campbell secretly relished a bit of drama in his daily work, and there was more of it to be found in trolleys, where, as an additional attraction, Maureen presided. Hadden, taking on Nurse McGraw and the sprained ankles, had been more than generous. Campbell spent the rest of the morning dealing with an assortment of sick people, most of whom needed thoughtful assessment, many of whom needed admission to the wards and one of whom, having had a massive coronary and arrested, resisted his best efforts at resuscitation and died in the department shortly before lunch.

After a half pint in the pub across the road and a quick lunch in the general mess Campbell went up to the Respiratory Intensive Care Unit to see how the Indian trader from the road traffic accident was getting on. The unit was high in the older part of the Institute, in an irregular garret with odd corners, gently sloping ceilings and deep dormer windows, perhaps an odd place to find the latest in high-technology life-support systems. It was one of the areas in the hospital where a rigid doctrine of sterility was preached, in the faint hope that a reasonable standard of cleanliness might prevail, so Campbell had to put on a paper cap and mask, a green gown and, having taken off his shoes, don a pair of loose disposable paper slippers.

The duty anaesthetist on duty (such units being the traditional province of gasmen the world over) was a pleasant, unambitious man from Campbell's year called Wilson, who greeted Campbell with a surprising question. 'Hullo there. Thought you'd be up. What's an Ismaili?'

'No idea.'

'We think it's some kind of fancy Moslem, but we're not sure.'

'Have you asked the chaplain?'

'Hadn't thought of that. Good idea. We were kind of worried. It's a bit off the beaten track and someone was wondering if they might not be like orthodox Jews. You know, more trouble dead than alive, because infidels like you and me can't touch them.'

'Is it as bad as that?'

'Oh, no. Just came up in conversation.'

'How is he?'

'His bicarbonate began to go down a bit about midnight so we really blew him over-night. And then this morning we began to wonder if we hadn't overdone it. As you know there are compliance problems with these crushed chests quite apart from the floating segment. But I've just repeated his blood gases and he's practically eucapnic now.'

'Oh.'

'And his conscious level's just what you'd expect, not that he'd any evidence of head injury, but we run them fairly flat so they don't fight the machine. You just let them up to see how they're going if you think there's a problem. But he's fine.'

'And his ankle?'

'A compound tib-fib. Wound toilet, four screws and a BKPOP.'

'So he's all right?'

'Oh, by no means out of the wood. But he should be fine provided he doesn't run into problems with his pulmonary contusion.'

From all that Campbell deduced that the patient, in a time-honoured phrase, was as well as could be expected. 'That's nice. The locum from Casualty said he was in capable hands.'

'Smooth black bastard?'

'A Pakistani. Dr Subhadar. He's been up a couple of times.'

'Something like that. And he's dozens of visitors already. Mainly brown blokes from Glasgow. You should have seen this place at one o'clock, with them swarming around in green gowns, paper hats and those Sinbad slippers. Looked like a hospital production of Kismet. Actually some of them you might have crossed the street to avoid in the jungle.'

'I'm glad he's doing reasonably well,' said Campbell. 'Nice guy. Tough about pain. And remarkably unbothered about his van going up in flames.'

'Oriental fatalism,' said Wilson. 'Or maybe the insurance. Did you know the police were interested?'

'Yes. About the accident. A couple of them came in this morning and took my name, rank and number as a witness.'

'Hmm. Might be just that. But I don't think so. They really wanted to talk to him. Which, of course, just wasn't on. When I explained the

46

man would have a tube in his windpipe for maybe three weeks, and probably didn't speak much English anyway, they went on as if I was making feeble excuses. Kept saying it was a most important inquiry and they would have to refer the matter back to the inspector in charge of the case. They'll probably go off and learn Urdu and come back with a semaphore manual for him tomorrow.'

Campbell had a look at the patient, who was under sedation, but as well looking as his colleague's report had suggested. He decided to ask Hakeem about the Ismaili business, and perhaps about the possibility of interpreting. And on his way downstairs he wondered if he had missed anything interesting at the scene of the road traffic accident the previous night.

TWO

'I know it's difficult for you, David.'

'Mmm.'

'But it's really difficult for me too . . . I'm honestly not used to this sort of thing.'

'Mmm. But you're very good at it.'

'It's not really me. Not really me as I think of myself at all. And I'm just not used to it. Everything was so simple before . . . all this. Before us. And it's not simple at all now.'

'No.'

'But it's simpler for you than it is for me. You don't have to lead two lives. I do. It's like being two of me. One for Jim and one for you. It's very complicated.'

'You're very good at it.'

'Before, when I thought about what it might be like to have an affair, you know, just as a sort of experiment in my head, I thought it would be difficult, but the really difficult things are things I would never have thought of in a million years. Silly things, that in my innocence of before two p.m. on the fourth of May I couldn't even have imagined myself thinking about.'

'Mm. What?'

'Oh well . . . sex. Coming round to see you, properly, I mean, and spending the whole afternoon in bed and going home, proper home that is, and looking at Jim and thinking he's nice too and then by bed-time hardly being able to wait until he's cleaned his teeth . . . And wondering . . .'

'Wondering what?'

'If he knew . . .'

'Don't know.'

'Don't know what?'

'Don't know if people would know . . . You know.'

'Do people know if people have?'

'Have what?'

'You jolly well know what I mean.'

'Oh. Treading a wet deck and all that?'

'What?' Jean sounded puzzled and surprised.

48

'It's a nautical expression, I believe,' said Campbell with scholarly detachment.

'Sounds horrible. What is it?'

'Like stirring your mate's porridge, but not so soon after.'

'David! Sometimes you sound really awful. Where on earth did you hear that?'

'Can't remember.'

'Ugh.'

'It's not something I've done,' said Campbell soothingly. 'It's just an expression I've picked up somewhere.'

'Anyway. Would you know? When he's treading me as a wet deck to use your horrible phrase, — would he know?'

'I honestly don't know.'

'I sort of wondered about that. So I have baths practically all the time. It's absurd.' She giggled. 'Our affair's been just one clean weekend after another. So then, of course, I think, will me having so many baths make Jim think things.'

'Is he all right now?'

'For sex?'

'I really meant generally.'

'Well enough to want to do all-night experiments on his frogs. He's not too bad generally, but not really all right for sex. Honestly, it's so complicated. Seeing you, well, screwing you, to use another of your horrible expressions, makes me want to screw him and he sort of knows that and sometimes apologises because things aren't really all right yet and says he's sure everything'll be fine when he's better And he's so sweet about it and then I feel very silly because I'm getting so much sex with you. So it's difficult for me too, which is what I wanted to explain. Knowing it's difficult for you too. Mmmm. And I love you anyway. Still. Which doesn't make it any easier.'

'Quite,' said Campbell, just to be annoying.

Jean giggled and nudged him in the ribs. 'I know when you're just trying to annoy me. Or make me less pompous about my problems. Which is usually the same thing. Oh. Cuddle me.'

'I am.'

'I know. But closer.' She took Campbell's left hand and cupped it over her right breast, and closed her thighs more tightly over his right. 'I'm not sleepy any more. What time is it?'

'Midnight, maybe.'

'Oh, David, I wish I hated you. Or you hated me or something simple like that.'

'I don't.'

'It's so complicated.'

Campbell felt very tired. They had been in bed since just after eight. And it wasn't as if Jean had to stay awake to go home as she often did because, for complex family reasons to do with frogs, she was staying the night. She snuggled back against him, her hair tickling his nose. He snuffed the nearest bits away from his nostrils. 'That's nice,' said Jean, in a small sleepy voice. 'Oh, I wish it were simple.' Half awake, Campbell lay with his arms round her, his hands disposed obligingly as described, listening with the patience and tolerance of a good marriage guidance counsellor, until he fell asleep.

Jean got up early next morning and went off to collect Jim from the lab. Campbell lay in bed for a while then got up too, and went through to wake Bones, because of the Thursday meeting.

'Sorry . . . Oh, hello, Maureen. Coffee?'

'Thanks, David,' said Maureen.

'Morning, Campbell. You were bloody noisy last night,' said Bones.

'Oh, sorry. Did it keep you awake?'

'Well, we weren't sleeping much, were we, love? Yes, thanks. Coffee. It's a bit early, though.'

'Thursday.'

'Oh. The meeting.'

'Yes. The kirk session. Sugar, Maureen?'

'No thanks.'

'Bloody hell,' said Bones. 'We weren't going to get up. Bloody meeting.' He turned to Maureen. 'Back at about ten past nine . . . love.' Maureen smiled. He had paused quite a long time before saying 'love'. Campbell wondered if he had forgotten her name. He left them and then went and had breakfast in the kitchen. He read the *Scotsman* for a few minutes and when he had finished went back to his bedroom and got ready for work. On the way out he met Bones in the hallway.

'Hang on a minute. Quick shave and some cornflakes and I'll be with you.'

They walked across the park towards the Institute. Bones was insufferably bright and chirpy, as he usually was when things like that had happened. Campbell confessed he had been somewhat taken aback.

'No reason you should know,' said Bones. 'Hasn't been going very long. She was on in trolleys yesterday afternoon and I said I'd meet her for a quick drink when I came off at ten.'

'I see.'

'Nice girl.'

50

'Really?'

'Yes. This could be the beginning . . . well, of something small. She might be a steadying influence.'

That would be a welcome development. One of the hazards of living with Bones was never knowing who you were going to meet at breakfast.

'Was that your Mrs Thing making all that noise last night again?'

'Yes.'

'I though her husband was getting better.'

'He is.'

'She makes a hell of a noise.'

'It's funny. She really doesn't know she's doing it. I've even threatened to tape record it.'

'I might drop her a note myself,' said Bones. 'She works in Endocrinology Outpatients, doesn't she?'

'Yes.' Campbell sensed that they were already quite far into one of those conversations. 'Any idea what's coming up at this morning's meeting?'

'Haven't a clue.'

'Milk, I suppose.'

'Probably. And the usual cautionary tales.'

'Done anything dreadful this week? I don't think I have.'

'Nothing I can think of.'

'That's the worst kind. No. Maybe not. For the really worst kind you get the old ''David, my boy, could we possibly have a quiet word'' as soon as he hears.'

'I suppose it maintains standards.'

'I suppose so.'

It was still only twenty past eight, but the pedestrian rush hour across the park had begun, as people streamed into town from the nearer southern suburbs: office workers, students and schoolchildren converging from the paths on to the broad leafy avenue that marked the eastern limit of the Institute's grounds. Bones and Campbell walked smartly. No one (except Dr McDiarmid) was ever late for Mr Gillon's Thursday morning meeting. His weekly 'Kirk Session' was a brief but religiously observed gathering of all the medical staff of his department, held at eight thirty so that whoever was on night duty could attend without losing much sleep, and because it was Mr Gillon's custom to start his working day promptly.

Hadden was sitting on his own drinking coffee when Bones and Campbell reached the room round the back. He was a big heavy man, whose armchair looked small under him, and whose hand dwarfed the coffee cup. He got up and switched the kettle on again.

'Could definitely do with another,' said Bones. 'Hardly slept a wink all night.'

Hadden ignored that. 'Young Campbell?'

'Yes, please.'

'This milk looks as if it's getting a bit mature.' He opened the bottle and tipped it over a cup. It did not pour. He shook it a little. A solid plug of cream dislodged and the milk rushed out and overflowed the cup. He swore violently, mentioning Sister by name, then went across for some paper towels to mop up the mess. 'Highland cow,' he muttered angrily, paddling the paper towels in the milk on the table, and throwing them soggily at the waste paper basket. Dr Subhadar, whose night on duty was just finishing, was watching from the door.

'How unfortunate. Especially as I had made ample provision of fresh milk via my police contacts. Here is the key.' He produced his little key again and opened a cupboard. 'And here is the milk. Fresh as a daisy.'

'More than I feel,' said Bones.

Dr McDiarmid came in at twenty-nine minutes past eight, looking much more tired than Dr Subhadar, who might well have been working all night, and Mr Gillon came in half a minute later. The consultant surgeon in charge was of above average height, a well-preserved wing three-quarter of thirty years ago, dressed conservatively but extremely well. He had a buttonhole of expensive-looking flowers. Campbell glanced at it as he passed.

'Iguanas, David.'

Campbell, who thought they might be orchids, must have looked surprised.

'Iguana Trust, David. An interesting share this morning. The orchids mark its onward progress. You could do worse yourself. Morning Graham. Morning Hakeem. Quiet night? Morning Andrew. Glad you made it. Morning Albert.'

J.G. was the only person in Edinburgh who called Bones Albert. True, it was his proper name and, as he sometimes pointed out, a common and well-regarded name in Oswaldtwhistle. But everyone he knew in Edinburgh called him Bones. J.G. sat down and laid his folder on a damp patch on the table, the remains of Hadden's puddle of milk. He looked at his watch and coughed. 'Not much from me today, really. One or two things from last week . . . The Tansey Health Centre business seems to be moving slowly towards a satisfactory solution. I met old Joe at the BMA Wines night — only reason I go is it's the one meeting in the year everyone else attends. Handy for that sort of thing — and he thinks his twenty-five man primary health care team can probably cope with the removal of our sutures provided there's nothing complicated and we guarantee to bale them out if there is. It took longer than he thought to get it through District Management and up to the Area Community Nursing Co-ordinating Committee. And he'd just missed the last meeting. Swears he hadn't forgotten about it.'

'Oh, and a couple of nice letters here. An American lady someone saw. I think it was you, Albert. She says the physician on duty (Bones made a ritual grimace, to indicate he thought of himself as a surgeon) Dr Barrelwood — that's the nearest we've had for a while, isn't it, Albert? — was really sweet with her allergy. Maybe you should go private. And another one from a rather embarrassed sounding lady who had diarrhoea. She particularly thanks the nursing staff so I'll pass it on to Sister.' It was J.G.'s habit at the meetings to throw in a little of this sort of thing before the bad news, whatever it happened to be. 'Which brings me to the vexed question of circular three four seven slant twenty-nine. The one about 'Allocation of Casual Non-Accountable Dietary Items: Clarification of Entitlement.' This, the milk memorandum, had been pinned to notice boards, enjoyed its brief hour before being snowed under by a steady accumulation of similar memoranda on similarly weighty topics, and then quietly been forgotten by almost the whole hospital. Only in Casualty had it proved to be a source of contention.

'I read it again to make sense of it. See if it says what I think it says. Beats me where this new lot find the words. Makes you realise how lucky we were in the old days, with a medical superintendent who didn't care about this sort of thing but could have written about it in English if he had. As I understand it the thinking behind it is that we're all the same as our portering colleagues now, and porters don't get free milk. Officially. So we, or in this case you, don't get free milk. Again officially. Which is more or less the position as it was before. The inscrutably worded circular three four seven slant twenty-nine simple restates this policy and as far as I've heard hasn't changed anything much around the hospital generally.'

He paused, and most present thought silent thoughts about Sister. Campbell glanced at the intercom to check that the light was off. J.G. went on, 'In the special circumstances of this department, however, problems appear to have arisen. As you know, with no in-patient beds our allowance of milk for patients is something of a polite fiction. Except perhaps for tea for people waiting a long time for ambulances, and of course for the bereaved. But it's a fiction that's been around since I was a houseman' — he smiled wryly — 'and that wasn't yesterday. And then there's the attitude of the nursing staff.' J.G. glanced at the intercom too. 'It may be that in the brave new world of reorganised nursing the supervisory staff covering our department, and I don't mean departmental nursing staff, having so little to do, spend their time gratuitously worrying about the implementation of such circulars as our friend three four seven slant twenty-nine.' He paused and looked round. 'And then again there may be other explanations . . .' Most of those present at the meeting had by now glanced at the intercom. 'So the best thing for all concerned might be to play the thing fairly gently until people stop thinking it's important. I'd thought at one point of having a quiet word with Sister myself to restore the status quo, and there was a time when I'd have had no hesitation about doing so, but in these enlightened days a consultant surgeon in administrative charge of a department might find himself in all sorts of awkward corners if he started telling Sister where to put her milk.'

Most people smiled at his turn of phrase. Hakeem did not. He sat forward in his chair, his lips pursed, and murmured, 'Very circumspect, sir, if I may say so.' Bones was slumped back with a fatuous expression on his face, presumably working out how soon he could be back in bed with Maureen. He certainly didn't look as if he wanted to prolong the discussion. Nor did Hadden, who stared glumly at the damp patch on the table.

'Agreed, Andrew?' said J.G. Dr McDiarmid started and refocussed and muttered, 'By all means.'

'There's a lot to be said for the quiet life.' J.G. flicked through the papers on his folder. 'I don't think there's much more from me. Oh.' He turned to Hakeem and said, 'Dr Subhadar, my profound apologies.'

'Sir?'

'For being so rude as to omit to begin our proceedings by welcoming you. You'll have met all the boys of course, but this is your first . . . ah . . . kirk session, to use a presbyterian expression, with us. So welcome, Dr Subhadar. I hope you enjoy working with us. And if I may mention it, I'm sure we all wish you well in your forthcoming joust with the examiners. Study going well?'

That was one of J.G.'s formal questions, expecting a monosyllabic answer or none, but Dr Subhadar was not to know this. 'I find your system of night duty most conducive to good study. The department is peaceful as a rule from one until seven. Not a mouse stirs and the occasional patient is welcome as a break from the books. I am reading your own Edinburgh textbook on pathology at the moment. A monumental work of great readability.' If it was the one Campbell was

54

thinking of it ranked bottom equal in the readability charts with Gray's Anatomy, but its peculiar orotund phraseology might appeal to this poor blackamoor.

'Glad to hear it,' said J.G., getting up. 'Vital stuff, pathology. Anything from you chaps? No? Good. Sorry for keeping you so long. I'll get out of your way and let you get on. Morning all.' He smiled at Bones, who looked suddenly guilty, then turned to Campbell. 'Yes, young David, isn't it about time you became a man of property. D'you invest?' Apart from a clutch of ill-starred birthday present premium bonds, not worth mentioning to an enquirer with an orchid in his buttonhole, Campbell had nothing to declare. 'Well, I should have thought you should be doing something interesting with the spare from your salary at your time of life. You bank it, I suppose.'

'Mainly, sir.'

'Just about the worst thing you could do. After National Savings Certificates.' Campbell felt secretly relieved at having cashed his on reaching the age of discretion. 'You should have a think about something a little more exciting. A good time for it too. These Iguanas have had a lively week or two and look like going up a good bit more. You interested?'

'Never thought about it.'

'Time you did. Maybe not them. Something respectably gilt-edged to begin with, and a little in the chancy stuff on top of it later. Think about it. Better than subsidising the speculations of the Bank of Scotland, who aren't going to cut you in on their profits on your money.'

'Thanks for the advice.' Campbell had once shared a telephone in a room in the Institute with a doctor who had spent most of his mornings conversing with his broker, but it had never seriously occurred to him that he might, in an appropriately cautious fashion, share in the hazards of the market.

'How's the job working out?'

'Fine. Interesting . . . Varied.'

'I was sure you'd enjoy it, and it's good to have you here. Perhaps we'll make a surgeon of you yet . . . Oh, Andrew. Could we have a quiet word?' Consultant and registrar left together and turned left towards J.G.'s office. Dr McDiarmid was looking less sleepy, and distinctly glum. Bones slipped out quickly.

Dr Subhadar was taking off his white coat. Campbell remembered the man upstairs in the Respiratory Intensive Care Unit and his conversation with Scott Wilson, the duty gasman there yesterday.

'Oh, Hakeem, I went upstairs yesterday to see the man from that accident.'

'That was kind of you, David. I went up myself also in the small hours of this morning. Between miscellaneous caseating lesions and sarcoidosis.' Campbell realised, not immediately, that he was referring to an interval in his reading programme. 'I found him as well as could be expected. Communicating very little, naturally, in the circumstances. But remarkably well, taking into account all he has been through.'

'Yes. The chap who was on for the unit yesterday mentioned there had been some communication problems.'

'I suppose there will be. In fact I have already offered to supplement the efforts of his relatives where . . . more technical vocabulary is required. These simple people, you know, are not accustomed to our ways and our extensive vocabulary.'

'Hakeem, you don't mind me asking what is this . . . Ismaili business anyway. You mentioned it a couple of times, and . . . I was wondering.'

Dr Subhadar looked thoughtful and then smiled. 'For a start it is not a business. Some people, some theologically mistaken people would describe us as merely a sect of Islam. And in a simplistic and, forgive me, commonly held western view, that may be a point of view. However, there is more to it than that.' Campbell did not have J.G's gift for curtailing this man's replies. He leaned on a work top and listened. Dr Subhadar sat down. 'It is a way of life, to state the matter simply. To use your terms, it might be described as something one is, rather than something one believes. It might help if I explained that our enemies call us the Jews of the Orient.'

'I see.'

'David, I hope you do not see.' He smiled threateningly. 'Only our enemies compare us to the Jews. True we have certain things in common. Our regard for family. Our charities and scholarships. Our business acumen. But I think after dealing with Jews you will find Ismaili people upright and trustworthy, not given to intrigue, and, if you look at our record down the centuries, a great and powerful support to the British Empire.' He smiled again. 'Unlike our friends the Jews. But to answer your question, simply, we are the children of the prophet. Our leader, of whom you have no doubt heard because his father the late Aga Khan was a close friend of your own Royal family, is the present Aga Khan. He is a spiritual rather then a temporal leader, but a considerable force in his capacity as a statesman. Incidentally I should also mention he is a munificent benefactor and happened to be the patron of the trust which so generously funds my scholarship.'

'So you have your own customs and language and that sort of thing.'

'Not really. We have customs dating from the earliest times of Islam, but I think you will also find that Ismaili people have been among the most advanced in acquiring the skills of western civilisation, from the first days of the Raj. As to language, the Aga himself speaks six or eight, being an international figure. I speak three. The majority of Ismailis speak mainly Urdu, but are adept at picking up other languages, as circumstances necessitate.'

Campbell thought of the van driver's Glasgow accent and said, 'Your own English is remarkably good, if you don't mind my saying so.'

Hakeem laughed. 'I don't mind at all. But I was hearing English from birth, as some families in Pakistan do, and all my education has been in English.' A twinkle came into his eye. 'Except, to be sure, for me secondary education at the hands of the Marist brothers,' he added, in purest Dublin.

'Marists?'

'Yes. In Karachi.' said Hakeem, reverting to his own voice. 'They took my father's money, taught me and believed what they wanted. But you need not fear I am a secret Celtic supporter. We Ismailis do not convert our beliefs. We remain what we are.'

'I see. Thanks. That's interesting.'

'So. It's a beautiful morning. But I must go to bed. Good day, David.'

'Goodbye, Hakeem. Sleep well.' Campbell felt he had found out a good deal about Ismailis, but not whether you could touch a dead one, which might have been difficult to elicit in casual conversation.

For obscure epidemiological reasons, to do with the availability of general practitioners, and with people's inclination to work or otherwise, Thursday was usually the quietest day of the week in the department. Mondays were always busy and sometimes chaotic, as people brought the weekend's backlog of accumulated miseries to the attention of the official services, and the disinclination to work seemed to be at a maximum. Tuesdays, Wednesdays and Thursdays were successively quieter and there was a little upsurge on Friday as the citizens got themselves medically tidied up for the weekend, in the knowledge that professional attention would be hard if not impossible to come by until the Monday morning, when services would be overloaded again.

Sometimes, in such doldrums as Thursday mornings, Campbell reflected on the less admissable functions of the Casualty Department. Officially the cases seen were in two categories: either they were the clinically imperative victims of accident and other acute emergencies, or they were referred by their own doctors having been seen and considered in need of urgent treatment beyond the scope of care at home under their own GP. In an ideal world the latter group would all have come with helpful letters giving concise and accurate details of the history and physical findings, and some note of previous medical history and current treatment if any. This seldom happened. Patients whom it would not be possible for even the most enthusiastically oriented Casualty Officer to regard as victim either of accident or medical emergency habitually rolled up to be seen, and J.G.'s standing orders dictated that they would be, though many had not even attempted to see their own doctors.

This larger, unofficial function of the department was to provide an open-access place of self-referral for all who wished to be seen by a doctor. Some simple souls confessed simply to have come up 'for a second opinion', some wished a delicate matter handled confidentially and some would have had difficulty finding a doctor any other way. The unofficial function thus served not only to provide medical cover for the city's transient population, from tramps to tourist, but also to protect certain of the lieges from the laziness, ignorance or inaccessibility of their general practitioners.

It was a delicate area. Not infrequently, when faced with the obvious consequences of neglect or mismanagement by an established and virtually invulnerable member of the profession, a casualty officer one or two years out of the egg had to treat the patient and save the day without being seen to rend the seamless garment of professional solidarity. It was sometimes tempting to enquire about details of previous contact with the GP but the safest thing to do was simply to manage the case in vacuo, minimise discussion of previous fumblings and dictate a neutral but gently educative note to the practitioner concerned, a task always most difficult when it was most necessary, in the chaotic Monday morning Minor Trauma session. Equanimity, thought Campbell, came more easily on Thursdays.

'Our commonwealth colleague's off, then.' Hadden reappeared in the coffee room, drying his hands. 'Looked as though you were there for the morning, in the ''Ismaili for Beginners'' course.'

'Quite interesting. I'd never come across it before.'

'Got a chunk of his life-story myself earlier, before you lot came in. He's on a slightly sticky wicket with the college. Yes thanks. More coffee. And have one yourself. A bit unforthcoming on how many shots he's had already at the wee test.'

'How many shots are you allowed?'

'As many as you want. This college reserves the right to take sixty pounds three times a year from silly buggers for as long as the cheques don't bounce. Don't the Physicians do the same?'

'No. Four attempts at Part One. I think. But I've never been into it. The matter never arose.'

'Ooh, clever. I'm surprised they don't change and run it as a growth industry the way the Surgeons do. Last time I was down there the place certainly looked as if it could do with redecoration.'

'Poor old Hakeem. But I expect the Aga Khan's paying.'

'That's another thing. Taking money from those poor Pakis probably counts as an invisible export. The College doing its bit. Backing Britain and all that. Seriously, Hakeem sounds as if he's got a problem. Reading between the lines this morning he seems to know a hell of a lot about the exam. Everthing except how to pass it . . . Thanks. Had problems with physiology, and for God's sake you don't need much of that to squeeze through. But OK on the parrot stuff, I expect. Tell you a hundred and one anatomical facts about obscure little muscles like extractor digiti minimi, and seems to revel in reciting polysyllabic pathology.'

'Fairly brave of him, sitting the exam after a week of nights.'

'Maybe. But it's not till Wednesday. Time to get your biological clock right way up again. And just now he can sleep all day and work all night. Not a mouse stirs, like the man said. And the cockroaches don't make that much noise.'

'Is there much about?'

'Not a lot. I've just tidied up Minor Trauma again. One chap with flu and a police inspector who unrolled his roll-up garage door on his big toe. First offence. I let him off with an X-ray and a warning. Honestly don't know whether this place is worse when it's too quiet or too busy.'

'Don't know. Any idea what J.G. wanted to see Andrew about?'

'No idea. He hasn't said very much for about a week. But I did hear that a fractured pelvis had slipped through and only got picked up when the radiologist checked the films the next day.'

'Difficult.'

'There but for the grace of God and by courtesy of the Medical Defence Union goes any one of us. His record's not all that good though. And he's not happy here. God knows why he wants to be a surgeon. It's as if he's always waiting for the heavy hand from J.G.

59

You know. Taken aside, fatherly hand on the shoulder, then "General practice, my boy. Have you thought of it. Good openings here and there. No shame in it. And you can rely on me for a reference . . . for general practice."'

'Does he do that?'

'Been known to.'

'Anyone we know?'

'Blair. Johnny Blair. Year above me. He's probably the last it's happened to. Little chap. Prematurely bald. No wonder.'

'GP now?'

'Ignored the good advice. Went off to the Navy. Sad tale. I think it's true. He was on one night, a Friday, and the place was busy. Hibs and Hearts were both playing at home and the pubs had shut and the place was filling up. Usual kind of thing, blood and vomit everywhere and the medical registrar standing in the middle of it all in trolleys lost in the mysteries of someone's ECG, with a football riot swirling round him. And a chap was brought in from the cells in the High Street. Typical story. Slipped on the steps. They must have thought they'd killed him otherwise they'd have left him till morning. Anyway, this chap was marched in with a cut head and his arm up his back, and sat quietly for a while then was put through in trolleys as a head injury for assessment, with a couple of cops still hanging close by to see he didn't escape or explain how he'd cut his head or do anything liable to cause a breach of the peace like that. Our Johnny was doing the needful: put out your tongue, how many fingers do you see and all that, when the chap suddenly went quite wild, yelled something about purple alligators and fleeing from the wrath to come, and leapt off the trolley. The gendarmes weren't too keen on this, but they were a bit slow and he got as far as the door of trolleys, just into the main corridor, when one of them got a hand on him and brought him down.'

'He fought quite hard and he went on fighting. The other cop leapt in, not careful or anything, and you know how when something like that happens all sorts of nasty people want to help. Porters, those ambulancemen with Rommel hats, all that lot want to have a go. Our hero was a big bloke, twice the size of wee Johnny who was by now standing well clear thumbing his Casualty Officer's Handbook, and thinking what might be the best thing to do. Meanwhile, they're all in a great big heap on the floor, with this chap in the middle thrashing around and shouting about everyone being damned, and not really assisting the police with their enquiries at all. I think there was even a chap who was supposed to be having a coronary, holding a leg or something.'

'Anyway, wee Johnny found the place and read all about acute psychosis and the nurse had drawn him up some haloperidol. The only problem was getting the man to hold his arm still for the nice doctor. He mentioned that to a few people in the heap and eventually somebody yelled 'Got him, doc,' and gave him an arm with nice veins all over it. He shoved in a quick mainline ten milligrams and breathed a sigh of relief. Everyone sort of got up and dusted themselves and said 'Great effort' and 'Tough bastard' and all this, then one of the policemen clutched his arm and dropped to the floor, out cold, and the lunatic scrambled to his feet and streaked off into the night.'

'Good yarn.'

'Yes. Don't know if it's true. But if it was going to happen it would happen to someone like Johnny Blair. Casualty wasn't his lucky job. Anyway he's off in the Queen's Navee, prescribing stoppage of rum as a sharp medicine but a cure for all seamanlike diseases'.

'So J.G. plans your career.'

'If you let him.'

'I think he's planning my finances now.'

'Well, he's got the connections ... Wee Johnny had some redeeming features.' Hadden took up his saga in his *BMJ* obituary voice. 'He used to take the piss out of Sister something rotten.' The light came on.

'Hello. Any doctors there?' Hadden glanced at Campbell to make it clear that the junior doctor present should answer such enquiries. 'Hello. Any doctors there?'

'Yes.'

'A crash box call. Came in just now. Multiple injuries. Be in in about ten minutes they said.'

'Thanks. We'll be ready.'

'Right. I'll let you know when it comes in.'

Hadden settled back in his chair, and Campbell did likewise. There had been a time, perhaps five weeks previously, when he would have gone round and hung about the front of the department or checked the equipment in the resuscitation room. '(He had done that only once: nurses' reaction had deterred him from ever doing it again). Now, a hardened veteran of six weeks on the Casualty scene, he was prepared to sit and wait, in the knowledge that the equipment was all in order, and that he would cope no better and no worse for having abandoned the comfort of his armchair any earlier than was strictly necessary. That did not, however, stop him from wondering what problems he might face when the victim arrived. Multiple injuries could mean anything from two broken toes to death in a welter of blood.

'You can take it,' said Hadden. 'Let me know if it's anything you're worried about.'

'Fine.'

'Who was that?'

'Who?' Hadden nodded at the intercom.

'Oh, I think she's called Mary,' said Campbell.

'The dark girl?'

'That's the one.'

'With a soulful expression that always makes me think she's got dysmenorrhea?'

'Yes. Her. I think she has . . .' Campbell couldn't remember how he'd come across that scrap of useless information, but was pretty sure it was true.

'Looks the type,' said Hadden. 'I used to work with a sister like that when I was a houseman. For two weeks out of every four she was a normal human being, well, normal for a ward sister in this place, then for a week she'd go manic and clean everything on the ward, then for a week she'd tear your arm off just because it was there. She'd given all of us hell for a whole ward round one day, and we were going for coffee, herself in the lead, and old Gentleman Jim Johnston standing holding the door open for us in his old-fashioned way as we trooped past in strict order of seniority. He was shaking his head slowly and muttering, ''Phases of the moon, boys, phases of the moon.''' '

'Hello. Hello. Dr Campbell.'

'Yes.'

'He's here. Could you come right away.'

'That was quick,' said Hadden. 'Let me know if you want any help.'

'Thanks.'

There were four people in the resuscitation room In addition to the patient, who was lying on a trolley in the middle, under the lights and the X-ray machine, there was the nurse, who looked even seedier than Campbell had expected, and two men in dark uniforms, with peaked caps and little silver badges on their shoulders. They didn't look as if they were going to go away. The nurse was taking the man's pulse. Campbell addressed one of the uniformed men. 'What's the story?'

'Found lying on the floor.'

'Couldn't get up,' the other man added.

'Three floors down from his own corridor,' said the first man. 'Must have climbed the wire.'

'Nice popular chap too. Nobody had it in for him,' said the other.

'His pulse is just over a hundred, Dr Campbell.'

'Thanks, nurse.' Campbell turned to the man in uniform again. 'So he fell three storeys.'

'No. He jumped.'

'Unconscious?'

'Not when he was found.'

'Lying long?'

'Don't think so. There's always people going through that bit.'

'Thanks. Do you want to go and wait in the waiting room?'

'Can't.' The man who appeared to be in charge pointed to his colleague's wrist, which was attached to that of the patient by a pair of handcuffs. 'He's dangerous.'

'I see. OK. Thanks.'

The man was a middle-aged prisoner, described as dangerous, who had fallen three floors in circumstances that it was someone else's job to elucidate. And he had not been unconscious. Campbell went to the head of the trolley and looked at the patient's face.

'Just leave me alone. I wanted to do it. I wish I was dead.' The man's voice was faint and his lips pale and dry.

'You're in hospital now,' said Campbell. 'I want to examine you.'

'Don't bother. Just leave me, son. I think I still might die.'

'I'm sorry you feel like that, but I still want to examine you. Where does it hurt . . . most?'

'Look, son, if I was dead it would all be over and it wouldn't hurt at all. Can you not just leave me alone to take my chance?'

The man wasn't going to help, so Campbell just got on with examining him, starting at the top. He checked the scalp for lacerations, or other evidence of head injury, then gently moved the man's neck and ran his hands over his shoulders, arms and chest. The patient moaned softly and distantly, indifferent to what was going on. His clothes were rough and smelly, battledress trousers and top, dyed deep prison blue, and a coarse twill shirt. Campbell pulled the clothes away to look at the man's belly.

'His BP's a bit down, Dr Campbell.'

'How far down?'

The nurse showed him a chart. The blood pressure was low but not alarming. Campbell laid the head of his stethoscope against the pale, slightly greasy skin of the man's abdomen and listened, holding his breath.

'I'm not very clean, son.'

'That's all right.'

'He's cleaner than some,' said the doppelganger on the other end of the handcuffs. Campbell frowned intently over his task to make the warder keep silence.

He listened carefully, for as long as was comfortable, took a deep breath and listened again. There were none of the normal sounds of the healthy abdomen. It was absolutely quiet. Campbell put away his stethoscope and felt it again. There was nothing remarkable, just a soft, normal-feeling belly with no lumps in it, and no tender places, but, given the story of a long fall and the abnormal absence of bowel sounds, there was a fair chance that something serious was wrong. Without being an expert on falls from the third floor, a casualty officer of ordinary experience and knowledge could hazard a guess that the man's liver or spleen might have been damaged by the impact, and either could bleed quite fast enough to make the unfortunate patient's wish come true fairly quickly.

'Could we put up a drip, nurse?'

'Ready when you are. Which side?'

'This side.' It would be easier to put up a drip on an arm without handcuffs and a prison officer attached to it.

'I'll get out of you way,' said the unattached officer. 'All right, doc . . .? And I'll be just round the corner if you need me, Kevin.' Campbell put his tourniquet round the prisoner's free arm, a little surprised to discover that prison officers had christian names and used them in the presence of dangerous criminals. He did not find a vein first time, and had to ask the nurse for another cannula. She handed him one, with an expression of disapproval as though to remind him that these things cost money.

'Can I sit down, please?'

'Hang on a minute, please . . . That's OK. Run it now. Open it up. Right up. Good. Thanks.'

'I really would like to sit down,' said the prison officer. Campbell looked up. The face under the glossy black peak was so pale as to be almost green.

'There aren't any chairs here,' said the nurse. 'It's a resuscitation room.'

The man moaned quietly and his knees folded under him. He fell untidily to the floor and lay there with one arm up, the hand dangling limply from its steel bracelet.

'Bloody hell,' said Campbell. The man on the trolley tugged at his doppelganger.

'Are you all right, Kevin?'

It was all getting a bit complicated. Campbell was beginning to feel that he could, without any loss of face, get some help with this increasingly difficult clinical problem. After all, even the nurse was looking quite poorly. He left the drip running and went over to the intercom and pressed the button marked 'Minor Trauma'.

'Mr Hadden?'

'Try round the back,' said the voice of Nurse McCraw. Campbell pressed a button labelled 'Room Nine'.

'Graham?'

'Hello, lad.'

'There's a prison warder hanging around somewhere. Could you get him round to resuscitation quickly please. And if he won't come ask him for the keys for the handcuffs. And if you would perhaps come round yourself anyway, when you've found him.'

'This isn't the first of April or anything.'

'No. I'm afraid it's for real.'

'OK, lad. See you shortly.'

'Thanks.'

Campbell went back to the jailer on the floor. He was too young for a heart attack and in any case looked like a straightforward faint: he was pale, out cold and his pulse was very slow. The author of the celebrated advice about loosening all tight articles of clothing had probably never thought of handcuffs, but help with that problem was just around the corner, so to speak, so Campbell contented himself with slackening off the man's collar and belt, and turned his attention to the prisoner on the trolley once more.

'Is Kevin all right?'

'Fainted.'

'He's not one of the worst. Just started.'

'What about you?'

'I was trying to kill myself. And it doesn't seem to have worked.'

'Any pain in your belly.'

'It's not bad. My legs are worse, And my back.'

'Where in your back?'

'Low down. And it's worse when I try to move my feet.'

'Well, young Campbell, what's going on here?' Hadden bent down to unlock the handcuffs.

'Campbell indicated the man on the trolley. 'He's supposed to be dangerous . . . And he's fainted.'

'I'm not dangerous,' said the man on the trolley. 'Not even to myself. I've tried.'

'What's the story?'

'Jumped from the third floor. Not knocked out. His belly's quiet and he says it's sore.'

'Anything to feel?'

'No.'

'Fractures?'

'Haven't found any,' said Campbell. 'Yet.'

'Let's have a look,' said Hadden.

'I've been over his neck and arms. Nothing. His back and his legs are sore.'

'That's what you'd expect. Bloody sore. Let's see.' Hadden slid a hand under the prisoner. 'Sore there?'

'Hellish.'

He gripped the man's pelvis and gently squeezed it. The man grimaced and writhed painfully. 'Are your knees sore?'

'Yes. And my feet.'

'They usually do their calcanei, their tibial tables and the lumbar vertebrae. Sometimes their hips. Best just to X-ray more or less everything. Got a drip up? Good. Give him some blood, because with that lot he's either lost or's going to lose four pints, even disregarding his belly, which might be worth another three or four.' That was an impressive tally, considering most people had only about eight to start with. 'Did you take blood for cross matching?'

'Yes. There should be plenty.'

'Good. I'll organise the X-rays if you go and ring BTS and do the forms and get a porter to take the stuff down right away. At the rush. You got his name and all that.'

'No. The warder'll have it though. Where did you find him?'

'At the desk. And don't worry about this one. He'll crawl to the touch-line when he wakes up. You got some plasma made up, nurse?'

Campbell started on the BTS forms while Hadden buzzed the X-ray girls on the intercom. ('And bring plenty of plates. There's not much of him I don't want pictures of.') The man on the trolley was now looking very pale indeed.

The conscious prison officer was at the desk talking to the clerkess. He had recovered his composure, was chatting up the girl, and appeared to be doing quite well. Was there no lower limit to the appeal of a uniform?

'Excuse me,' said Campbell. 'Have we got a name for this man?'

'Sure, doc . . . Just giving the particulars to this young lady. He's called Hislop. James Hislop. Not a bad lad, either, considering what he's in for.'

'Really. H.Y.S. or H.I.S.?

'H.I.S. Attempted murder.'

And failed suicide, thought Campbell, writing in the man's details including his normal place of residence, which could be taken for granted. 'What age?'

'Fifty-four.'

'Thanks.' He scribbled in the other blank spaces on the BTS form. Most of them got 'Not Known' or 'Not Applicable'. ('State number, date and outcome of previous pregnancies. Give full details of any complications.') The important thing was to get blood for the man quickly.

The porters were having tea when Campbell disturbed them, but then porters were almost always having tea. The oldest one smiled. 'An urgent one, doc? No trouble. Young John here will be right with you.' Young John took another mouthful of tea and got up, with a resigned expression on his face. Campbell tried to make the job sound sufficiently important and interesting to merit doing quickly. 'A multiple injury from the jail. Probably needs about six pints.'

The porter, a sallow youth with dead eyes, looked at him pityingly and sauntered off with tube and form. Campbell wondered if, given occasional issues of official free milk, they might run sometimes.

Back in the resuscitation room, X-ray screens surrounded the trolley, and the radiographer in the control box in the corner had taken temporary command. Her camera, suspended from the ceiling, tracked over the patient and its focussing light shone on successive squares of him, as her assistant slid the plates in and out of the slots under the trolley. The lights and warning buzzes, the assistant armoured in her dark grey lead lined apron, and the detached microphone voice from inside the control box produced the ambience of science fiction, in a distant technological exercise strangely at odds with the broken unhappy man at its centre, in his prison clothes. On the drip stand the original clear saline had been replaced by a bottle of opalescent plasma, golden in colour and half run through already. Hadden was talking on the phone in the corner. The prison officer who had fainted was now fully recovered and stood sheepishly by, the vacant handcuffs trailing from his wrist.

'Can we just leave him like that till we see what the pictures are like and what's come up?' The X-ray girl had come out of her box.

'Fine,' said Campbell. 'How long?'

'Four or five minutes for the first ones.'

'OK.' He returned yet again to the man on the trolley. The nurse was taking his blood pressure again.

'It seems to have levelled off,' she said, taking the stethoscope out of her ears. 'Hundred over sixty. Pulse is just the same too.'

Campbell picked up the clip board and marked the reported readings and the time. From the fluid chart he learned that the bottle running in was the second unit of plasma. Hadden must have been quite worried about the man's blood pressure. Attached to the chart was another printed form with a simple line drawing of a man, face on. It was used in the department for recording injuries graphically and quickly. The face of this cypher, the casualty man, the anonymous and universal victim, bore an expression of dumb acceptance, not unlike the prisoner patient's. His hands were by his sides, palms forward, and his feet at a slightly awkward 'attention'. Hadden had annotated him with double lined crosses and question marks, casualty shorthand for possible fractures, at heels, ankles, knees, hips, pelvis and lumbar spine. Casualty man could take it. There were hundreds more forms in a pile on the desk.

The man on the trolley moaned, and Campbell wondered first if he'd had anything for pain and then if there were any good medical reason for not giving a shot of something nice. The possible abdominal injury might be more difficult to assess after a powerful analgesic, but that problem had to be considered in the context of the pain from all his other injuries. He scribbled on the treatment chart and handed it to the nurse.

'Could you give him some morphine. Fifteen please.' The man moaned again and Campbell bent over him to assess his abdomen once more before the injection. It was less soft, and when he listened it was quiet, just as before. The nurse opened the dangerous drugs cabinet, high on the wall: a small white metal cube with a red light on top which came on when the door was opened, and another yellowish light inside which lit the nurse's pale thin features and her hands as she reached inside. She took down a small cardboard box and slid it open.

'Check this, please, Dr Campbell.'

'Right.' Dangerous drugs were always handled by staff in pairs, usually both nurses, who recorded the removal and use of each dose, and signed a register that was checked regularly to prevent loss or misuse of substances at once therapeutically indispensable but also subject to abuse and therefore commercially attractive, even in Edinburgh.

Campbell checked the number of vials in the box and the number recorded in the register while the nurse snapped the top from the vial, drew up sterile water for injection from another vial and added it to the airy white crystals in the first. She drew it up, expelled it and drew it up once more to mix it, the small practised movements of her pale hands, under the lit cupboard, with the open book still lying there making a little ritual of preparing the drug for injection, abruptly terminated when she closed the door and locked it, and put the loaded syringe in a stainless steel dish and walked back towards the patient.

'Just a wee jag in your bottom, Mr Hislop.' On hearing that, Campbell went over for a quiet word. The site of injection chosen was traditional but not sacred, and in this case, where to move the man at all would be painful, and where there was local bony injury as well, it would be preferable to put the stuff in the flesh of his arm or shoulder. The nurse had started to undo the man's rough blue trousers.

'Nurse?'

'Yes, Dr Campbell.'

'Could we just put it into his deltoid. Might be less disturbing.'

Casualty staff nurses were a tough and special breed who did not take kindly to being advised on essentially nursing matters by junior medical staff. Her face set and she replaced the patient's clothing and then turned and started to roll up his sleeve, saying 'Whatever you think best, Dr Campbell,' with a trace of what might have been sarcasm. She flicked the skin with a cleaning swab and deftly inserted the needle, half-pushing, half-throwing it, with a skill Campbell had long envied but never mastered. She drove the clear fluid into the mass of shoulder muscle and smiled acidly. 'Will that be all right, Dr Campbell?'

He had not meant to offend her. Quite often nurses did things automatically, on the tramlines of their rigidly authoritarian training, without taking much thought for variations in individual circumstances. She went over to the book and glumly signed her name in the space which recorded who had administered the drug.

'Sorry, nurse. He's mostly fractures from the waist down. More comfortable to use his arm.'

'Of course, Dr Campbell.'

Hadden marched in with a fistful of X-ray pictures and switched on the row of viewing boxes on the end wall. Their lights flickered and came up. He slammed the films one by one up into the clips above the screens then stood back to view the collection, his face lit by the glow of the fluorescent light. Campbell joined him for a muttered conference. The staff nurse hung back, still looking offended.

'The poor bugger's got just about the lot. What Every Young Orthopod Should Know About Compression Fractures. Look. Both calcanei, that one displaced. And both ankles look a bit messy. That knee, the right. He's done the tibial table and sheared a condyle above. And his pelvis. Look. There and there. And a crushed lumbar vertebra. Third. No. The fourth.'

Considering the speed at which they had been produced, the pictures were very good. From left to right on the white-lit viewing boxes they told a tale of skeletal destruction, starting from the heels and extending in grisly series right up into the spine.

'What's his future?' Campbell asked.

'Well, for a start he'll be about two inches shorter. But he'll walk again, after a while. And he's going to need a lot of nifty carpentry right away. I've rung the duty orthopod bod already. It's funny, these chaps do end up a couple of inches shorter, when it's all over.'

'Poor bugger.'

'Has he had anything for the pain?'

'I gave him fifteen of morphine.'

'Good lad.'

'I worried about his belly, though.'

'Oh, no. He needed the morphine and they'll have to open his belly anyway. My money would be on a liver. Or maybe a spleen. I've rung the duty surgeon. Has any blood arrived?'

'Don't think so.'

'We should probably sling up some more plasma. How's his conscious level?'

'Not too bright.'

'Hm. Let's see.' They went from the X-rays back to the patient.

'Mr Hislop,' said Hadden in a loud but respectful conversational voice. 'Mr Hislop.' The man's eyelids flickered and opened. 'How d'you feel?'

'The pain's not so bad . . . Light-headed. A bit.'

Hadden picked up the BP chart and reached over and speeded up the drip. 'Mr Hislop, I've asked a couple of specialists to come down and see you. You're going to be all right, but you're going to need an operation. Probably soon.'

'I'd rather be dead,' said the man faintly.

Hadden reached for the clipboard and jotted down the X-ray findings, then came over and joined Campbell, who was still looking at the plates. Hadden stood back and looked at them again, then closed in, starting on the left, with the pictures of the man's feet, and working slowly along the row.

'We've found so much that we must be missing something.'

'What else do they get?'

'Well, they sometimes do their hips. Fractures or fracture-dislocations. And neck injuries, maybe just whiplash, but sometimes compression fractures, are on the cards. He's really been smashed up. What's he in for anyway?'

'Attempted murder.'

'Poor sod . . . Oh, that's interesting. Look. He's taken the tip off one of the transverse processes of that lumbar vertebra. And there in

70

the same picture, look at the muscle shadows. Clear on the left, blurred on the right. Not a great soft-tissue film, but it makes you think about a big collection of blood in there.'

'Quite correct, Graham.' A third persons had joined them silently and now spoke. 'I suppose we'd better tackle that before our orthopaedic colleagues begin more time-consuming tasks on less life-threatening injuries. What age did you say he was?'

'Fifty-four,' said Campbell.

'Thank you, David. So we all must stop what we're doing and scrub up and go into theatre with a fifty-four year old murderer.'

'Attempted murderer, Mr Laird.'

'Thank you, David.' Gavin Laird, who had been an embittered surgical senior registrar a year previously, was still a senior registrar and perhaps more embittered. He smiled a small chilly smile. 'That knowledge adds greatly to the privilege of saving his life. Is he cross-matched?'

'Six pints on the way.'

'Thank you. And bowel sounds?'

'None.'

'Head injury?'

'No evidence of it.'

Mr Laird smiled again. 'You're getting cautious in your old age, David. A year ago you'd have said simply ''No'' ... Ah well. And you mentioned this patient's name on the phone, Graham?'

'Hislop.'

'Ah yes. Mr Hislop. Address, Her Majesty's Porridge Factory. And we know his attempted occupation.' Gavin, despite being a man who rarely did anything unkind, retained his irritating habit of sounding capable of any enormity. 'His lodgings cost us sixty-five pounds a week, I've heard. But of course a bed in here runs at about a hundred and twenty. So the sooner we get him fit to go back there the better.' He talked quietly and civilly, scanning the X-rays, then pointed to a tiny fleck of detached bone in the man's neck, which neither Hadden nor Campbell had noticed. 'Some trivial ligamentous injury to the neck.' He smiled again. 'Lucky to have got away with just that.'

Hadden and Campbell followed him across to the prisoner, and watched as he examined the man's abdomen with great skill and gentleness, and talked to him with the utmost civility. Then he glanced over the various charts on the clipboard and asked the junior doctors if the orthopaedic surgeon was expected to be much longer. Hadden said he didn't know, but that he had left the man in no doubt as to the urgency of the case.

71

'Perhaps you could give him a ring again, Graham.' Because both Campbell and Hadden had worked under Gavin a year before, they recognised that as an urgent order. Hadden complied immediately.

'Did Mr Hadden say which orthopaedic surgeon he'd spoken to, David?'

'No.'

'Ah well.' He looked at the charts again then slowed down the rate of flow of the plasma. 'Pity to drown the poor chap simply because the orthopod hasn't turned up.'

Hadden was still on the phone when the orthopod arrived. He was breathless and apologetic. He appeared to know Gavin, but not to like him, and they stood in front of the X-rays at a polite distance, discussing the case, then came and took the clipboard away and discussed it further.

'Gavin-baby doesn't change much,' said Hadden.

'Pity.'

'Still, I suppose even quite a nice chap could get like that just from working with Ravelston Orr for as long as he's been there.'

'Who's the orthopod?'

'O'Rarity. But at least he's white, as Gavin might say.'

Surgeon and orthopod returned from their fluorescent-lit conclave. 'Mr O'Rarity agrees that the abdomen needs a little daylight in it as a matter of urgency, and he can chip away at the rest all afternoon if necessary. So if you can kindly persuade the porters to move him . . . And send the blood up when it comes, or better still divert it at source. Thank you, David.'

All four doctors left the prisoner, who was having his blood pressure taken for perhaps the tenth time by the nurse. As they did so the prison officers returned to assert their authority. The senior one released his colleague from the vacant handcuffs, and then went over and applied one bracelet to his prisoner's wrist, and the other to the frame of the trolley.

'Interesting chap,' said Hadden as they walked back along the main corridor of the department. 'You learn something new every day. That neck thing that Gavin picked up. It's advertised in the books as an occupational hazard of clay-shovellers.'

Campbell felt that he had not shone in his immediate management of the case, and that he would feel better if he told someone so. 'I was a bit slow finding his fractures.'

'You started at the wrong end, lad. Comes with experience. Though I suppose you'd have noticed if he'd fallen three floors on to his head. And then everybody forgets how much blood goes west in fractures.

There's a cheerful little table about it in one of the big books if you're interested.'

'Thanks. Nothing in trolleys?'

'No. So it's back to the suffering millions in triviatrics, I suppose. I'm sure they just come in there out of the rain.'

'Dr Campbell.' A clerkess from the front desk ambushed him as they passed. 'There was a phone call for you. She said it could wait if you were busy and I said you were. Dr Moray in Endocrinology Out-patients.'

'Thanks, Hazel.'

'Are you still keeping up your interest in that lady's glands?' enquired Hadden, without malice. 'I thought it was all drawing peacefully towards its close.'

'That's probably what she's phoning about.'

Campbell went on to the room at the back and Hadden turned off to Minor Trauma. Jean seldom phoned the department, so seldom that she thought she could be quite open about it, giving her name to the girl at the desk as she had just done. When she did phone it was usually about something important. There was no one in the coffee room and Campbell found himself dialling her extension without having to think what the number was.

'Hello.'

'David, I've got a patient. I'll ring back. No. You ring me here in five minutes.'

'Fine. Bye.'

'Bye.'

Back in Minor Trauma Campbell picked up the clipboard of notes concerning a fat lady with a sprained ankle. At the next cubicle Hadden was writing about another sprained ankle. He muttered from the side of his mouth, 'The end came suddenly and as a merciful release.'

'Hm?'

'That was quick. Is it ''No letters, no flowers, please''?'

'Piss off,' said Campbell, very quietly so that the patients wouldn't hear. The lady with the sprained ankle averted her eyes. Campbell, slightly pink, put on his doctor voice and asked the usual questions about how her unfortunate injury had been acquired. He scribbled the X-ray card, wondering what Jean wanted to talk to him urgently about, and got the side of the injury wrong, an error he noticed only as he handed the card to the X-ray girl, who looked rather supercilious while he changed it.

73

The next patient was a little old lady with a hat consisting mostly of shiny black beads, and embellished with a selection of wax fruit. Her teeth did not fit very well, and she smacked her lips a lot in an effort to control them. She apologised several times for coming up, before getting round to what was wrong with her, and her story began slowly, with a complex preamble concerning a milk bottle and a cat, and her customary evening routine, interrupted on this occasion by the appearance of a strange tom. The climax of the tale revolved around the defence of her tabby's virtue, a close-run thing, to hear her talk, then, rather as an afterthought, she mentioned that she had fallen and hurt her wrist.

'I see,' said Campbell. 'Which wrist?'

'The right one,' she said, still holding her handbag on her lap with both hands. 'Oh . . . Would you like to see it?'

'Yes, please. If you don't mind.'

'Not at all. To tell you the truth, it's quite painful. Kept me awake for a large part of the night.'

'Could I see it?'

'Yes, of course.' She stuck out a bony wrist, obviously deformed by a fracture just above the base of the thumb.

'You fell with your hand out?'

'Yes. Trying to save my pussy.'

'I see. Any other injuries?'

'Oh, no. Just my wrist.'

Campbell gently palpated the bones of the wrist. There was a step-like discontinuity in the normal contour of the radius. He quickly checked the pulses and then tested the cutaneous sensation in her hand. 'Feel that? Good. That? Fine. We'll get it X-rayed and then set it for you. When did you last eat?'

'What?'

'When did you last have something to eat? It's for the anaesthetic. They don't like doing it too soon after a meal.'

'Dear me,' said the lady. 'I didn't know about this. I never thought I'd need chloroform for a wee thing like this.'

'Nowadays it's something nicer than chloroform. You won't feel a thing and you'll be fine, and fit to go home after an hour or two lying down.'

'But I'll get home tonight . . .' she said distantly. For some reason Campbell envisaged battalions of rampant tomcats assembling in her mind's eye. 'There's pussy to think of.'

'Oh, yes . . . You'll be fine by this evening.' Campbell scribbled the X-ray card, getting the side right, then remembered about phoning

74

Jean. 'When did you have breakfast?'

'Oh. The usual time.'

'When would that be, roughly?'

'About seven. I have an egg and . . .'

'Oh, well. That'll be fine. A quick X-ray now, then later a little injection to give you a sleep while I straighten it for you, then a plaster on your arm, and in a few weeks you'll never know you've had it.'

'Weeks? In a plaster? Me?'

'That's the best way of dealing with this sort of thing . . . Miss Warrender,' said Campbell firmly, glancing at the notes again to get the name right. 'I'll arrange it all now.'

The lady's injury was an absolutely standard problem, to be dealt with according to a standard procedure. The particular fracture, whose familiar name immortalised one Dr Colles, of whom nothing else was known or remembered save that he had described it, was a misfortune which awaited old ladies who fell on their outstretched hands. It was said, though Campbell himself had never seen this, that the first sharp frost of winter could harvest a crop of as many as a dozen, who might all arrive in the department at once. The fracture was recognised by the characteristic deformity produced by the displacement of the lower fragment of the radius, which give to the wrist a fancied resemblance to an old-fashioned dinner fork. It was treated by manipulation under anaesthetic, to restore the fragments to the alignment intended by God and Gray's Anatomy, and a plaster slab applied to keep it so until it healed.

There was no hurry. The further down her breakfast egg could travel, the less of a risk it would constitute to her respiratory tract during an anaesthetic. A quiet half hour on a trolley, with a dreamy trip into temporary oblivion at the end of it, while Campbell sorted out her arm, would suit all concerned quite admirably, if an appointment could be confirmed with the duty gasman, and the traditional operating area, the clean turret, booked with Sister. These arrangements could be fitted conveniently round coffee and a return phone call to Jean. Campbell made his way round the back.

'Hello, son.'

'Hello, Ronnie. You on here today?'

''fraid so, David. This morning anyway. Not that it's busy. Just waiting for a possible meningitis a GP rang me about half an hour ago. Said it would be in in about twenty minutes. How's things?'

Ronnie Bertram had been Campbell's mentor in younger, happier days. As registrar when Campbell had been a houseman, he had filled the duty room with pipesmoke, homely wisdom and gems of medical lore ('If you don't put your finger in it, you'll put your foot in it,' 'Never let the sun set on a consultant's mother-in-law,' 'Beware of the last patient before coffee time,' 'Bleeders come first,' etc.) and passed on to Campbell the simple skills of basic doctoring: how to put up a drip, how to cast a veil over neglected investigations, how to pass on bad news and how to keep senior staff away from ill patients. Later, as an honorary lecturer, a status he acquired by a legendary coup of manipulative diplomacy, he had consoled Campbell, then miserably becalmed in the doldrums of a research appointment and then, when the time came, had provided tactical advice which had greatly expedited his escape. Now, as receiving physician, he was on duty for acute medical admissions from Casualty, seeing patients referred direct to him by their GPs and those passed on to him by department staff as too difficult to diagnose or too dangerous to discharge.

'Got any trade for me?'

'Don't think so. Trolleys is quiet. And nothing for you from Minor Trauma.'

'Busy along there?'

'Got a Colles'. Just going to ring the gasman. And book a turret.'

'Sorry. Am I keeping you back?'

'No . . .' Campbell would have rung Jean first, had Bertram not been there. Duty prevailed. He phoned the exchange and asked them to get the duty gasman to call the extension. In a few seconds he rang in, and when told about the problem asked what Miss Warrender had had for breakfast and when, and whether she would have any objection to taking part in a small clinical trial. Campbell told him about her breakfast and said he didn't know about the trial, and the gasman, sensing that Campbell would not be keen to extract informed consent for a research procedure about which he knew nothing and cared less, said he would see her himself, and gas her at the time requested.

'Can I make you some coffee, David?'

'Thanks.' Dr Bertram, an experienced receiving physician, was making himself at home in the department. He switched on the kettle and walked out of the rest room in the direction of the kitchen. Campbell buzzed Sister on the intercom.

'Sister.'

'Yes, Dr Campbell.'

'Can I have the clean turret in half an hour for a Colles', please?' There was a long, grudging pause.

'Could you not make do with the dirty turret, Dr Campbell.'

'It's not a dirty procedure.'

'All right, Dr Campbell, no need to shout.'

'Thank you, Sister.'

Bertram come back. 'What's that stupid bitch been up to? There's a bloody great brass padlock on the kitchen fridge.'

'What?'

'Honest. Like Shirley Temple's chastity belt. Or the bloody Bastille.'

Campbell hoped Sister was listening. 'Something to do with milk, I believe.'

'I knew she'd go mad. She's had the look for ages. They're not British up there, you know . . . They just pretend they are, for the National Assistance, ochone, ochone, and the Hill Farm Rough Grazing Drainage Subsidy.'

Even though the intercom light was off, Sister could still be listening to this outburst of lowland backlash, because the call had been initiated from the doctors room end. Campbell pointed to the cupboard where Hakeem had hidden the milk, put a finger to his lips and pointed to the intercom. Bertram looked puzzled, then understood. He poured milk into the two cups of coffee muttering, 'If I didn't know you'd just started here six weeks ago, I'd say you'd been here too long. Do you have a lot of this sort of problem?'

'Fair amount lately.'

The phone rang and Campbell picked it up. It was Jean.

'You're off this afternoon, aren't you?'

'Yes.'

'So am I. See you at two.'

'Where?'

'Your flat.'

Campbell began to say, yes, that would be nice, but Jean had put the phone down. He reached for his coffee.

'What's she keeping in there?'

'Official milk.'

'What's that I put in our coffee?'

'Unofficial milk.' Bertram looked suspiciously at his cup. 'You know. Private milk. Non-NHS milk.'

'Oh. I see. To do with that circular about milk.'

'Yes.'

'You know it doesn't actually mention milk?'

'Doesn't it?'

'No.'

'I don't know. I haven't read it. I'm surprised you have.'

'Oh, I haven't, but somehow a copy got sent to old Creech. Because he's in administrative charge of the unit, I suppose. And it really gave him something to get his teeth into. He wrote to the district administrator, asking for information about the background to the circular, and got a four page letter and a sheaf of photostats, really just saying it was about milk. Then he queried a couple of minor points in that lot of bumph, and got another letter, this time about six pages, quoting extracts of committee minutes in detail, and with a Home and Health Department circular appended. That really made his week. Then he wrote asking for a distribution list and when he got the answer he disappeared into his office with his pocket calculator, and came out a couple of days later and showed us all a letter he'd drafted to the district administrator, all about making certain assumptions as to secretarial costs, stationery and distribution and so on, but assuring the bureaucrat concerned that the expense of the whole exercise, circular and correspondence, was equivalent to the cost of about two hundred gallons of milk so far, and had he thought of any satisfactory way of proving his efforts were cost-effective.'

'Good for Henry. Nice to know he's busy and happy.'

'Oh, he's fine. Rosamund's not doing too well, though.'

'Oh?' Rosamund had supervised Campbell's research misadventure.

'Some difficulties about original work for publication . . . Not original enough.'

'Really?'

'So the referees thought. In fact one chap who was sent it to read thought he'd published the stuff himself, and wrote to her saying so. Tense, it was, up there for a while. Fortunately the other chap had something to hide too, and when Rosamund found that out they arranged a kind of Mexican stand-off, and the two of them got together and published the third chap's work jointly. And then she had some difficulty filling your post.'

'I'm not surprised,' said Campbell, who had wasted six months in the wilderness in pursuit of scientific glory for Rosamund.

'In fact she's getting a bit paranoid about her staff generally. Even me. Wore the good suit to work the other day, because the other one was at the cleaners. She must have suspected I was sneaking off quietly somewhere for an interview, because at tea she said something dark about hoping nobody else was thinking of doing a Campbell, as she put it. So you're famous, son. The one that got away. And we're all jealous.'

'I've got no regrets. It's nice to get up in the mornings and not have to pretend I believe in faecal vitamins.'

'You're looking well on it, David. I'm having doubts myself again. In fact on Sunday there we left the kids with their granny and sneaked off to look at a nice wee practice down near Ayr. Golf. and a lovely school for wee Karen. Nearly didn't come in on Monday . . .' From his pockets Bertram produced an assortment of matches, pipe cleaners, and the sundry gadgetry of his hobby, and began a leisurely and elaborate pipe-ritual, expanding as he did so on the delights of life in general practice, as he was wont to do regularly, though he had never, to Campbell's knowledge, done anything definitive about ending his career in hospital medicine.

'Dr Campbell,' Sister whined once more from the intercom. 'The anaesthetist's been waiting for quite some time . . . Dr Campbell.'

'Is that the silly bitch who locked up the milk?' said Bertram, whom Campbell now suspected of being conversant with the communication system of the department.

'Thank you, Sister,' said Campbell.

Campbell and Bertram got up.

'Ah, well, mustn't keep a busy casualty officer from his work. Wonder what's happened to that bloody meningitis. Must have been migraine after all, and gone away before the ambulance came.'

'Now, Miss Warrender, just a wee jag in the back of your hand, and I want you to think of something nice. You don't mind the flavour of onions, do you?'

'What, doctor?'

The anaesthetist smiled professionally. 'Some people get a funny taste like onions in the back of their mouths with this stuff I'm using to put you to sleep, but I'm sure it won't worry you if you know it's going to happen. Anyway, never mind the onions, just lie there and think of something nice. What's the nicest place you've ever been on holiday?'

'Oh, we always went to Elie as children.'

'Lovely little place. Perfect for families. No pain in your hand?'

'No, doctor. Of course we always had a house of our own, over-looking the East Bay.'

'Loveliest part of Elie.'

'Lovely . . . Oh, dear . . . Onions . . .'

'There you are, Campbell. You could take her tonsils out with your bare hands and do her piles as an encore and she wouldn't twitch an eyelid.'

'Thanks, Bill.'

The clean turret, where they were working, was one of the two small operating theatres attached to the department. These theatres, fitted with basic anaesthetic and resuscitation equipment, were used for minor procedures on day patients, and were known as the turrets because they occupied the bases of two round Scottish baronial towers adorning the corners of the pavilion which housed the department. In the dirty turret, boils were lanced, septic toenails avulsed, and abscesses drained with fine pre-Listerian abandon, while in its clean counterpart, certain standards were maintained, and only patients whose injuries were clean, or closed like Miss Warrender's, were dealt with there.

The clean turret was certainly the more pleasant of the two. Unlike its north-facing partner, gloomy, smelling of patients, cleaners and cleaning, and referred to by Hadden as 'the abattoir', it was a sunny, airy place, well lit by daylight for most of the morning and afternoon. Sunlight sparkled on the pipes and knobs of the gasman's little machine, as he leaned forward to put a mask over his patient's face.

'How did she do this, anyway?'

'Last night. Trying to save her cat from sexual assault.' The gasman looked intrigued. 'By a tomcat,' Campbell added. 'Nice old girl. More worried about her pussy than about herself.'

'D'you hear that, nurse?' said the gasman, looking at the staff nurse in a way that made Campbell wish he had phrased that differently. 'A nice old-fashioned girl.' Campbell did not know the anaesthetist well, but gained an impression that the smoothness he had displayed initially with Miss Warrender did not reflect his true self. The staff nurse blushed. She was new to the department and, since her royal blue uniform retained its straight-out-of-the-box brightness, presumably only recently qualified.

'How is she?' said Campbell, to restore order.

'Your patient is ready, sir.'

'Thanks, Bill.'

Campbell had reduced perhaps ten or twelve Colles' fractures since coming to the department, and one or two more before that, as a student. The task was well within his competence, but not so familiar as to be dull. There was always minor variations in the degree of deformity and the quality of bone encountered, and it was an intriguingly physical task, requiring a certain amount of force and a bit of delicacy too. There were various little tricks to the manipulation, if it turned out to be anything other than straightforward, and if the fracture didn't look and feel right after a first attempt, you could go back again, as long as the patient was comfortably gassed, and have another go. Afterwards, a check X-ray showed the true position of the bones, and provided a permanent and undeniable record of success or failure.

'Have you seen this done before, nurse?'

'Just once. But I was so busy not fainting that I didn't take much in.'

'All right now?'

'Oh, that was ages ago.'

Upstaged by Campbell's adoption of the combined roles of surgeon in charge of the case and tireless clinical teacher, the anaesthetist got on with his job quietly, and took the patient's blood pressure.

Campbell picked up Miss Warrender's wrist. 'See how it's broken. There. A sort of step in the bone, with a hollow in the arm above, and that lumpy bit there that's supposed to make her hand look like . . . a dinner fork. You can see how falling on, say, the heel of the hand would snap the end of the radius, there, and push that bit back. Like that. And you can see it in the X-rays there. Now, if you'd like to hold her elbow back as I pull on her wrist. Firmly. Like that, and try not to let it rotate. Fine. I'll just pull the fracture apart, tweak it around a little and see if it pops back together the way it should be.'

There was a little more to it than that, but it was difficult to explain and Campbell preferred to wear his slender orthopaedic learning lightly. The nurse held Miss Warrender's arm back as Campbell gripped the wrist, with both hands, palms downwards, and pulled. There was an uneasy, crunchy feel as the ends of the fracture came apart, then he bent the wrist backwards and outwards a little and let the lower fragment of the broken bone settle gently back into place, or rather into what he hoped was its right place.

There was soft tissue swelling round the site of the fracture, which made the result of his efforts harder to assess, but in general it was a better looking wrist than it had been. The hollow and step had gone, and if there was any resemblance now to an old fashioned dinner fork, it was now only a very slight one.

'That might be it,' said Campbell. 'Like to feel it, nurse, before we put the slab on.'

'Yes, please.' The nurse ran her fingers over the straightened forearm. 'I see.'

The gasman, holding the mask on the patient's face with one hand, and keeping a finger on the carotid pulse in the neck at the same time, was beginning to look impatient. 'When Sir Percival Pott, or is it Sir Benjamin Brodie, is pleased to draw his fascinating teaching case towards a close, is it his wish that his humble servant the anaesthetist wakes the old faggot up, or d'you want her asleep for a check X-ray and another pull?'

'Sorry, Bill. I'm honestly not sure about this one. Rather have a quick pic, if you don't mind. I'll get the girl in.'

'I'll go,' said the nurse, who looked as if she might be glad of a breath of fresh air . . .'

'Nice little piece,' said the gasman even before she had closed the door. 'Wouldn't mind running through a few manipulations with her, under appropriate relaxation.'

'I've seen her before somewhere. I think she juniored where I did my surgical housejob. Sister liked her because she could spell.'

'How long's she been here?'

'Weeks at most. Since I came.'

'What's her form?'

'How would I know?' said Campbell. 'I only work here.' Over the previous year he had found himself increasingly detached from the great romantic teaching hospital merry-go-round, and had begun to feel a little critical of its febrile, mindless pace. Or was he simply jealous of Bones' latest adventure?

'I bet she does,' said the gasman. 'Those fragile saintly ones always go like rabbits.'

The door slid open again and the girl in question came in. 'She's just coming. The machine was along the corridor.' She was followed by a girl radiographer pushing a small X-ray machine.

'Hello, David. Oh. It's Miss Warrender. I did her first picture.'

The X-ray camera was mounted on a wheeled frame almost too big to come in through the theatre door. There was a lot of awkward shuffling and manoeuvring in the turret, with the staff nurse passing dangerously close to the anaesthetist as she went round to the other side of the patient. The X-ray girl had plugged her machine into a power point on the wall, and was looking round for something. 'Sorry,' she said. 'Silly me. Forgot to bring the plates along. Won't be a minute.' She left and the gasman settled down to embarrass the staff nurse further. Campbell checked the wrist again. It was straight enough to yield a certain workmanlike satisfaction, to be confirmed radiologically, of course.

'Is she all right?'

'What?'

The staff nurse was staring at Miss Warrender's face. 'She looks terrible.' By a very nursey reflex, commendable in one so young, she picked up the patient's uninjured wrist and took her pulse. 'Did you know her pulse is about forty?' she said accusingly, addressing the anaesthetist.

'Christ.' He whipped his stethoscope from his neck up to his ears and pumped up the blood pressure cuff wrapped round the patient's right arm. Listening to Miss Warrender's elbow for the sounds of her pulse, the gasman looked suddenly very worried. The column of mercury in the sphygmomanometer dropped slowly and steadily, far below the usual levels, without showing the tell-tale quiver in time with the patient's heartbeat.

'What's her pressure, Bill?' said Campbell, trying to make it sound casual.

'Around sixty systolic. If it's anything . . . Has she any cardiac history?'

'No. Good previous health.'

'Drugs?'

'None.' Campbell had taken a brief history, concerning previous health and medication, from Miss Warrender. A conscientious anaesthetist would have repeated this before undertaking to gas her. 'D'you want an electrocardiograph?'

'Isn't there one here?'

'No, but I can get one.'

'Thanks. And I'm going to shove a tube down her, just to be on the safe side.'

The staff nurse had started to tilt the table, to put Miss Warrender's feet above the level of her head, so that such circulation as she had would be concentrated where it mattered. Campbell pressed the intercom button for Sister's office.

'Sister?'

'Yes, Dr Campbell.'

'An ECG machine in the clean turret, please. Quickly.'

'Is it urgent, Dr Campbell? The porters . . .'

'Very urgent.'

'All right, Dr Campbell. I'll see what I can do.'

'D'you want a drip up, Bill?'

Miss Warrender's head was right back, and her mouth open. The anaesthetist was peering down her throat, with a laryngoscope in one hand and a red rubber endotracheal tube in the other. 'Thanks, if you don't mind. Her neck's a bit stiff and this tube . . .'

The staff nurse, despite the novitiate shade of her uniform, was doing well; she had unwrapped an IV giving set and plugged it into a bottle of saline, and was running it through.

'Thanks, staff . . .' Campbell re-inflated the sphygmomanometer cuff and tried to find a vein in the uninjured forearm. Miss Warrender's hand was pale and cold, and the veins practically empty. With a bit of coaxing a fragile blue line just below her elbow filled out a little. He rubbed it gently.

'Small cannula? Or a butterfly, Dr Campbell?'

'Smallest Argyle, please.'

'Got a pink one.'

'Thanks, staff.'

'Got her,' said the gasman, straightening from his task. 'These rocky old necks are a nuisance. But at least we've got an airway. What's her BP doing?'

'I'm trying to get a drip up . . . Can it wait a second?'

'Sure. We can use the other arm, when you've finished with that cuff.'

The vein Campbell was working on was a difficult one, but the best available. It was narrow and poorly filled, despite the tourniquet above, and lay just under the skin, which meant that it would be slithery and mobile and difficult to cannulate with the IV line on its guiding needle. And the best bit of it, a straight section just below the elbow, was only an inch long. Not a beginner's vein, he thought, stroking it to try and dilate it a bit more, but a nasty uncompromising one-shot vein of the sort you found on people with really shut-down peripheral circulation, who were the people who needed intravenous fluids most.

The nurse handed him a cannula from a pink container. He gave the vein a last encouraging pat, lined things up and speared in. Very very slowly, dark blood oozed back into the hilt of the needle.

'Looks all right.'

'Thanks, staff.' The nurse handed him the brimming end of the tube from the saline bottle. He drew the needle from its surrounding cannula and joined the giving set tightly in, just as blood welled up and dropped on to the patient's pale clammy skin. 'Open up.' He looked up at the drip chamber just beneath the bottle. Saline trickled through it, not rapidly but quickly enough to assure them that the line was well into a vein, not simply oozing into subcutaneous tissue. The door opened again. 'Oh,' said the X-ray girl, 'D'you still want that second picture now?'

'No thanks, Val. Perhaps if you can get your machine out . . . No. Could you please go and find out what's happening to an ECG machine that's supposed to be on its way along here.'

'Has she gone off?'

'A bit. Thanks, Val.' She disappeared again and Campbell left the nurse to look after the IV line, taping it down and splinting the elbow, while he started to shift the X-ray machine out of the turret. Even if Miss Warrender did not get any worse, it would be difficult enough to look after her with half the confined floor space of the theatre taken up by the camera and its even more bulky frame.

84

'Good idea,' said the gasman.

'What d'you think's happened?'

'Well, her systolic's still under sixty. And she's really flat. I've stopped everything and she's on pure oxygen and by rights she should have started to come up. An ECG would be the most important thing, I suppose. Her pulse is still way down.'

Miss Warrender was in her seventies, and though it was rare for previously fit seventy-year-olds to have trouble under anaesthetic, it was possible that she had been unequal to the stress, and had had a coronary while being induced, or while Campbell had been pulling her fracture.

'Hello, son.' Bertram appeared from nowhere and helped Campbell heave the X-ray machine out into the corridor. 'Having a bit of trouble?'

'Thanks, Ronnie. Yes, in a word. Previously fit seventy-something-year-old duck with an uncomplicated Colles'. Circulatory collapse while we were sorting her out under gas.'

'Not on any pills?'

'No.'

'Pulse?'

'Slow.'

'Got an ECG?'

'Just getting one.'

'Likeliest thing. Did she actually arrest?'

'No. Always had a pulse. As far as we know.'

Bertram entered the turret and nodded politely to the gasman. The nurse smiled.

'Hello, Lesley.'

'Hello, Dr Bertram.'

'Hmm.' Bertram took the patient's pulse for himself, and felt her skin with the back of his hand. 'BP?'

'Just under seventy. Coming up,' said the anaesthetist. 'On pure oxygen now, but she's still flat.'

'And no previous history?'

Campbell said 'No' and the gasman looked shifty.

'I see,' said Bertram. The door opened and the radiographer came in carrying a big blue portable electrocardiograph. 'Good. Let's wire her up and have a look at what's going on.' The anaesthetist tended the patient's airway while staff nurse, medical registrar and casualty officer applied the ECG leads in record time. Bertram ran a trial strip, tested the voltage calibration then spun the lead selector and pressed the 'record' button.

Technically the trace was less than perfect, but it was good enough to let them see the most likely cause of the trouble. In the first lead there was a gross abnormality. Instead of the neat narrow flicker of ink given by a normal heartbeat, each pattern was broadened and slurred, with a trailing hump and a deep downward deflection at the end. The rhythm was regular but very slow.

'Nasty. We'll just flick through the first six leads and not bother with the chest ones. Looks awful like a big anterior, with a sinus bradycardia. How's her conscious level?'

'Flat,' said the gasman.

'Pupils?'

'Big. Slow but reactive.'

'How d'you feel about giving her some atropine?' The anaesthetist turned his tray of emergency drugs and broke the top off a vial. The staff nurse helped him draw it up, and he injected it slowly into the rubber connector in Campbell's IV line. He was looking very worried.

'D'you want to shift her, David? She'd probably be better off in intensive care.'

'Could we take her through to resuscitation and put her on monitor first. Just in case. This place scares me stiff.'

'OK.'

'Val, is there a trolley out there?'

Getting a trolley alongside the operating table was another difficult manoeuvre, achieved less lightheartedly than the entry of the X-ray machine. Together they lifted the patient, limp and inert, from table to trolley, with the ECG leads trailing, and put the machine on the shelf underneath. Slowly Miss Warrender was wheeled from the clean turret, with the staff nurse leading, her bottle of saline held high above her shoulder. The anaesthetist, on the other side of the trolley, steered and kept watch on the endotracheal tube. Bertram and Campbell brought up the rear.

Their passage through the department to the resuscitation room caused hushed interest. Stray members of the public stared, and staff in a position to deduce the significance of the little cortege correctly assumed from the personnel, route and equipment involved that a minor surgical case had gone severely wrong.

They drew up in the middle of the resuscitation room. The gasman checked Miss Warrender's blood pressure, Bertram took her pulse again and Campbell ran off another strip on the ECG machine. The rate had speeded up after the atropine injection, and it remained regular. The staff nurse hung her bottle of saline on a drip stand and went over and pulled a screen across the entrance.

As Bertram left the patient to go across to the phone in the corner, the pale staff nurse who had been in the resuscitation room earlier that morning pushed the screen aside and walked purposefully towards the patient and addressed her colleague from the clean turret. 'Hello, Lesley, what brings you along here?'

'This lady had a coronary. While she was having her wrist straightened.'

'What's her name?'

'Miss Warrender. She's seventy-five and . . .'

'Thanks, Lesley. What's she got up?'

'Just saline. And she's had atropine.'

'Has she had anything for pain?'

'She hasn't been conscious yet.'

'Thanks, Lesley. I think I'll cope.'

While waiting for Bertram to find somewhere to put Miss Warrender, Campbell observed this item of territorial behaviour among recently qualified teaching hospital nursing staff out of the corner of his eye. At the end of it the clean turret nurse retreated without saying goodbye. The figure on the trolley was as inert as ever. Campbell suddenly remembered that she had come in originally with a broken wrist, and that the position of the fragments had been at least satisfactory before the more recent drama had begun. He picked up Miss Warrender's left wrist. All things considered, it was still in fairly good shape, and he wondered about immobilising it for her in the resuscitation room, before any further treatment or transfer within the hospital was comtemplated. As he held it, the figure on the trolley showed sudden and welcome signs of returning vigour. She coughed and spluttered on her tube, and her colour went quite quickly from pasty white to a dull, boozer's pink.

'She's coming up,' he remarked to the gasman, whose attention was wandering again. Miss Warrender, as though to reinforce his remarks, choked convulsively and suddenly coughed up the red rubber tube and its retaining balloon. The anaesthetist, who had been looking vaguely in the direction in which the clean turret had retreated, turned round as Miss Warrender's splutterings rose and changed, as the tube emerged, into hollow stertorous coughing.

Bertram had come back. 'That's fine, dear,' he said. 'You'll be all the better for a good cough. How's her pulse, Bill?'

'Is there a bed in ICU, Ronnie?'

'No problem, David. What about a monitor, staff?'

The gasman, recalled once more to his duty, took the patient's pulse and blood pressure. 'She's coming up a treat,' he said, with satisfaction.

'How d'you feel, Miss Warrender?' The patient's face changed slowly as she woke up and focussed. She looked up at the gasman and coughed. 'Excuse me,' she said in a faint hoarse voice. 'In all the times I've been to Elie, I've never had onions like that.'

Campbell tried hard not to laugh, and the staff nurse threw him a reproachful look. 'Has she had anything for the pain, Dr Campbell?'

'I don't even know if she's had any pain . . . But I'll find out.'

'Miss Warrender,' said the gasman, 'Have you had any pain?'

'Onions have never agreed with me,' she whispered, 'I do have a little discomfort.'

'Where?'

'It's just heartburn. But quite severe, to tell you the truth.'

'Would you like her to have something?' said the staff nurse.

'Maybe some Cyclimorph,' said the gasman.

'Will you check it, Dr Campbell?' The staff nurse opened the DDA cupboard and the little red light on top came on.

'What about the monitor?' said Bertram. 'And we'd better have a defibrillator too.'

'Over there . . . Under the arrest drug tray.'

'Thanks, staff.' Bertram brought the portable ECG monitor and the red shock box across to Miss Warrender's trolley and began to connect up leads, without disconnecting the first lot of leads to the ECG machine wired on already. 'Sorry to bother you with all these wires and things, Miss Warrender. It's just a precaution.'

'I think there's been some mistake . . .' she murmured. 'I came into the Institute this morning with . . .' Her voice trailed away and the colour drained from her face.

'Bloody hell,' said the gasman. 'She's off again.'

'David, could you give a hand here. She's gone off.' Bertram continued to wire Miss Warrender up to the monitor, which was a cool and sensible thing to do. Campbell could thump her chest, compressing the heart to maintain her circulation, and the gasman, who specialised in that sort of thing, could slam another tube down and breathe her if necessary. And they had a drip up already. If someone had to have a cardiac arrest in the department, thought Campbell as he pounded her thin chest at the approved rate, it was as well for them to have it in circumstances like these.

'Steady on a minute, David, I'll just see what's what on the monitor.' Campbell stopped and stood back with Bertram to look at the little display screen. At first there was nothing to see, then a fluorescent blip wandered in from the side, trailing a chaotic, wriggling line. Bertram stopped and twiddled the knobs until the trace ranged

88

horizontally across the middle of the screen. It remained a chaotic scribble. He ripped open Miss Warrender's blouse, pushed her bra up towards her neck and squirted electrode jelly on to the front and left side of her chest. 'Stand back, Bill. OK, staff? Is this thing charged up?' The staff nurse nodded and he took the two electrodes from the red shock box, put them on Miss Warrender's chest, one at the front and one on the left, and pressed the discharge button. She jerked and arched back and then flopped flat again. Bertram stopped to inspect the results of his handiwork on the monitor.

'Modified rapture. She's back in sinus bradycardia. Atropine, staff?'

'Right.'

'And we'd better have some bicarbonate up instead of the saline for a while.' Campbell changed the bottles on the giving set while the staff nurse drew up more atropine for Miss Warrender.

'Terrible things onions,' mused Bertram. 'How are you getting on, Bill?'

'Her neck's practically solid, but we're getting there . . . That's it.'

'Fine.' Bertram put the atropine into the giving set. 'Let's get her off to ICU before she thinks of anything else.' Bertram disconnected the leads from the ECG machine, leaving Miss Warrender wired only to the monitor. 'D'you think this thing's got a cut-out? Might have blown it's insides out. Sorry, staff.'

Campbell remembered something from much earlier in the morning. 'What was that you said about a trial of something, Bill. Is she in it?'

'Sort of,' said the gasman, connecting a portable oxygen cylinder to the endotracheal tube. 'We're doing something on two intravenous induction agents. Comparing side effects. It's supposed to be double blind and all that, but only one of them tastes of onions. She had the safe stuff.'

Jean arrived at Campbell's flat at one minute past two, and kissed him perfunctorily, in what Campbell thought of as being the manner of a dutiful wife, then she paused and looked at him thoughtfully. 'What's wrong, David?'

'What?'

'Something's wrong.'

'Yes . . . A patient this morning. An old girl with a Colles'. She did it last night and came in this morning, and while we were reducing it under gas she had a big MI and we got her into resus. room and then she arrested.'

'Is she all right now?'

89

'No. She's dead. We got her started again and down to ICU, and they kept her going for another hour or so. But she died just after one. I went down there to see how she was, and they were just wheeling her out.'

'Oh, David.' She put her arms round him. 'How awful.'

'A straightforward Colles'. The gasman had just put her out and I pulled her wrist and it looked not too bad and I wanted an X-ray to be sure, and someone noticed she looked terrible . . .'

'A coronary?'

'Yes. A big anterior. Really big, they said in ICU.'

'Previous history.'

'None.'

'Did she have relatives?'

'Don't think so. Miss Somebody. Miss Warrender. She lived alone. She had a hat with wax fruit. And a cat.'

'Did she know? Did she have a lot of pain?'

'I don't think so. She sort of half woke up, and said something about onions and then went flat. I had just written her up for something when she arrested. Ronnie Bertram was there and he was great. He was on as receiving med. reg. It was a good arrest, if you know what I mean, with everybody doing the right things.'

'But she died . . . Oh, David.'

'I know you can't stop people having coronaries, and as Ronnie said, she could have had it over a scone tea in Jenners' and everyone would have said what a nice way to go. But when you've seen someone, and actually decided on something and done it, and then they die an hour later, it's not the same as reading, ''suddenly, at tea in Jenners''.'

'Will . . . anything happen?'

'You mean in the department? Or legally? I don't think so. I rang the procurator fiscal, and he said practically the same as Ronnie, and I told Mr Gillon too, and he was sensible and reasonable, and said these things happened. But . . . I still feel my name's on it.'

'Who was the gasman?'

'Bill somebody. A bit of an oaf. And I suppose it's more of a blot for him than it is for me, in a way. He was sort of slow to pick it up. In fact the nurse he was trying to chat up noticed first.'

'Nobody's going to know that,' said Jean, being suddenly rather practical. 'And everybody knows you're careful and sensible.' She held him tighter then said, 'I haven't had any lunch. Have you got any food?'

'Neither have I. I sort of forgot with all this. There's some paté and stuff. Oh, Jean.' They kissed again, and Jean seemed less absently marital about it. They had a drink and lunch and did not talk about Miss Warrender any more. Jean was quiet over coffee and Campbell moved his chair closer to hers. They held hands without saying anything for a while, then went to bed and made love quietly, not chatting and joking as they usually did. Time passed silently, in slow comforting crescendoes. They lazed and arched together, thinking sad, individual thoughts, and were eventually separated not by exhaustion or satiety by the harsh intrusive sound of the doorbell.

They ignored it at first. There was a pause then it rang again, more insistently and frequently. They looked at each other and Jean said, 'I bet it's the Mormons.' Campbell laughed. Someone knocked heavily at the door and a man's voice shouted 'Police'.

'Bloody Hell. I'd better get up. Oh, Jean.' He kissed her and got up and put on slacks and a shirt, rather than face the forces of law and order in a dressing gown having come straight from bed with Jean. She looked suddenly miserable, pulled the downie round herself and lay on her front, watching him. 'Don't be long.'

'If I buy a double ticket for the police ball, will you come?'

'Don't be long, David.'

There were two policemen, in plain clothes. The taller one said, 'Are you Dr David Campbell?' and showed an identity card. They invited themselves in and Campbell showed them into the lounge. Jean had switched on the radio in the bedroom.

'Take a seat, please.'

The junior policeman moved one of Bones' backnumbers of *Playboy* from the sofa as though it were something much, much worse, and they all sat down.

'Dr Campbell,' the senior policeman began, 'I'm Detective Sergeant Lowther and this is Detective Constable Rowe, CID.'

'Hello.'

'I'm sorry to bother you when you're off duty, and sorry if we've come at an inconvenient time' — he was looking at Campbell's bare feet and sandals — 'We tried the Casualty Department and wouldn't have come here if it hadn't been something a bit out of the ordinary. I should say from the start that it's not to do with anything arising from your work in the department . . .' The detective constable was glancing round the room, perhaps looking for other evidence of Bones' depravity. 'You've already been contacted by the uniformed branch, I understand. In connection with an accident which you attended . . . informally. And I believe you did useful work in getting the driver out

91

of the van in question.'

'Oh. That. An accident at Westburn?'

'Yes. On the evening of the twenty-seventh. Tuesday. We're follow-ing up one or two odd things in connection with that accident and we hoped that as one of the first on the scene you would perhaps be in a position to help.'

'I didn't see the accident,' said Campbell.

'No, but you had quite a lot to do with what happened afterwards.'

'Yes. We got a chap to get the ambulances and so on. And helped to get the man out. And the police came along quite soon afterwards . . .'

'Yes . . . quite. What particularly interests us is whether you noticed anything . . . shall we say, odd, anything strange, about the accident, the van, the driver. Anything that might have caught your attention.' The sergeant spoke slowly, choosing his words deliberately. He was fortyish, a little overweight, and wore the plain clothes uniform of raincoat, sports jacket, club tie, etc., right down to the shiny brown shoes. His manner was patient, methodical and confident. The constable watched him carefully, as though to be reassured that you didn't have to be clever to succeed in the CID. Campbell remembered a lot about the night they were interested in: the shiny boot through the windscreen, Jean's hand and voice, the smell of petrol, the man wetting his trousers and the little man who had unloaded the back of the van not knowing the risk he was running, but none of these were the stuff with which policemen's notebooks were filled. His own giggly elation when the driver was laid on the stretcher was the strongest single impression Campbell retained from the incident.

'What sort of thing are you after?'

'Anything suspicious. Anything at all.'

Campbell tried to run through the things they might be interested in: the accident, stolen vehicles, stolen goods, and nastier things that did not seem immediately relevant to the case in hand. (A white slave ring centred on Dumbarton Road, Glasgow?)

'We took a lot of stuff out of the van. And just dumped it on the verge. Just boxes of . . . oriental goods. Oh. And there was one odd thing that didn't strike me at the time. A chap who helped.'

'What sort of chap?'

'Thin. A bit dirty. A decent kind of ordinary bloke who'd actually tried to get the driver out before . . . before I stopped.' Campbell felt extremely uneasy about his impending revelation and perhaps a suspicion of this aroused his questioners' interest. Both the detectives were looking at him. 'He seemed . . . quite keen to leave before the police arrived.'

92

'What was he driving?'

'An old lorry. A light lorry with some scrap on the back.' The policemen looked very serious indeed and Campbell wondered what else he should have noticed about the man. Then the sergeant laughed. 'You're right,' he said. 'He's a villain.'

'Who?'

'Shuggy. He's called Shuggy Henderson. Wholesale and retail stolen goods. And scrap. We knew he was there.'

'He was very good.'

'Oh, we're not picking him up for anything to do with this. He just gets lifted once a year anyway. Like tatties.' The constable laughed, partly at his superior's joke and partly at Campbell's embarrassment.

'No, we're not worried about Shuggy. Glad to hear he helped. Bear it in mind next time we go round for him. No, what we'd like to know about is anything you noticed about the van, the driver, the load.'

'The driver was Indian,' said Campbell. The sergeant frowned slightly and the constable glanced round to see if the sergeant thought the witness was showing insufficient respect for his position. 'You know what I mean. And most of the odd things about the accident followed from that.'

'What odd things?'

'All the odd things like the driver's accent, and the funny stuff in the boxes — nice stockings, fancy goods, oriental toiletries, as he said.' The constable was smiling and the sergeant looked serious and interested. 'Some of it smelt pretty strange. And the oddest thing of all, to me anyway, was the way the driver wasn't too bothered when his van went up in flames.'

'That's what we're interested in,' said the sergeant, still doing his slow, patient, labrador-of-the-law thing. 'A van that smells funny and bursts into flames, and a driver that isn't too bothered about it all.'

Campbell had the authentic detective-story sensation of almost having worked out for himself what was going on, but feeling at the same time that it might be easier to turn over the page. The sergeant did just that. 'Apart from the official stuff in the cardboard boxes, we think that the van was stuffed, lined, upholstered, loaded with marijuana.' In his own exhaustive way, the detective seemed to get more syllables out of that last word than most people did. Diction apart, Campbell was quite taken aback by this suggestion, and must have looked it. 'But we're obviously going to have trouble proving it now. We've had Alsatians wagging their tails at the smell on those boxes, but you've got to have something in a wee plastic bag to show the jury. And those Ismailis . . .' Again his pronunciation verged on the laborious. 'It's like talking to a bunch of Irish tinkers. Half the time they make out they don't understand what you're on about, and the other half they're as tight as wulks.'

The policemen got up, together, and Campbell got up too. With his hand on the door handle the sergeant asked, 'You didn't happen to smell . . . any substance such as majijuana when you were working in the van, Dr Campbell?' Somehow the two policemen were standing close on either side of him, and it crossed Campbell's mind that he might be under invitation to imperil his immortal soul.

'I'm not sure I should recognise it. And there was a terrible smell of petrol and all those funny soaps . . .'

'Of course not.' The sergeant opened the door and they all moved into the hallway. 'Interesting people, these Ismailis. Good afternoon, Dr Campbell. Sorry to have disturbed you.' He was looking at Campbell's bare feet. 'But thank you very much.'

Jean was dressed and sitting on the edge of the bed when Campbell went back to her. He sat down beside her, and told her what the policemen had been interested in, and why it had taken so long. She said she had been on the point of going. They sat for quite a long time on the edge of the bed, then Jean undressed again, saying as she did so, 'It's not easy for me, David.'

THREE

'While it is of course not possible to be completely confident about such things as the examination for the first part of the Fellowship of the Royal College of Surgeons of Edinburgh, I think I could say now without undue immodesty that I have as sound a basis for meeting the examiners as the next man. My systematic reading of the various subjects has been thorough, and supplemented by dipping into the journals on the lookout for the sort of things the examiners might also be on the lookout for before the exam. For example, David, I wonder what clinically obvious congenital anomaly you might find in association with reduplication of the first part of the duodenum?'

'Nothing that springs to mind.'

'No? Well, you are unaware not only of the mental processes of surgical examiners but also of the nature of the information which their minds select and retain. I was reading in the *British Clinical Review* this morning, while waiting for an anaesthetist, that this interesting anomaly has been described in a patient with one bat ear! Jex-Blake, McGibbon, McFarquhar, Stangoe and Rabindramurthi; *BCR* 23, page two one nine, and only this month. So! An important abnormality lies hidden in the abdomen, a trap for the surgically unwary, which might complicate the presentation and indeed the management of any duodenal pathology, and all the time it is advertised by one sticking-out ear, as plain as the nose on your face! It is this sort of thing that they are interested in, to select the outstanding candidate from the merely competent fellows who have worked at their anatomy, and digested their pathology, but lack the flair and inspired attention to detail which are the hallmark, if I may say so, of the man of promise in surgery. And it is the same in the basic sciences. I dare say for every hundred candidates they meet who can describe the processes of inflammation in the adequate fashion, they meet only one who knows that Metchnikoff, who described the whole jing-bang, had a Scottish grandfather. And of course your examiners are for the most part Scotsmen — you will note I do not commit the solecism of calling them Scotchmen.'

Hakeem paused for a sip of coffee and puff from his cigarette, which he held curled in the little finger of his left hand, drawing the smoke through his closed hand to the space formed by the inside of his thumb and his first knuckle. Campbell remembered something about good Moslems not letting tobacco touch their lips. 'So you see, David, that although the examiners and I have had our minor differences in the past, it is not for lack of attention to detail on my part. Between ourselves, I feel that this, if you are familiar with the expression, is it. So tomorrow I shall go forth, and in Mr Gillon's words, joust with the examiners. Go into the lists, and come out on *the* list. Though of course I shall not know until the weekend.'

It was all rather tedious, and a little bit sad. If this chap was as old as he looked, and had started medical school at the usual age, he had spent a long time in a foreign country chasing a piece of paper. Without wishing to sound cruel, Campbell inquired, 'So this isn't your first shot?'

Hakeem took a thoughtful puff through his hand. 'Frankly, David, no. In one instance I was woefully unprepared with regard to anatomy. Perhaps it was the over-confidence that came from being chosen from my people and sent forth to Britain as an Aga Khan Scholar. I was unable, in the heat of the moment, to describe the nerve supply to the superior constrictor of the pharynx.' He paused and smiled at this folly of his youth. 'It is of course innervated by a branch of the accessory nerve. An elementary point as I am sure you are aware, but perhaps what one might call first night nerves got the better of me, and I am afraid I went quite to pieces. In London.'

'You tried the London Fellowship.'

'Initially yes. But after that and one other misfortune, concerning the Henderson-Hasselbalch Equation, and an advantageous offer of employment north of the border, I came to Scotland. To tell you the truth, I prefer it in many ways. Compared to England, it is much more like Pakistan. The people are more thrifty and industrious than their neighbours, and clearly rank in the aristocracy of the world's races. With regard to England, I think you will find my comparison of Pakistan and the Republic of India instructive. So of course I find Scotland more congenial. I have made many friends here, for example. When I was working at Hillhouse General Hospital, near Glasgow, the senior surgeon was most kind to me. I think I became even as one of his family. He had served in India with the Imperial Forces and many an evening we swapped stories over a chota peg. In the operating theatre he would call me the Wise One, and I used to call him McGrogan Sahib. Ah, we had good times at Hillhouse, and he would have been an invaluable influence in the college this week.'

'Oh?'

'Yes, indeed. He knew many of the best men in the Edinburgh

College, though of course he was also a fellow of the sister college in the West. Unfortunately he has retired, or perhaps I should say he *was* retired. A good friend to me, David, a man with a profound understanding of the world, from the eastern and the western points of view. A great loss to the profession as a whole, and to me in particular at this moment.'

'What happened to him?'

Hakeem rolled his eyes, looking round the room and checking the intercom twice. 'He had enemies. Small men with mean local ambitions who may have been jealous of the amount of time he spent with me rather than with them. They chose to put it about that he was unwell, playing down his considerable surgical achievements and making much of what was only a spot of whisky between friends with a common interest in the orient. He drank no more than any sahib would, and as the persecution increased he had many worries, but these small men, mean-minded physicians and administrators led, regrettable to relate, by his own junior consultant, made much of this, and one or two surgical misfortunes of the sort that will occur when a man is turning out a decent volume of turnover, and caused him to be put on sick leave. Naturally the stress of all this evil conspiracy played havoc with my chances in the exam at Glasgow, and it may even be, though I am not taking it so far as to make it a formal allegation, that these same small-minded men who harried like jackals around McGrogan Sahib may also not have been above putting a word in against me in certain quarters in the Glasgow college, though I would be grateful if you would regard that piece of information as being divulged only in the strictest confidence. Anyway, all that is in the past. My friend is out of hospital. Not working, you understand, and only a shadow of his former self, broken by these intrigues of his enemies. It is a great pity, David, because both as a surgeon and as a teacher he could stand with the best in the country. I hope you will not think me immodest, but I think I can say I owe my expertise in a whole range of surgical techniques entirely to the man I call McGrogan Sahib. I was his senior house officer for more than two years, with no registrar whatsoever, and only Glasgow-trained Indians as my house staff, but between us we pulled the weight of an entire surgical team. When he had assured himself of my basic skills I commonly started his lists and always finished them. I was his first assistant, as such often entrusted with his entire Monday list. He used to remark that for me fellowship would be not a matter of examination, but of mere recognition, as my daily work with hernias, veins, piles, appendicectomies, even breasts and the occasional gall-bag, would testify. Had he chosen to endure the calumny and stay at his post I am sure I would not now still be jousting with mere first part examiners. But there we have it. A matter for great regret.'

'I've never worked in the West,' said Campbell, 'but I've heard that these hospitals round Glasgow are very good for cutting experience.'

'I tell you, David, it was chop, chop, chop.' He glanced round again and leaned forward. 'This job is like a study leave. This morning I have seen about twenty people, with eight of them needing treatment of one sort and another, five of whom were dealt with by the nurses. I myself have sewn up a hand, the sort of thing the students got at Hillhouse, put on a below-knee walking plaster and taken a peanut out of a school-boy's nose. By this time . . .' — he looked at his watch — 'in an average day at Hillhouse I might have seen ten new referrals at out patients, plus twice as many follow up cases, or, on an operating day, stood with my friend merrily taking out a stomach and two or three gallbags, to say nothing of a few hernias of my own to begin with. I think I can say we were a good team, old Sahib McGrogan and I. He used to say that in other circumstances we could have gone off back to Karachi togethere and made our fortunes in surgery. McGrogan and Subhadar, the ladies would say, what a marvellous job of surgery they made of my gallstones, for that is the way they talk there. Do you know that I even named my first child after him?'

Campbell, only half listening, was nonetheless intrigued. If the boy Hakeem had been teased about his name at school, what would little Ali McGrogan Subhadar not have to endure?

'I see you smiling, David. No, I did not call my son McGrogan Subhadar, but used, with his permission, the first name of the Sahib in its Moslem form. Mr McGrogan is called David, as you are, and my son is called Daud, which is not unusual, for as you know, King David in your Bible, the son of Jesse and the father of Solomon, is also in the holy texts of Islam as a patriarch.' He pulled out his wallet and produced a small square colour photograph and handed it to Campbell. 'My son and heir.'

A chubby olive-skinned baby of indeterminate sex, muffled in bright green so that only his eyes, nose, ears and cheeks were visible, sat in the middle of a largish room, the floor of which was covered with toys, including a vast rambling layout of expensive looking train set. 'The head of the household while I am away, though his mother and my brothers, his uncles, are for all practical purposes taking the running of things while I am abroad on my surgical training scholarship.'

'Very nice,' said Campbell, giving back the snapshot. Dr Subhadar smiled proudly and put it back in his wallet.

Campbell had just come on duty. He was on the week of late duty, which meant coming into the department in the early afternoon and leaving when the night man came on at nine thirty. It was an agreeable routine, with mornings off and enough time left over afterwards for some sort of social life. The only drawback was that it did not fit in very well with Jean, and he had not seen her for several days. Some time before, when he had just started in the department with a week of late duty, she had made a practice of slipping in for brief visits to his flat on her way to work, or even driving round the park for a quick and early lunch, combined with what she called 'seeing him properly', but their customary late afternoon and early evening assignations, the best time of day for fairly married girls with jobs and husbands, were now quite ruled out.

None the less, it was very pleasant to be off in the mornings. He had got up late, lounged in a bath, strolled out into town with the airy sense of freedom that comes from being officially idle when most people are working, bought some paperbacks and spent half an hour in a coffee shop flicking through them, before returning at a leisured pace to the Institute, lunch and work. Not that there was much work to do. The morning Hakeem had described had been quiet for a Tuesday, and very little had come into the department since two o'clock. Campbell sat fairly contentedly in the doctor's coffee room. It would have been more pleasant to read the paperback about the lost BBC television crew eating their Peruvian porters than to listen to poor old Hakeem, but Campbell felt that some departmental good was being achieved thereby. The man was lonely and worried and needed someone to share his fears and rationalisations with. And the tales from the Wild West of Scottish surgery had been interesting. He resolved to ask Hadden if he had picked up any ripples of the McGrogan affair from less biased sources.

'Hello, could we have a doctor for Minor Trauma, please,' said the intercom. Hakeem got up and said, 'As a penance for boring you with my personal worries, David, I shall go to what your friend Mr Hadden calls the department of triviatrics.' He turned and said 'I am coming' to the intercom, and its light went out. 'And perhaps you will tell your friend Mr Hadden that I am a graduate of the University Medical School of the University of Karachi, and not of Swettipore, wherever that may be. I am not sure that any town of that name exists, and I am certain there is no such medical school.' He walked out, leaving Campbell to his paperbacks. He started the top book half way through, in the middle of an argument between members of the crew about how much detail from their ordeal should be filmed, then lost interest and began to wonder about Hakeem's last remark. The 'Swettipore' line had the authentic ring of a Hadden jest, but Hadden would never have risked causing offence by voicing it within the earshot of its putative graduate. The light came on under the intercom, and Campbell realised that the most likely course of events was that Hakeem had been eavesdropping on some bantering conversation of Hadden's, in another part of the department.

'Hello.'

'Hello.'

'Dr Campbell?'

'Yes.'

'Could you come round to trolleys, please. There's a patient here you might like to see right away.'

'Coming, Maureen.'

Campbell left his paperback and walked round to the trolley room. A large woman was standing in the entrance, apparently waiting for him. She was about forty, dressed in the manner of affluent matronhood and carefully made up. She blocked Campbell's path and smiled a determined smile of formal greeting.

'Dr Campbell?'

'Yes?'

'She's got no worries, you know, doctor. Not a thing in the world to worry about. She's a happy, active girl, and well above average in her classes. No social anxieties of course. A nice boyfriend and we haven't got any money problems and George, my husband, has just been promoted again. And she gets on really well with Fraser, that's her brother. I was flabbergasted when the phone call came through from school. But I can assure you she's got no worries.'

'I'm sorry,' said Campbell. 'I've only just been called round. I'd like to have a word with the staff nurse.' Maureen was hovering just behind the large lady. 'Would you please excuse me?' Campbell and Maureen retreated down the trolley room towards the desk, and the lady disappeared behind the only set of drawn screens in the trolley room. Through the occasional pauses in her continuing discourse, Campbell caught the sound of sobbing.

'An overdose,' said Maureen. 'Aspirin. A lot.'

'How much?'

'She thinks fifty at least. But it's hard to get near her.'

'What age is she?'

'Sixteen. Fifth year at school.'

'When?'

'About three quarters of an hour ago.'

'Anything else?'

'No.'

'Oh well. We'd better get on with it. Can we get rid of mama?'

'I've been trying, David. She doesn't take hints.'

They went back to the patient and went behind the screens, where the large lady was leaning over a figure with her back to her, who had the pink cellular departmental blanket pulled right up over her face, and was crying bitterly. Campbell picked up the clipboard and said authoritatively, 'Would you excuse us, Mrs Anderson?' The lady looked surprised. 'Could you wait outside, please?' She looked puzzled and hurt. The girl on the trolley continued to sob. 'Could you wait outside please,' said Campbell patiently.

'But my daughter's very upset.'

'Could you wait outside, please, Mrs Anderson?' The lady looked at Campbell and the staff nurse and gave up. 'I'll be just outside when you need me, doctor.'

'Thank you, Mrs Anderson.' She went away, looking over her shoulder at the girl on the trolley, who was still sobbing, and hiding her face. Campbell checked the clipboard again. A schoolgirl, aged sixteen, had taken a very large overdose of aspirin. She had been registered in the department for only five minutes, and had taken the tablets perhaps three quarters of an hour before that. It was a common emergency, to be dealt with quickly in the department by a method that was rather more unpleasant than was popularly supposed.

'Miss Anderson.'

There was a muffled sob from beneath the pink blanket.

'Miss Anderson, it's important that you tell me about what you've taken. What sort of tablets were they?'

'Aspirin.' The figure on the trolley sobbed and shuddered again. 'And I wish I was dead.'

'How many aspirin?'

'Nearly a bottle full.'

'Where's the bottle?'

'She's got it.' The staff nurse slipped outside the curtains.

'When did you take them?'

'End of the lunch break.'

'When's that?'

'Quarter past one.' That made it nearer an hour and a quarter. The nurse came back with a little brown bottle. 'About twenty left from a hundred.'

'Was the bottle full when you started?'

'Yes. I'd just bought it.'

Campbell knew most of the things he wanted to know about the patient, but had not yet seen her. 'Pulse and BP?' he asked Maureen.

'Normal BP. Pulse one ten.'

'Can I take your pulse again please?'

The inert and hidden figure made no reply but offered no resistance when Campbell took her wrist. The pulse was still as Maureen had recorded it, and more importantly, some sort of clinical contact had been established. Campbell decided to push on a little further with this slightly unusual encounter. He checked the girl's first name from the clipboard. 'Sheila, how do you feel?'

'I wish I was dead.'

'I didn't mean that. Have you any pain?'

'A bit. My tummy.'

'Can I look at it.' The lump under the blanket was silent. 'Turn over please.' Very slowly the girl turned over and lay on her back. She took the blanket away from her face as she did so, and sobbed again when she saw Campbell and the staff nurse.

'What do you want?'

'I'm trying to help you.'

'I don't want help. I want to be dead.'

'We can talk about that after we've helped you,' said Campbell. 'Where's the pain, Sheila?' Maureen took the blanket right off. The girl was red-eyed and dishevelled, but looked as if, in less disadvantageous circumstances, she might be pretty. She was in school uniform minus blazer. 'Where does it hurt?'

'There,' she said, rubbing her belly.

'I want to examine you. Sit up, please.' In a dazed slow way she complied. The staff nurse took off her blouse and loosened the band of her skirt. Campbell shone a pen torch in the girl's eyes, and told her to put out her tongue, then listened to her chest and told her to lie down again. 'Sore there?' he asked, pressing her midriff.

'A bit.' She sobbed again. She was looking up at him, her face slack with misery and her hair moist and straggled with tears. She had a little bit of lipstick on and it was smudged. Her respiration rate was increased.

'Sheila,' said Campbell. 'I'm going to wash out your stomach.' She started to sniffle and sob again. 'It might upset you but it's absolutely necessary and the sooner I do it the more it'll help you. Is that all right?'

She nodded miserably, biting her lip.

'We'll move you to a little room along the corridor, and then do it for you right away. It might be a bit uncomfortable but I'll be as gentle as possible. And it helps if you don't struggle.'

She looked up at Campbell. 'What would happen if you don't?'

'You'd get very ill, and feel really terrible. And then lose consciousness. But that won't happen because we'll not let it. OK staff?'

Maureen mouthed 'dirty turret' in the interrogative, and Campbell nodded.

'Is there someone else on up there?'

'Staff nurse McCraw. I'll ask her to get things ready.' She went across to the intercom, pressed a button and spoke softly and closely into it. While she was doing that Campbell said, 'd'you want to tell somebody why you did it, Sheila?' The girl burst out into hysterical sobs.

'All right. Never mind. Perhaps you'll want to talk to someone else about it later.'

Maureen came back to the patient and Campbell went outside to explain to Mrs Anderson what was going to happen. She did not seem very receptive to outside information but interspersed assertions that the girl had no worries with rhetorical questions as to why she had done it. Campbell felt his duty was to inform her and get on with the job, and she appeared surprised when he left her to follow the girl's trolley down the main corridor. She made as though to follow too, but Campbell stopped her and showed her to a waiting room.

Nurse McCraw had done well in the limited time allowed. The dirty turret was cleared for action. Its operating table was parked outside and its floor was covered with polythene sheeting. The mixer tap was running full bore and she was filling big steel jugs with warm water. Campbell started to explain to the girl what the procedure involved.

'I'm going to put a rubber tube down your thoat,' he said, making it sound as gentle as possible, 'then wash out your stomach with warm water to bring up the pills. It'll make you want to be sick, and if it does just be sick. I'm sorry, it's all a bit uncomfortable but it's the only way to help you.' She looked at him with disbelief, and Campbell got the impression that she had just begun to trust him, and was now suspicious again. 'We'll tilt the trolley, and I'm afraid it's best that you're sort of strapped in so you can't fall.' Her face showed betrayal and despair.

The nurses, acting with a rapport and expertise born of frequent practice, descended on her and wrapped her in the blanket again, so that her arms were immobilised and only her head and neck were free, then they fastened the broad leather straps across the trolley and tilted it so that the girl's feet were eighteen inches or so above the level of her head. Campbell checked that the door was shut.

'That everything?' said staff nurse McCraw.

'Oh, the basin.' Maureen put a big steel basin on the floor near the head of the trolley.

'Tube, please.' Campbell was handed a red rubber tube almost an inch across and about two feet long. The end was open and perforated, and moistened with clear jelly. 'Sheila,' he said, bending over the girl, 'I want you to try to swallow this.' Her mouth was resolutely shut.

Sometimes, if patients were violently determined to resist, it could all be very difficult, with broken teeth (patient's) and bitten fingers (doctor's) but this girl did not look the type. She would be unwilling but not violent, and it would all be over soon.

'Open your mouth.'

She did so and he slid the tube in, risking his fingers to get it central in the back of her throat. 'Now try to swallow.' Whether the patient swallowed or not, the tube, having got that far, almost always went right down. The girl coughed a little, and wriggled under her blanket as it disappeared slowly and without undue resistance.

'Try to relax,' said Campbell. 'Breathe through your nose. Funnel, please.'

Staff Nurse McCraw handed Campbell a large polythene funnel which he connected to the free end of the rubber tube. 'Thanks. That's the worst bit, Sheila. Now I'm going to wash the pills out.' He lifted the funnel above the level of the girl's body, picked up the first jug and slowly poured in several pints of warm water. She retched and spluttered, and Campbell held the funnel in the same place for a few moments, then lowered it and the water, cloudy now, welled up to fill it. He poured it into the waiting basin. Blurred, disintegrating white fragments, the remains of several aspirin tablets, settled from the turbid water.

'Did you have any lunch?'

The girl shook her head.

'That makes it much easier for everybody,' he said reassuringly, and picked up another jug of water. The girl lay passively, not even coughing any more, but retching silently as Campbell washed her out with six or eight gallons, jug after jug until no more tablets came up and the returning water was clear, then he took up the tube, and the staff nurses released the girl from her straitjacket. She sat up and coughed a lot and Campbell listened to her chest again. She was tearful and silent as Maureen washed her face and combed her hair and helped her on with her blouse. After a long time she said, in an oddly composed way, 'I'm sorry to put you to all this trouble.'

'I'm sorry to have had to upset you with all that,' said Campbell, 'but it's the only way we can help once people have taken tablets.' She smiled damply then looked as if she had just remembered something. 'Where is she?'

'Who?'

'My mother.'

'In the waiting room. D'you want to see her?'

The girl started to cry again and Campbell felt foolish. 'You don't have to see her right away if you don't want to. And I'm going to get a couple of other doctors down and they might be a few minutes. You could perhaps just wait here with one of the nurses, if you want to.'

'I don't want to see her,' said the girl. 'Not just yet.'

'Oh?'

'She's as bad as he is. She knows and she lets him.'

Campbell had the feeling that further details might not be the sort of thing a simple bone-setting, skin-cobbling casualty officer could concern himself with. The routine was that patients who had taken overdoses were washed out by the casualty officer and then seen by the receiving medical registrar, and the duty psychiatrist, if he could be found.

'I've had enough,' said the girl. 'And I'm not going back for more.'

Whether it was Latin homework, compulsory bible reading or corporal punishment, Campbell felt that someone else could come to grips with the details. 'I'll just go and phone for those other doctors I mentioned. Meanwhile you'll be all right with staff nurse. Won't be a moment. OK staff?'

'Doctor, can I talk to you?'

Campbell paused and the nurses looked at him.

'Fine.'

'I want to tell somebody why I did it.'

Fifteen minutes later Campbell went round to the back of the department to make a few phone calls in relative privacy. Hadden was sitting reading a file of duplicated typescript. He looked up and enquired, 'Are you thoroughly familiar with your role in World War Three, young Campbell?'

'Not really.'

'You should read all about it in this,' he said. 'I think you take the first hundred major casualties excluding burns. But don't worry, they'll clear ward sixteen and you'll have a houseman and two staff nurses to help you.'

'Thanks, Sounds as if it can wait.'

'I think so. You busy?'

'Sort of. A nasty one.'

'Anything in particular?'

'Family life in Barnton. Presenting as an overdose.' Campbell picked up the telephone and dialled the exchange and asked the operator to get the receiving registrar to ring his extension. 'Kid of sixteen. Took about eighty aspirin to get away from it all for a while.'

'Is she all right?'

'Should be. Good washout. She hardly turned a hair and we got a clean return quite quickly.'

'What was her blood level?'

'Hell. I forgot. I better go back and do that. And I suppose she needs to see the duty psych.'

The phone rang and a rather youthful male voice said, 'Receiving medical registrar.' Campbell described the basic clinical problem of the overdose succinctly, and the voice, to which he could not put a name, and which offered none, asked him a number of silly questions designed to demonstrate a knowledge of aspirin poisoning. Campbell found this irritating, as the man would have to come down to see the patient anyway. Fortunately the interrogator did not ask about blood levels, and the phone call ended without Campbell's omission coming to light. He then turned his attention to getting some psychiatric help for the girl.

Attempting to involve the duty psychiatrist in the management of a case was one of the least rewarding tasks that could come a Casualty Officer's way. The rota was a complex and untidy one including about thirty of the city's current crop of trainee psychiatrists, and no individual did the duty often enough to become good at it or even familiar with it. Perhaps as part of the working out of the odd cravings that impelled people towards psychiatry in the first place, the partici-pants in the rota took badly to the discipline of availability. Some refused to carry the bleep provided, on the grounds that it might interrupt meaningful silences, and some (presumably as a semi-overt token aggression against a hierarchically structured authoritarian work-situation) simply forgot all about it when their turn came up. But in theory at least, a psychiatrist was available twenty-four hours a day seven days a week for patients deemed by Casualty staff to require their urgent attention. Fortunately he was not often needed.

The game of hunt-the-psychiatrist usually began with a long pause while the operator at the Institute's main switchboard found the rota and worked out who was supposed to be on duty. The next step was to track him down by bleep or phone. During working hours psychiatrists seemed to organise for themselves an endless series of telephonically inviolable meetings and groups, though a few strategically placed secretaries consented to hold messages which lay in wait for people rushing between smoke-filled rooms. For out-of-hours calls, telephone numbers were left, where psychiatrists were seldom to be found. If, having passed the first couple of hurdles, a casualty officer happened to find himself in telephone conversation with the duty man, the game proper had scarcely begun. What might seem to a simple casualty officer to be an urgent and inequivocal case for psychiatric help might be deemed, depending on the sectarian enthusiasms of the expert, anything from a crime to a transparent manipulation. Only very rarely was it a psychiatric problem. Usually a time-consuming conversation ended in a glib evasion of clinical responsibility. Urgency was dismissed as panic, reason was met by slippery rationalisation, and anger (an emotion not unknown to casualty officers dealing with psychiatrists in emergencies) was sometimes handled with an infuriating coup of chop-logic that left the caller feeling that everything was his fault. Actually to obtain the physical presence of a psychiatrist in the department was a very rare achievement.

Somewhat to his surprise, Campbell found himself talking to a psychiatric registrar after only about five minutes. 'Incest?' he said. 'I'll be right down.'

'Humph,' read Hadden, as Campbell put the phone down. 'The head porter and the deputy chaplain will be responsible for the organisation of a temporary mortuary in the laundry. Four hundred cases only . . . And you, me, Bones and the Dormouse will work continuously, except when Hak relieves us for half an hour at three hour intervals, for periods of up to twelve hours. And there's nothing about free milk . . . I wonder how they manage these things in Moscow.'

Campbell returned to the dirty turret to take blood from the girl who had attempted suicide. Maureen was still with her, and they seemed to have hit it off together. The girl was smiling and relaxed and bore few signs of her ordeal. She looked more like someone who'd been for a brisk run followed by a shower than the victim of self-poisoning followed by therapeutic assault. She greeted Campbell as if she knew him quite well. When he told her what he wanted to do she made a face then grinned.

'I don't mind,' she said. 'Nothing could be as awful as that tube.'

'Sorry. Hold your arm straight out please.' Maureen compressed the girl's upper arm while Campbell slid the needle in just below her elbow, and took off ten mils of blood for the test. 'It's just to make sure that everything's OK.'

'I'm fine,' said the girl. 'Except I'm hungry.' Maureen said something about asking an auxiliary to make some toast, and the girl looked pleased and said thank you. There was a knock at the door, and she suddenly became a frightened schoolgirl again.

'Come in.'

The door slid open and a short, sallow man with lank ringlets of greasy hair and black leather jacket came in. 'I'm sorry . . .' said Campbell.

The man came very close and said 'Duty psychiatrist', and lowered his head. 'We spoke on the phone just now,' he added reproachfully. 'Have you finished your bit? Perhaps we could be left alone.' Campbell and Maureen exchanged glances and went out of the turret, Maureen first. As they did so the psychiatrist advanced on his patient with a child-molesting smile.

The girl's mother was waiting in the corridor outside. She looked anxious and stopped Campbell once more.

'There isn't going to be any trouble, is there?'

'I think we've got all the tablets up. I've just taken some blood to make sure she hasn't absorbed enough to hurt her.'

'Yes. Good. There aren't going to be any difficulties though, are there?'

'Well, usually people stay in overnight, just to make sure everything's going to be all right. I've asked someone from the medical side of the hospital to come and see her . . . and another doctor's with her now.'

'That man . . .?'

'Yes,' said Campbell. 'It's best that everyone who's done something like that gets seen by a specialist. Quite often they can help a lot.' It was Campbell's private view that as a general rule they hardly ever helped, and that this chap in particular, from first impressions at least, might turn out to be a positive menace. The woman smiled brightly and said, 'Well, she's got no worries to speak of,' with less conviction than formerly. They left her waiting in the corridor.

'All sounds a bit ghastly,' said Maureen when they were out of earshot.

'I bet he's a church elder, dirty old bugger. Nice kid though. She'll probably be fine when he stops.'

'D'you think so?'

'Probably. But we'll see what the expert thinks.' Maureen returned to trolleys and Campbell went round the back with a quick coffee in mind. As he switched on the kettle Hadden put down his reading material and said, 'Thanks, lad. No sugar. Diet. I suppose the thing to do is keep smiling and remember you're British. ''The deputy chaplain will liaise with the burgh cleansing department to arrange non-denominational services for agnostics, atheists, infidels and unidentified radioactive crisps of possibly human origin''.' Campbell suspected Hadden was making that bit up. — 'Nothing like a war for bringing people together.'

'Where d'you find that?'

'In the Disaster File. Serves me right for opening it. The Pandora's Box *de nos jours*. Thanks, lad. It's terribly fifties. Ladies in green hats will dispense tea from blast-proof urns, and Vera Lynn records will be made available to all wards and departments. Can't see it myself. I think I'll be a radioactive crisp. One of the largest found. Nicely basted, though. How's your aspirin eater?'

'I guess she'll pull through. The psych looked a bit of a fright. One of the ton-up rocker kind.'

'Change from the beads and bangles lot.'

'I suppose it might have been that silly bugger who challenges you to be embarrassed by his stutter.'

'What's the problem?'

'Family nasties.'

'What sort?'

'Come to daddy. And mummy's a pretty nasty bit of work too.'

Hadden returned to his analysis of how the Casualty Department would react to being put on a war footing. Ten minutes later the psychiatrist pushed the door open and looked round. 'Come in,' said Hadden.

'Oh, hallo, mate.' Campbell was being addressed. He invited the psychiatrist to sit down and offered him some coffee.

'Thanks a lot . . . Well . . . There's a slice of life, then. Like the News of the bloody World. Dirty old bugger. I'd have him in the clink. Sex education? Something too important to be left to the state in schools? I'd kick 'is arse. And like she said, her mum's just about as bad. Suits her book. You know. Lovely husband, doesn't trouble her at all. Thanks.'

'What'll happen?' Campbell asked.

'Not a lot. Well, not much chance of him getting what he deserves. But of course I'll pass the word round my mates at the New Club and he'll have to resign. No, the beaks don't really go heavy on this kind of guy. Even the working classes just get a bit of a ticking off from a social worker. ''Proceedings potentially more damaging than the regrettable episode now over'' and all that. This bugger'll sit boring the arse off some poor shrink like me, with how it's all due to his strict religious upbringing, twice a week for six months then the whole thing'll be forgotten about. If it were up to me he'd be breakin' stones somewhere hot, but I'm only the duty psychiatrist.'

'What about her?'

'Boarding school.'

'What?'

'Yeah. Pity. Locking her up for something he's done. But it'll separate them. They say it's habit-forming. Can I write something in the notes? Nuffink lurid. Just ''Seen by duty psych. Social work reports awaited. Letter follows.'' '

'Fine. Thanks very much. And thanks for coming so quickly.'

'Don't mention it. All in a day's work. Change from agoraphobia and bloody piss-heads.' He finished his coffee and went away, leaving Campbell and Hadden to continue their analysis of the department war plans.

'I don't know if I'm so sure now as I was about this guy. When did you last see him? Oh, yes. The first night he was in. Yes, he was fine then, just coming down quite nicely from the complicated stuff overnight, when his blood gases went kind of funny, and I'd been up half the night twiddling with things. Yes, he was coming along fine for about twenty-four hours, rolling nicely along, just this side of a wee touch of respiratory alkalosis, and quite pink and healthy, well, as pink as these chaps go, and perfectly healthy. Peeing fine and all that and really doing all the things you'd expect from a crushed chest, given the fact that he'd a couple of fractures as well. Then he started to go off. You know. Just off. Nothing you could hang your hat on, just a vague feeling that you sometimes get with these chaps before anything goes wrong with anything you can actually measure. He just looked a bit dry and wee bit more floppy than he should have been on what we were giving him, but nothing more specific. The sort of thing you don't notice until somebody points it out. Anyway, he just began to look a bit off even before there was anything you could put your finger on. I suppose experience comes into it. Charlie Sim, or even the boss, would have picked it up earlier. But there was nothing measurably wrong with him. Then his temp began to creep up. Nothing wild, just a shift from mainly below the line to mainly above the line, and I thought at first it was just one of those post traumatic reactive temps people sometimes get with nothing really going on anywhere, and no

110

bugs to grow or anything, at least not from anywhere you can think of. But it went on, and then we picked up an odd thing on the chest X-ray. That's it there on the right-hand viewing box. No. It's not. That's the other guy. But his looked not unlike that. Well, more so yesterday. But anyway, we picked up just a flick of patchy consolidation on the chest X-ray, a fluffy bit of muck in the right mid-zone, just below the horizontal fissure, actually, just more or less overlying the upper border of the fifth rib, we thought. We had him sucked to see if we could grow anything from the secretions or even the catheter tip, but it can't have been bronchial, or hardly at all, because everything was as clean as a whistle. Well, just about. So we thought it might just be a little bit of fluid, you know, oedema after the pulmonary contusion, but it wasn't really typical so we decided just to watch it and see what happened. Where was I? Oh yes. That was Wednesday or maybe Thursday morning, and of course they get X-rayed every day as long as they're on the machine, and the next picture showed the same patch, only a bit bigger, and in the one after that he'd started a similar wee patch in the right lower zone, so we thought, oho, we're bound to grow something now, and had him sucked out again and . . .' Dr Wilson spread his hands in eloquent despair.

'Nothing,' said Campbell, to hasten his story to its end.

'Not a bloody thing, would you believe. And his temp still just swinging round the line, usually above, and sometimes below. So of course we looked for infection elsewhere, and cultured his urine — he had a catheter in of course — and re-X-rayed his fractures to see if it was them that were beginning to fester. And of course we wondered if he'd a clot of blood rotting away quietly somewhere, like behind his liver. But we didn't come up with a damned thing.'

Campbell shifted from one foot to the other in his paper overshoes, feeling uncomfortable in his face-mask and silly paper hat. He had just run upstairs while the department was quiet and while Hakeem and Hadden were still around, to find out how the driver of the now suspected van was getting on, and how heavily the police were leaning on him and his associates. 'So how is he now?'

'That's what I'm sort of getting round to telling you,' said Dr Wilson. 'He's bloody ill, as a matter of fact. He really cooked himself up, and went up to forty-one even with tepid sponging, we thought from his chest, then suddenly everything we cultured came back positive. His urine was jumping with various beasties, and we got coliforms in his spit, well, in his bronchial secretions, and we even got a positive blood culture. At long last.'

'Where's it coming from?'

111

'It's a really nasty one. Bacteriology seem to have been phoning me up every couple of hours to tell me something new about it . . . Oh, *where* is it from?'

'Yes.'

'Oh. We haven't found out. But it's everywhere now. It's a Pseudomonas, they think, and he's dripping with it. That's why he's in there.'

'I see. And how is he now? What's his future?'

'Bloody ill. Like I was saying. And it's not just that, the drugs he needs now are a bloody dangerous collection of poisons. For that Pseudomonas.'

'What's he on?'

'Well, we started him on Ampiclox, as soon as we had the first result . . . but when the sensitivities started to come back we began to think about changing him to . . . No. I tell a lie. *Before* the sensitivities came back . . .'

Campbell had known Scott Wilson for a long time. He tended to talk a lot when he was worried. It appeared that the driver was dangerously ill. 'What's he on now? Gentamicin?'

'Right. But he's not the easiest of people to keep a steady blood level in. Since his kidneys packed up.'

'Did they?'

'Oh, yes. Didn't I mention that? His urea's been climbing steadily since his second day in here. We wondered what was doing it. We thought about trauma to begin with, but I suppose infection's got more to do with it now than anything.'

'You dialysing him?'

'Not yet.'

'Thinking about calling in the kidney men?'

'Thinking about it. Unless his blood urea's gone down the next time it comes back.'

'I see.'

It had begun to sound as if the small matter of a police investigation about cannabis might already be accounted among the patient's lesser problems, but Campbell was curious to know what was happening, not least because he had been hauled from bed with Jean to assist the police with their enquiries. 'And what about the police?'

Dr Wilson looked blank and worried, as though Campbell were suggesting that the police might be after him for letting their suspect die. Campbell helped him. 'Remember you said the police had been up.'

'Oh, that.' He sounded relieved. 'Yes. They've been up a couple of

112

times. Funny. They even asked if we happened to have kept a specimen of his admission urine. I don't know what they were getting at. I mean to say, Moslems don't drink.'

On the way down from the respiratory intensive care unit Campbell met an unusual group on the stairs. Five men, all Indians or Pakistanis or whatever, presumably the relatives of the van driver, ascended the Institute's largest and most imposing staircase, past busts of ancient physicians alternating in the window sills with carefully arranged flowers. They were chattering animatedly. The men were of various ages and dressed in a remarkable diversity of styles. A smooth youngish man wore a dapper office suit and a tie perhaps denoting some school, club or association. Behind him was a grey-bearded man with a skullcap, who wore an embroidered jacket and baggy white pantaloons. The remainder of the group were clad in a selection of mixed and intermediate styles. They talked rapidly in their own language and one of them was laughing. As Campbell passed they fell silent and re-arranged themselves into a single line proceeding quietly upstairs as though to some religious observance. The smooth young man in front smiled at the doctor descending the staircase.

Back in the department, Campbell took a quick scout round its various rooms, mainly to ensure that he could go round to the room at the back and begin *Flesh of Life* in earnest with a good conscience. Several patients sat in Minor Trauma, and a glance at their clipboards showed that all have been seen already. There was a middle-aged lady with a black eye and a split lip, a schoolboy with a sprained ankle and a nun with one arm in a sling. Staff nurse McCraw was handing a bottle of aspirin to a youth who looked as if he might have toothache.

'Everything all right, staff?'

'Yes, thanks, Dr Campbell.'

'I'll be round in room nine.'

She smiled, showing large yellow teeth. He had just got through the door when she called him back. He returned and she looked, for some reason, pleased with herself.

'There's a new man in. Just this minute. I thought you might want to see him right away. You know.' She smiled again. 'He's a hand.'

'Thanks, staff.'

'End cubicle.'

A man sat in the cubicle indicated, looking as pale as death. Usually if someone came in with a minor injury and appeared to be in any danger of fainting, they were taken into a sideroom and given a trolley to lie on until they felt better. Perhaps staff nurse McCraw was having one of her hardhearted days. Campbell picked up the clipboard with its blank casenotes. 'Hello. What's the trouble?'

The man unwrapped a large khaki handkerchief from his left hand. 'It's not very nice to look at.'

It wasn't. The hand was normal apart from the ring finger, which was very abnormal indeed. It was only two-thirds of the usual length, the tip was entirely missing and the middle third of the finger had been denuded of skin, muscle and tendons so that only the bone, slender and gleaming white, remained. The first third of the finger, for what it was worth, appeared normal.

'I see,' said Campbell.

'I've got the rest in my pocket,' said the man. 'My mate said you sometimes sewed things back on.'

'It depends. How long ago did this happen?'

'I came straight in from Fairmilehead. About half an hour, I suppose. See, here's the rest.' He fished in the right hand pocket of his jacket and brought out a tobacco tin, which he opened one-handed. Inside lay most of his left ring finger, with a few fragments of tobacco clinging to the raw rim of skin as it's base. He picked it up and blew them off. 'What d'you think, doc?'

'I'm not sure. Probably not much hope. How did it happen?'

'Pity,' said the man, putting the finger back in the tobacco tin. Staff nurse McCraw, who had been looking over Campbell's shoulder as he had been examining the patient, reached forward and snatched the tin with its contents from the patient as though it were a matter of established procedure and common knowledge that all severed fragments of human tissue automatically became hospital property. The man looked a little surprised.

'Don't worry,' she said. 'You'll get your tin back.'

'How did it happen?' Campbell asked for the second time.

'Working overhead. I'm an electrician, see? And I was wiring up a new house in that scheme just past the slaughterhouse, working up among the joists, and I was standing on this wee ladder, putting in a light fitting, and I felt the ladder go.' He paused and looked sadly at his left hand. His colour had improved. 'I grabbed at a joist. Done it before. You just dangle like Tarzan till the ladder falls clear then you let go and drop.'

'What happened this time?'

'Well, I sort of missed my grip. There was a nail in the joist, and it caught my ring. So there I was in a heap on the ladder, feeling like an idiot, and my mate says, ''Hey, Jimmy, where's your finger . . . Oh,

114

here it is,'' and picks it up. Out of my toolbag. ''Never mind my finger, I says, Where's my bloody ring. The wife'll kill me.'' '

'D'you find it?'

'Oh, aye. Hanging on the bloody nail. Anyway. You going to fix it?'

'Might be difficult . . . We'll get a hand chap along. A specialist from the orthopaedic department. You feeling all right?'

'To tell you the truth, doc . . . you know . . . it's not every day you lose your finger. I wouldn't mind lying down . . .'

Staff nurse McCraw had come back. The status of the severed digit had been clarified. It lay on a sterile gauze swab inside a clear polythene bag which she had marked in large black letters 'Left ring finger. Mr McCluskey.' She handed him his tobacco tin first. 'There's your tin.' She looked at him again then handed him the polythene bag. 'And you can hang on to this too, meantime. Don't lose it. The surgeon might want it.'

The man looked pale again. 'Perhaps he'd like to lie down, staff,' said Campbell. She eyed the patient with a certain coolness, as though his pallor had been contrived simply to inconvenience her. 'In that case I'll get you a trolley.' She helped him through to the side room, while Campbell went to phone the duty orthopaedic registrar.

Flesh of Life began with a potted biography of its author, Keith Somebody, a cameraman from Godalming who seemed to have spent most of his career on remote projects with all-male teams, in which surnames were never used. A series of Terences and Kevins blurred together in a variety of exotic places, and the first illustration was a picture of the author with a friend in Tangier. By page thirty-two cannibalism still seemed a long way off, and Campbell's interest had begun to wane even before the intercom summoned him through to trolleys. He put down his book with a vague why-me feeling, reflecting that being alone in that room was fine for getting on with reading, but left no chance of avoiding or even sharing work if the intercom called. Most probably Hadden and Hakeem were stitching at the other end of the department. The call did not sound urgent, and he strolled off round to the trolley room with no particular zeal or even curiosity, wondering, as he did so, if he could ever become as blase about casualty work as Hadden seemed to be. The pale nurse lay in wait for him.

'Collapse,' she explained. 'In a barber's in Castle Street. He's in a lot of pain.'

'Chest pain?'

'Yes. Quite bad.'

'Fine. I'll see him. Have we got a cardiograph organised?'

She smiled. 'I've sent the junior nurse along for the machine.'

'What age is he?'

'Fifties by the look of him?'

'First one?'

'Didn't ask. I just had a quick look and asked you to come round.'

'Readings OK?'

'Pressure's a bit up. Pulse normal.'

'Thanks.'

'Something for pain?'

'Well, let's have a look at him first.'

There were several patients behind screens in the trolley room. Most of the curtained spaces bore labels denoting that the occupants had been referred to specialists in the Institute by their own GPs, and although temporarily in the department did not come under the care of its staff. A blue label with CAS in big letters on it signified Campbell's patient. He parted the curtains.

'Good afternoon.'

'Good afternoon, doctor. Very sorry to trouble you. Especially if it's only indigestion.'

'What's the trouble?'

'A sort of twinge up here.' The man was middle-aged, well turned out and a little overweight.

'When did it come on?'

'Just about twenty minutes age. Quite suddenly. I was getting up out of the chair in the hairdressers — excuse the wee bits of hair all over me — and the man had begun to brush me down and suddenly I had the strangest feeling.'

'What sort of feeling?'

'Oh, you could hardly call it pain . . . More a sort of tightness. A feeling that it would really hurt if I took a deep breath.'

'Where was it?'

The man clenched his fist in front of the top few buttons of his waistcoat. 'To tell you the truth my first thought was that it was wind, and it would all go away with a good belch, if you'll pardon the expression, which might have frightened the barber but done me the world of good.'

'Then what happened?'

'I honestly don't know. The next thing I knew I was waking up on the floor with the barber leaning over me.'

'Sweating?'

116

'What?'

'Did you sweat?'

'I think I did.'

'Sick?'

'No. Just this feeling of wind that wouldn't break, and a bit of squeamishness.'

'Was the pain just in your chest?'

'Mainly.'

'Where else?'

'Oh. A bit into my throat.'

'Arms?'

'No. But my left arm feels a bit heavy, now you mention it.'

'How long were you out for?'

'Oh, not long. You know. I'm not sure.'

'Any idea at all?'

'Maybe about a minute.'

'How's the pain now?'

'Oh, I don't know if I'd call it pain. It's a sort of discomfort.'

'Still there?'

'Yes.'

'Did you feel breathless?'

'A bit. With the tightness across my chest.'

'Ever had anything like this before?'

'No . . . I'm fairly fit as a rule.'

'On any pills?'

'Just something for my blood pressure. Until yesterday. I meant to go and renew the prescription. Beta something.'

'How long have you been on it?'

'Six months or so.'

'Were you warned about stopping them suddenly?'

'No . . . Is it dangerous?'

'Hmm.' From the story it was possible that the sudden withdrawal of the drug could have precipitated a heart attack. 'How d'you feel now?'

'Not too bad. Any idea what's wrong?'

'We'll need one or two tests. A cardiograph certainly, and that shouldn't be long. Then perhaps I'll ask a colleague to see you.'

'Here we are then.' The pale nurse bustled into the curtained space, carrying a little stainless steel dish with a loaded syringe on it. 'You will remember to write this up, won't you, Dr Campbell.'

'What?'

'Cyclimorph. For his pain.'

'Oh. Yes.' Campbell could not recall having ordered that drug in specific terms, or indeed making any positive recommendations about treatment for this patient, but it happened to be appropriate enough. She rolled the man half over, loosening his clothes to expose a buttock.

'You'll remember to write this up, will you, Dr Campbell?' Campbell watched her prepare the skin with an antiseptic swab. She lined the syringe up over the target and said, 'You're really supposed to write it up before it's given.' There was a short pause. Campbell watched the nurse, who looked up at him and smiled, as though conscious of some minor lapse from protocol. She seemed rather too aware of being observed. Her hand trembled slightly as the needle entered the man's pale, fat buttock. Slowly she injected the drug, pressing the plunger home to ensure that the last drop went into the patient. From the corridor outside came the sound of someone whistling. Campbell parted the curtains in time to see the horizontal figure of the electrician on his trolley proceeding towards the door. Presumably the orthopods had come and claimed him. The man who had just had a coronary said, 'Is that someone whistling "The Wedding March"?'

'*Flesh of life?* Is that the thing about a bunch of queers who ate each other in Patagonia?'

'Sort of, sir . . . I think it was mainly porters they ate.'

Yes, that's it. Porters. In Peru. I remember flicking through something about it in one of those colour supplements. Any good?'

'Not very impressed so far.'

'Canoe accident or something.'

'I think they were climbing. I haven't really got into it.'

'Used to read Shakespeare myself. Some of it's actually damned good.'

'Really, sir?'

'Yes. During the war. I'd no idea what a war was going to be like, so I didn't take a damned thing to read. It was dragging terribly — nineteen forty-one, I suppose — and my ma started sending out some of the historical ones. I used to read them between cases, and when we were waiting for something to happen, which is what you do in a war, by the way, for most of the time. I don't suppose you've read much Shakespeare.'

'Not much, sir. A bit at school.' In class readings Campbell had usually been given parts such as 'a townsman' and 'third soldier'. Even Philostrate, in 'A Midsummer Night's Dream', his only named part, had turned out to have only two lines at the beginning, and three more at the end. There had been little stimulus to pay attention while his classmates had haltingly mangled the intervening drama. 'And seen one or two of them on stage, of course.'

'Some of them are damned good, and not what you'd expect at all. I remember one I got just after Arakan, all about chaps sending chaps' heads around in parcels to their next of kin. Can't remember the name of it. Lent it to the chaplain and never got it back . . . D'you know why doctors don't read nowadays?'

'No, sir.'

'Because without war and TB there's no enforced idleness left for the profession. When I was your age home was a three ton truck, with a touch of surgery to break the monotony about once a fortnight. And of course dozens of chaps used to get TB from the patients, and push off to some sanatorium with a bagful of Proust. D'you ever read Proust?'

'No, sir.'

'Neither did I. But I always swore I would if I got TB.' Mr Gillon put down *Flesh of Life* as though to signal that the literary section of their conversation was over. 'How are things in the front shop?'

'Fairly quiet. Just packed a coronary off to intensive care. I think the others are stitching people from Minor Trauma.'

It was JG's custom to visit the department like this, about twice a week, never when it was so busy that he got in the way, or so quiet that the absence of activity was embarrassing. He would spend perhaps twenty minutes with whoever was around, before disappearing into his office to clear his desk. Sometimes he came with a specific question or message, but more often his mission was simply to take the temperature of his little empire, talking to the medical staff and the nurses, listening to what they had to say, and using information to anticipate trouble, and defuse little departmental crises informally. Along with the more structured Thursday morning kirk sessions, they were the main instrument of his benignly paternalist regime.

'Would you like some coffee, sir?'

'Thanks, David. No sugar.'

Campbell filled the kettle at the wash hand basin, wondering if there were any milk available. J.G. sat down. There was something punctilious about his behaviour, reflecting perhaps a military approach to civility. Without knowing much about these things himself, Campbell put it together as another carry-over from his war: senior officer visiting junior officers. J.G.'s behaviour in the room was always restrained, correct and quite unpatronising. By maintaining around himself the aura of a guest he added something to his undoubted

119

professional authority. And his careful abstention from almost any contact with patients was probably another way of making his juniors appreciate the full weight of responsibility delegated to them. They worked *for* Mr Gillon, not with him; and in return he offered a confident acceptance of their competence, and the feeling that, in time of trouble, he would bail them out if it were humanly possible. His usual style at the end of the Thursday meetings ('Old buffers like me should pop along and let you young fellows get on with the job') reinforced all this. And in the background was always the darker side of his authority and responsibility, the hand on the shoulder and the polite 'Could we have a quiet word, old chap?' which followed any lapse from grace.

The kettle boiled and Campbell made two cups of coffee, then looked round, as casually as possible, for some milk.

'I've no objection to having it black, if black it must be,' J.G. said, smiling.

'We've had problems.'

'Sorry to hear that. I thought it might have all settled down. Just noticed the lock on the fridge on my way past just now. Pity.'

From a lesser man that might have been an invitation to bitch about Sister. From J.G. it meant simply that, an occasion for regret, which need not be discussed. 'How are things apart from that, David? Got your next job fixed up?'

'Not yet, sir.'

'Got your eye on anything?'

'Something with medical experience, I think.'

'As opposed to surgical.'

'That's it.'

'So we haven't succeeded in saving you from a lifetime of physicianly doubts and despair.'

'Not yet, sir.'

'Thought about surgery?'

'Well . . . I'm enjoying this job.'

'But you've got the first half of your physician's ticket, haven't you?'

'Yessir.'

'I once watched Sir Monty McAlastair taking twenty minutes to decide how many minims of foxglove extract to give some poor old biddy who was dying before our eyes. Set my face firmly towards the knife. Never regretted it . . . I suppose they still deliberate, but do it all in milligrams now.' J.G. grinned fiercely at his little joke. 'I thought I might have saved a soul when I took you on from old Creech.'

''fraid not.' Even if Campbell had been a surgically oriented Shakespeare addict, it is doubtful if J.G. would have treated him any differently. His faintly military amiability was enjoyed by all who worked for him. He sipped his coffee, then looked up and said, 'How are you getting on with Dr Subhadar?'

Campbell sensed that J.G. had suddenly come to the business part of the meeting.

'He seems very sensible, and competent. And he's done quite a lot.'

'I was wondering . . . how you find him.' Both checked the intercom.

'Worried.'

'I thought so. About the exam.'

'Yes.'

'Between outselves, he was just a little . . . oriental . . . about how many times he's taken it previously.'

'He's certainly had more than two shots. And some hard luck, I gather.'

'And he got stuck with a real problem at Hillhouse,' said J.G. Campbell wondered how much J.G. would divulge, or indeed knew, on the subject of McGrogan Sahib. 'He could have found himself in serious trouble, I gather. Old Groggy took some hellish chances towards the end.'

'Hakeem mentioned one or two things about Hillhouse.'

'Have you seen last week's *BMJ*?'

'Which bit, sir?'

'Groggy. Mr David Murdo McGrogan. The late David Murdo McGrogan.'

'Really? What did he . . .?'

'You wouldn't guess from the glowing tribute. A lot of balderdash about suddenly at home, after a long and brave struggle against illness. Cut his wrists in the bath a week last Tuesday.'

'I didn't realise . . .'

'Poor old sod. Edinburgh graduate too. Went west in the fifties. Used to turn up at the College here fairly regularly. God knows how he got home sometimes. Hadn't seen him for a while then I heard about the recent troubles . . . Action being taken and so on. He was an odd one. Never looked drunk all day, but was. And dropped all pretences at night. He rang me up a couple of weeks ago, saying a colleague from the new commonwealth would probably roll up for a locum job, and mention his name, and that the man was pretty good as these chaps go. Oddest thing was he couldn't remember what his chap was called. Sounded sloshed. Maybe Ali something, he said, and couldn't pass the first part of the fellowship. Then Hakeem turned up and mentioned his name. That was the last I heard of him, until that obituary.'

'I don't think Hakeem knows.'

'Knows what, David?'

'That Mr McGrogan's dead. And he seemed to think very highly of him. Even called his son after him.'

J.G. burst out laughing, then said, 'Shouldn't laugh.'

'I nearly did. But it turned out it was only the Moslem form of David.'

'Poor chap,' said J.G. 'Hakeem I mean. In his way he probably kept old Groggy in business long after he'd stopped earning his pay. Misplaced loyalty. I suppose you and I can sit here and say he should have turned him in to the psychs, but I don't know if I'd have done it myself in Hakeem's shoes. Tricky one.' He stood up. 'Hope to God he slips through the exam this time.' Campbell got up too and J.G. stopped on his way out and said, 'I hope you lads are keeping a friendly eye on him.'

'Yessir.'

'You could mention that to the others.'

'Yessir.'

'Oh, and one other thing, David.'

'What's that?'

'You remembered the Iguanas?'

Campbell had no idea how to go about buying shares, and must have looked it.

'You should have a word with your bank manager,' said J.G. 'If you'd done it when I first mentioned it, you'd have made yourself a few pounds already. Thanks for the coffee.'

'Hello . . . Jean?'

'Oh. Hello.'

'It's me.'

'Mm.'

'Is it inconvenient?'

'Not terribly.'

'What?'

'No. I mean it's not really not.'

'Oh.'

'Yes.'

'Is there someone in the room?'

'Yes.' After a pause Campbell heard Jean laugh, then she said, 'There was until just now. A nurse. But she's gone. I think adulterous phone calls must embarrass her.'

'How are you?'

'All right. And Jim's fine.'

'Oh.'

'Yes. He's really well. We went for a walk last night. And he felt all right afterwards. Everything's coming back to normal.'

'Oh. And how are you?'

'I'm fine. One of my patients didn't turn up. So the nurse came in and told me about her marriage problems. Makes us sound quite simple.'

'Oh?'

'She found drawerfuls of dirty books and frilly knickers and things. Then they had a row. Because he hadn't really been going to the Masons. And they were men pictures. Poor girl. She's about the same age as me but she treated me as if I were old enough to be her mother.'

'Comes with the job.'

'I think so. She doesn't know what she's going to do. She likes him and she's not too fussy about sex. And no kids yet.'

'Sounds sad.'

'They only had their row last night. I'm the first person she's told about it.'

'Is that the one with red hair and a big chin?'

'Yes. Her.'

'Who asked me once if I was a patient.'

'Yes.'

'He probably only married her because she looks like a boy.'

'She said that herself just now.'

'Should go far.'

'Yes.'

'Jean.'

'What, David?'

'We haven't seen each other for ages.'

'Mm. I know.'

'Not even . . . improperly.' He heard her laugh. 'It's been ages.'

'I know.'

'And it feels even longer.'

'It's not easy when you're on your late duty. Wives have to be home at a decent hour.'

'I know.'

'And they can't go out without a proper breakfast.'

'Perhaps not.' Campbell reflected that they could before, in fairly similar circumstances. There was a long silence, then Jean said, 'Last time was nice.'

When Jean talked about the last time it meant she was thinking about the next time. Campbell was relieved.

'Yes. It was nice. Except for the policemen.'

'Gosh. I'd forgotten about them. I sort of listened to the radio. Then got up.'

'I know.'

He heard her laughing. 'Then went back to bed. I really didn't mean to. Oh, David.'

'Oh, Jean.'

'David . . .'

'What?'

'Tomorrow . . . If I don't feel like having a proper breakfast . . . can I come round and have a quick coffee with you instead?'

'Please do.'

'Thanks for inviting me.'

'No trouble.'

'Bye.'

'See you tomorrow.'

'"Everyone had liked Pablo. Though not the youngest of the porters he had always been the blithest and readiest to laugh. His easy grin, lopsided and puppyish, had brightened many a moment of exhaustion on the long trek up from the road-head. Tramping along in our slow sweating line, I had often noticed the firm curve of his calves. Still now forever . . ." Bloody hell, Campbell, you want to watch it. People might think things. And there's *my* reputation to think of. What would people think if they knew I shared a flat with a guy who read books like this? Anything in trolleys?'

'A gallbag sent in as a coronary.'

'Oh, bloody hell. "Dead flesh does not bleed. Though obvious after even just a moment's thought, this observation struck me with the numinous force of a revelation, as Jon's knife slid into the firm cold muscle by which Pablo had until so recently earned his daily bread. As he carved gently, almost reverently on, the fleshliness of the flesh yielded to the cold fact of the knife, and became meat. From his leg and poor shattered head, I averted my eyes."'

'Bonsoir and 'allo,' said Hadden. 'And for tonight we 'ave as usual ze fillet de Pablo au poivre, or of course Pablo bourguignon. And

124

for zose who wish somezing special I 'ave a real treat. Pablo tartare, a finely ground and delicately seasoned preparation of raw, freshly-caught mountain 'alf-caste. Our chef 'imself choose, wiz ze eyes, 'ow you say, averted.'

'They've probably all got worms,' said Bones, catching on to the altered drift of conversation. 'Warning by H.M. Government. Eating half-castes may seriously damage your health.'

They all laughed, then there was a sudden awkward silence, led by Hadden, who had noticed Dr Subhadar standing in the doorway. He was wearing a shiny blue sports jacket in a strange man-made fibre, with an open-necked shirt and rather dashing cravat. He smiled without conviction.

'Good evening, all.· I am sorry to put such a damper on your merriment. Doubtless some private joke, Dr Barnoldswick.' Bones looked round in surprise at the mention of his name, which was almost never heard in full and correctly pronounced.

Hakeem had gone off at five, leaving the department to Campbell and Hadden until Bones had come on at nine thirty to relieve them and take over for the night. Campbell wondered if, under the strain of the impending exam Hakeem had become hopelessly confused over the rota and had turned up under the impression that he was on duty overnight. The awkward silence reasserted itself and after a little while Hakeem spoke again. 'I just dropped in to see if by any chance any of you were proceeding across the road.'

'Very shortly, thank God,' said Hadden. Campbell indicted similar sentiments and Bones said something about having just come from there, and wishing he could go back, before reverting to the customary brief handover. 'Anything apart from the gallbag sent in as a coronary, Campbell?'

'Oh, one or two bods in Minor Trauma.'

'Anything difficult?'

'Don't think so. A query bony injury left elbow awaiting X-rays. A couple of early pub people. One might need stitching. A lip. See what you think. I thought it might be all right without. 'I've done the notes. And there was a call from the police. Someone coming in from the cells.'

'Fell down those stairs?'

'Might have been that. I don't remember.'

'OK Campbell. Poke off to the pub and fill your boots. I'm in charge. Let 'em all come. We never closed and all that. What idiot sent in a coronary as a bloody gallbag?'

'It wasn't that. It was the other way round. Probably because he wasn't very bright.'

'Who? The GP?'

'No. The patient. Can't really describe his pain, and says yes to whatever you ask about it. It's all a bit veterinary. But his ECG's normal and he jumped a mile when I prodded him in the gallbag.'

'I'll buy it,' said Bones. 'You getting somebody to see him? A vet?'

'Next best thing,' said Campbell. 'A surgeon.' Bones made a face.

Hadden got up. 'Let's go, Hakeem. Come fill the cup, what boots it to repeat how time is slipping underneath our feet. To the export trough. Bones, if you can't cope I'll be across the road.'

'Very good poem that,' said Hakeem. 'I learned it at school, though of course the Marists played down the drinking element for local consumption.'

Hakeem, Hadden and Campbell left the department by the main door, where a little queue was building up at the reception desk. A familiar vagrant, suspended between two policemen, was giving the clerkess on duty whatever name he was using at the moment. Behind them a thoughtful looking young man in an anorak stood nervously, as though he might at any instant change his mind and flee from the Institute forever. Behind him a teenage girl with a horrendously variegated tank top and pink hair was vomiting over a friend. In due course Bones would sort them all out.

On the way across to the pub, Hakeem and Hadden, having discovered a common interest in the best known work of Edward Fitzgerald, began to declaim alternate verses, starting from the beginning. It made an odd street scene. Hadden, large and bear-like, brow furled and arms going like a preacher's, rumbled his verses with an affected and grotesquely rural Scottish accent. '". . . a thousand scattered into clay; and this first summer month that brings the rose shall take Jamshyd and Kaikobad away."'

'"But come with old Khayyam,"' — Hakeem's voice, much lighter but authentically oriental and curiously compelling, drew an astonished stare from a man eating chips at a bus stop, — '"and leave the lot of Kaikobad and Kaikoosru forgot: let Rustum lay about him as he will, or Haitim Tai cry Supper — heed them not."'

Verse for verse, they kept at it like tournament tennis players, tossing the poem back and forth between them like a challenge, vying with each other to draw meaning from its obscurities, to roll their tongues round its curious names. They continued their exchange in more conversational tones in the pub, while Campbell got drinks. Religious objections to alcohol on Hakeem's part proved as nominal as

126

those to tobacco. All three had pints of export, and drank quietly through the poem until the last verse, which went to Hadden, who by that time had an empty glass to match its dying fall.

It had been quite a feat of memory, and both seemed to draw great satisfaction from it, listening while the other recited, alert for any lapse and silently rehearsing the next verse. Campbell, to whom only fragments remained from a superficial acquaintance many years ago, was most impressed and said so. Hakeem demurred. 'A reprehensible old cynic, I think you will agree. A hedonist and a nihilist. But what language. ''The nightingale cries to the rose, that yellow cheek of hers to incarnadine.'' What magnificent English. They do not write poems like that nowadays. And of course it owes everything to a culture very close to my own, though no one seems to know for certain who the terrible old fellow was.'

'Aye, they broke the mould,' said Hadden. 'Same again, Hakeem? You've earned it.'

'Oh, no thanks, Graham. Tonight I must have an evening of relative sobriety.' For Hakeem to use Hadden's first name was new, but perhaps understandable in the context of their just having triumphantly recited seventy or so stanzas of purple poetry together. 'Perhaps a half.'

'I shall instruct the surly tapster accordingly. And you, young Campbell? Fill the cup?'

'Thanks.' Hadden went off to the bar.

'Tomorrow is the big day, David.'

'Well, you're probably doing the best thing. A quiet pint and an early night. Worried?'

'Who wouldn't be? However much I study, however much I know, what can I do about prejudice?'

'Prejudice?' Campbell wondered if he were to be subjected to further details of the manoeuvrings which had led to the resignation and ultimately to the suicide (still unknown, he thought, to Hakeem) of McGrogan in Hillhouse.

'Yes, David. Even here. Even within the department itself.'

'Oh, I don't think so, Hakeem.'

'Oh yes.' Hakeem's eyes rolled white as he glanced round the pub for secret policemen, Klansmen and bugging devices. 'Strictly between ourselves, David, I have a distressing experience of Mr Gillon himself today. Only this afternoon, when I was stitching in the clean turret, I had occasion to use the intercom to call Sister on some small matter of suture material — the wrong thing, a useless cat-gut, had been laid out — and perhaps I pressed the wrong button, or perhaps the infernal machine was simply misfunctioning, but somehow as I was pressing, the voice of Mr Gillon came clearly through, saying "I've no objection to having a black", which I suppose is all very well. He had no objections. But when he went on to say "If a black it has to be". Which worries me very much because whereas the previous statement, while crude and objectionable, is not in itself a clear statement of prejudice, it *becomes* a clear statement of prejudice by virtue of the qualifying remark which follows. "If a black it has to be." '

'Doesn't sound like J.G.' said Campbell. J.G. always called blacks 'our colleagues from the new commonwealth'.

'I assure you, David. I assure you most solemnly, as sure as I have ears to hear. I heard it myself, today, in this very department where I am doing my best to carry out an honest day's work.'

'We all appreciate you're being here, Hakeem. Everyone's very pleased with you, as far as I know. I don't know how we'd have managed if you hadn't turned up.'

'You are very kind, David. And so is Graham Hadden, unfortunate jokes apart. He is a knowledgeable and cultured man.'

'He was talking about coffee, Hakeem.'

'What? What are you saying?'

'Mr Gillon. This afternoon. There was no milk. I made coffee, and told him there was no milk. So he said he'd have it black if it had to be like that. "I'll have *it* black, if black it has to be." It's funny. It half clicked when you were saying it just now.'

Instead of laughing or smiling at this harmless explanation of his fears Hakeem looked more worried than ever. He clutched Campbell's sleeve and said, 'Are you sure, David? Are you sure?'

'Yes. Of course. Now I've remembered it, it's obvious. And it's all because of Sister.'

'What is?' said Hakeem, looking by now utterly fraught. 'What?'

'Oh, you know. The milk. How it's all locked up now.'

Hakeem shook his head gravely. He looked greenish pale compared to his usual colour, and very troubled. His outfit, which, Campbell now realised, was a carefully if tastelessly chosen ensemble for an evening in a pub with the lads, looked suddenly awful too: the blue polyester jacket too bright, the green stripe of the Vivella shirt quite wrong, and the cravat, a paisley pattern in purple and crimson, a disaster. Hakeem moistened his lips and swallowed. 'Oh, David, you have almost reassured me. "I've no objection to having it black, if black it has to be," ' he murmured, to try this new theory out for himself. 'Yes. Perhaps Mr Gillon said that. Coffee. Just coffee. Not doctors.' He giggled wanly. 'I hope you are right.'

He revived somewhat with the return of Hadden bearing beer. It was clear that Hadden was not to be a party to Hakeem's fears, and a brave face was put on. He raised his half pint glass and said, 'Cheers, Graham, Fellow of the College — I hope, dare I say it, *our* college in the not too distant future . . . I admire the tie so much.'

Hadden was wearing the college tie, an undistinguished navy blue affair, embellished with crests, small and obscure, depicting a pale upright corpse and various tools of the surgical trade. He looked down and pulled it out from beneath his waistcoat. It was grubby and beerstained. 'I ought to have it laundered,' he said. 'Or at least weeded. For the honour of the college.'

'I look forward so much to wearing that tie myself one day,' said Hakeem. 'Do you know that even in Karachi, when surgeons foregather for conferences and the like, the Edinburgh tie we are looking at is often conspicuous among the selection, if not predominant.'

'How are you for tomorrow?' Hadden enquired abruptly.

Hakeem took a quick sip of beer. 'All right, I hope. The written paper tomorrow I am relatively happy with. It is simply a matter of knowledge, factual stuff and the very objective format of the multiple choice questionnaire: ''The following statements are true of midline lethal granuloma'' and then the little boxes of ''True'' and ''False''. For a candidate who has read widely, can think clearly and above all has the ability to make up his mind, such questions present few problems. It is the oral that I fear, for there the candidate is exposed to the whims and caprices of a sometimes prejudiced examiner . . .'

'Hang on, Hak . . .' After a pint and a half Hadden had reverted to the unwelcome familiarity used by Bones when talking to Dr Subhadar. 'Hang on. In these things there's a lot to be said for not knowing.'

Hakeem looked puzzled. 'But how can the college give rewards for indecision. Surely it is the business of a surgeon to be able to make up his mind.'

'Up to a point, Hak. But they don't give prizes for guessing. You know about the marking system. It's all on page one of the wee book you write the answers in.'

'I've read that,' said Hakeem. Campbell wondered how often, in total, he'd had cause to.

'Well, like it says, marks will be deducted for wrong answers.'

'Of course. But I like to think that if I know a thing, I know it. So, with my pencil I fill in the little box, true or false. And because I have read widely, there's not a lot that comes up, as a rule, that I don't have a pretty firm view on.'

Hadden put down his pint. 'Best of luck, old son. I think I scraped through on a thorough knowledge of my own ignorance, if you see what I mean. I knew what I didn't know, and answered the rest. And I suppose a bit of luck came into it. Reading up on gummatous bloody leptomeningitis the night before.'

'Had you read much?' Hakeem asked.

'Opened the odd book. Auchinleck's Pathology used to give me a terrible thirst. But no kidding, Hak. Don't guess.'

'Thank you for your kind interest, Graham. I will let you know how I get on. Mr Gillon has kindly given me a few days off to sit the written and the oral and to do a spot of revision in between. So we will meet again.'

'You going?'

'Soon I must go. Meanwhile we can talk of other things. What is the present position in the milk crisis?'

They discussed Sister's shortcomings for some minutes, in terms of increasing ribaldry. Hadden's hypothesis that she never had a proper father, only her mother's village milkman, would have accounted for much were it to be proved. At an appropriate interval Hakeem got up to go. He was smiling, almost carefree, perhaps grateful for the company and attention enjoyed on the eve of his exam. Campbell, sensing another hint of oriental formality, got up to bid farewell, and so did Hadden, bumping the table and spilling a lot of beer.

'Best of luck in the wee test, Hakeem.'

'Thank you, David.' They shook hands.

'Best of luck, Hak.'

'Thank you, Graham.' Hakeem bowed slightly to each, smiled and went out.

'Fucking awful jacket,' said Hadden, settling down to a third pint. 'No wonder they keep failing him.'

'Is that what it is? Funny how he dropped in tonight. I wouldn't. Not before an exam.'

'I invited him. It's be nice to Hak week. J.G. passed the word down. Went to some trouble to find out what had gone wrong in Glasgow. Silly bugger answers all the questions. Gets enough right to pass, and then the penalty points for his bad guesses fail him. "Just buy him half a pint and tell him to stop guessing." Decent of him, I thought.'

'Good old J.G.'

'Up to a point. But he's right about Hak. Poor bugger's been at it too long. Thinks he know all about the exam just because he's failed it six times.'

'Six?'

'Apparently so. Here and there. Dublin next, I suppose, if he ploughs it here this time. Maybe a change of scene would help. But you can see how he does it. Works himself into a frenzy of polysyllabic pseudo-omniscience and then charges at it like a bloody catamite.'

'A catamite?'

'You know. Those Moslem stormtroopers. Kamikaze stuff. Kill a crusader and go straight to paradise.'

Campbell knew what he meant but was pretty sure they weren't catamites. 'Hashemites? Circassians?'

'No. Janissaries. That's the fellows. But enthusiasm alone is not enought, as Mary Baker Eddy might have put it. It may be all very well for wiping out Christians, but to become a Fellow of the Royal College of Surgeons of Edinburgh, a little teeny weeny bit of self-awareness is regarded as at least desirable.'

The pub was fairly full, and most of those present were in some way connected with the Institute, even if the link amounted only to a vague ambition on the part of a bank clerk to chat up a nurse. Since its opening a few years before (previously the premises had been occupied by an undertaker, equally dependent upon the Institute for his trade) the succession of managements installed by the brewers had come to realise that no matter how indifferent the service or unpleasant the premises, the proximity of a large teaching hospital was sufficient to guarantee them against any commercial penalty. The staff was commonly found chatting round the till while customers stood white-knuckled at the bar, held back from shouting for service only because of the impression it gave of addiction to alcohol. The various knick-knacks installed at the outset to give the place atmosphere had been dusted perhaps three or four times in as many years, and on top of the juke box, in a hideous pastel striped vase, stood the only bunch of *withered* plastic flowers Campbell had ever seen.

The beers were sharp and gassy and, apart from the lager, all tasted the same. Spillage was recycled with ruthless unhygienic economy, and even the bags of peanuts seemed smaller than in other pubs. But still the place thrived. It was the natural venue for minor occasions originating in the Institute and requiring alcohol. Large groups came in at five and drank till six or seven, and a trickle of doctors on call and nurses going on or off duty kept the place going until the pre-closing time rush, which was now in full swing.

Perhaps because they knew that beer, by virtue of the appalling slackness of the service, was going to become increasingly hard to obtain, Campbell and Hadden drank fairly quickly, and were passing

131

the half gallon mark when a third person joined them. It was Wilson, the gasman from the respiratory intensive care unit.

'Hello, chaps. May I join you?' He was drinking his usual pint of lager, which Campbell always suspected of being tainted with lime, there being no accounting for the ways of gasmen. 'Hello, Campbell. Hello, Graham. How's things in the front line? Bones on tonight? Tough about that chap of yours wasn't it?'

'What chap?'

'The one who died.'

'The driver? The Indian?'

'Yes. The crushed chest.'

'Did he?'

'Oh. I thought you'd have heard. No real reason why you should, I suppose. But he did. About half past four.'

'What happened?' said Campbell, checking to see that he had a full pint glass in front of him.

'Septicaemia.' Wilson took a long gulp from his pint and put it down. Campbell waited. In the event it was Hadden who spoke next.

'That Indian chap you scraped off a road somewhere, young Campbell?'

'That's the one,' said Wilson. 'I don't know how much David's told you about him, Graham, but he came in on Tuesday night. No. I tell a lie. It was probably Wednesday because I'd just started nights so it must be just under a week ago. Anyway this chap came in with a couple of fractures, nothing serious, and a flail chest and did reasonably well at first. Well, reasonably well for a . . .'

At the end of his tale, which more or less coincided with the end of his pint, Dr Wilson excused himself, having someone else with whom he wished to discuss a case. As he left Campbell was jolted by his own reaction to news of the Indian's death: he wanted to tell Jean. He would do that when she came round for coffee before work the next morning.

Next morning Jean did not come round. Campbell waited as long as he could without being late for work, and was a little short with Bones when he was handing over. Later in the morning Jean phoned the department to tell him that she hadn't been able to come round because she had had to drive her husband down to the station for the nine o'clock train. She seemed vague about future arrangements, and when Campbell asked her when Jim was coming back she told him firmly that she was picking him up from the station again at five.

132

FOUR

'Just as well you're early, Campbell. There's quite a lot to tell you about and I'm not going to hang about. I've got Maureen organised to pick me up at nine thirty sharp. You all set?'

'Can I put my white coat on?'

'OK. I'll just tell you about one or two that might just bounce back. I sent home a guy with chest pain who thought he'd had a coronary, and his GP thought he'd had a coronary but I examined him and I'm pretty sure it's not. I tried to find the GP and tell him but he wouldn't listen. I got his wife on the phone and she said was it urgent and I said I didn't ring people up at home at nine o'clock on Friday nights about rubbish and she went on a bit and then he came to the phone, and I think she must have been trying to keep him out of it because when he came on he sounded pissed and he said the man was an old friend of his and he thought the best place for him was intensive care and who did I think I was anyway. I was trying to find out why he thought the guy had had a coronary so that I could explain to him why I didn't.'

'What's he got then?'

'I'm coming to that. So this bugger on the phone got really stroppy and said that if a friend of his phoned up with severe chest pain he took it on trust so I said what was he like when you examined him and he slammed the phone down. Then he rang in about two minutes later to say that he'd been in practice for twenty-two years and when did I qualify, so I said that the point was that I'd examined the patient, and he called me an insolent young puppy and put the phone down. So it might bounce back.'

'I see. What's wrong with the patient?'

'That was part of the problem. I couldn't remember what it's called. But I knew what it was . . . The rib thing.'

'Oh. Costochondritis?'

'Yes. That's it. So I gave the chap some Distalgesic and told him it was nothing to do with his heart and he seemed quite pleased, but said he was surprised he wasn't going into intensive care. But I told him he'd be all right and that I'd write to his GP. But you can do that.'

'Why?'

'Because you can remember that costo thing.'

'Tietze's Syndrome?'

'What?'

'Same thing as costochondritis. Another name.'

'Smartass physician. So you can do the letter. I've written in the notes. He's tender over the first two left ribs. Classical picture, except I couldn't remember what the damn thing was called. He was quite grateful. Thought he was booked.'

'Anything else?'

'A wino with lice.'

'What about him?'

'Told him I'd get him an appointment with dermatology.'

'And send it to his no fixed abode?'

'Smartass again. He's in custody.'

'They don't usually kick up a fuss.'

'Well . . . He's in custody and he's got a headache. Couldn't find anything . . . So I told him I'd get an appointment for his skin condition. They took him away. I don't think there's much to his headache. Nothing that slipping on those steps won't take his mind off.'

'Poor old sod.'

'So he might come back . . .'

'Thanks.'

'And there was a ski instructor with the clap. Wanted fixing up before seeing some bird at ten. I told him VD out-patients on Monday morning and strap it to his leg till then. They must really get stacks . . . Even in summer. Like an occupational hazard.'

'Is he going to come back?'

'Shouldn't think so. I just thought you might be interested.'

'Anything else lying about?'

'An RTA. Three of them. Two fractured. One lacerated. The girl from the front seat's a bit of a mess. I've asked the plastics guy to come down and embroider her face together again. Apparently quite pretty. And the orthopod's taking the other two. Driver's cracked his pelvis and the guy that ran into them's done his femur. Motorcyclist.'

'Is he OK?'

'I put up blood. He's pink and he can wait. D'you want to go round?'

'If you don't mind.

It was still only twenty-five past nine. Campbell preferred to come in early for nights, especially Fridays, because peace of mind later, when things got busy, depended on having a good grip on what was going on right from the start. Bones' white coat was smeared with blood and he looked more dishevelled and distraught than usual. 'Couple of drunks in here. Both brought in by the friendly blue van. Neither in custody. That one's sugar was a bit low, so I stuck up a unit of ten percent dextrose and it seemed to perk him up. At least at first . . . Triviatrics is quite quiet. I've seen most of those . . . Oh. She's new.' He nodded at a pale blonde girl with a face like a skull, whose hair was streaked with blood. 'Apparently there was something nasty happening at El Greco's. She might be from that. Hadden's stitching on an ear from there already. Or maybe he's finished.'

They proceeded up towards the turrets. A nurse was bandaging a gauze pad over the bruised and bleeding forehead of a young reveller, and in a side room, behind inadequate screens, a man with his trousers round his ankles stooped over a trolley while a nurse took aim with syringe full of penicillin. Hadden was in the clean turret. 'Ah, young Campbell. Good of you to drop in, lad, and let young Bones here off to give his maggot a gallop.' His patient, a very drunk drunk, lay snoring as he cobbled up a scalp laceration three inches long with the nimble dispassion of a sailmaker. 'If the last two hours is anything to go by, we could run out of catgut before the punters run out of drinking time . . . How's the other end?'

'Sorted out,' said Bones, meaning that he was going off duty soon. They left Hadden to his stitching and walked along to the trolley room. A policewoman escorting another bloodied girl stood politely at the desk while the porters grappled with a young man whose hair was dyed shocking pink. He was agitated rather than violent. The porters were trying to sit him down in one of the department's wheeled chairs. 'Looks like one for you,' said Bones as they passed. 'It's twenty-eight minutes past nine . . . And there are a couple of people in trolleys I haven't mentioned. No. Three. But nothing difficult. No. Four. But I don't know anything about the fourth one.'

They were standing in the middle of the trolley room. Most of the curtains were drawn, and most had labels pinned to them indicating that the patients on the trolleys inside had already been assigned to someone else's care. At one space there was no label. 'Who's that, staff?'

'A regular.' The staff nurse on duty was the pale thin one whom Hadden suspected of always having dysmenorrhea. 'Hello, doctor Campbell.'

'Hello, staff. Is he ready?'

'Not yet. I thought we'd clean him up a bit.'

'Thanks. I'll see him soon.' Campbell and Bones turned to leave the trolley room.

'So that's it, old son, and the best of luck. We're off for a drink and a meal somewhere and then we're going on to a couple of parties. And I'm not sure we'll be using the flat much over the weekend either.' The staff nurse had returned to the desk but was still following their conversation with interest. Bones lowered his voice a little. 'Maureen's just got a double bed. Lovely girl.'

Back in the coffee room Campbell switched the kettle on. Bones took off his white coat, put on his suede jacket and cap and sat with his feet on the table. 'Come on, woman,' he said to nobody. 'It's half past nine and I'm fed up with this place.'

'Is there any milk.'

'About half a pint. There.' He pointed to a cupboard. 'I don't know how fresh it is. I'm into black coffee.'

'Want some?'

'Be going any minute. But yes please . . . What's that rib thing called again?'

'Costochondritis.'

'Thanks . . . Viral, isn't it?'

'Probably.'

'Doctor Campbell,' said the intercom. 'Your patient's ready.'

'Thanks, staff.'

'Don't worry about my coffee,' said Bones. 'I'll make it myself.'

On the way round to trolleys Campbell met Maureen going to collect Bones. She was indeed looking lovely.

The staff nurse on duty in trolleys handed Campbell a wad of dog-eared pale blue clinincal notes, about an inch thick. 'He's a regular,' she said, adding, in a quieter voice, 'He's on the B list.' The B list, or black list, was an informal category of patients who for some reason or other were noteworthy in their abuse of the services of the department. Their record cards in the index had a small 'B' on the top right hand corner, and their case notes were filed separately. No one was very sure who ran the B list, or what exact qualifications were required before a patient's name was added to it. Once, on a quiet night, Campbell had browsed through the box of files, and concluded that the recurrent characteristics of its occupants were multiple atten- dance, social instability and at least a suspicion of malingering. Most had no regular GP, and therefore nowhere else to go, but this did not seem to be regarded as a mitigating circumstance. Many had no permanent addresses, or were listed as c/o one of the city's model lodging houses. Some had a variety of names, and were carefully cross-indexed under them all. Any casualty officer's collection of the most unforgettable patients he had met would certainly have included

136

one or two from its ranks.

The sheaf of notes referred to one John Houghton, with an address which, though unremarkable to the innocent eye, signified the city's most desperate night shelter. 'You probably know him,' said the staff nurse. 'The basket man.'

'Oh. I didn't know his name was Houghton.'

'No,' said the staff nurse. 'That's his real name.'

'Usually calls himself Howie, doesn't he?'

'That's him Houghton, or Howie. And sometimes Doig. But always John.'

'That's me, dear,' said a voice from behind the curtains. Campbell opened them and went in. It was indeed the down-and-out he had had in mind, a bedraggled rogue of considerable charm who toted a bundle of canes round the pubs, together with a sample of his wares, a little rattle in the form of a small enclosed basket with a cane handle and a bottle top inside. For the price of a pint he would run one up on the spot, commenting on the wit, charm, good looks and generosity of his benefactor and the unsurpassed beauty of his girlfriend, couples being his softest touch. Campbell had seen him here and there, in pubs or in transit, around the town for years and even, in his green youth, purchased one of his rattles. The boom time for his trade seemed to be the Festival, when he was not above wearing a tattered army kilt, with the American market in mind. His winter quarters, like those of the ducks in Central Park, remained a mystery.

'Hello, Mr Houghton . . . What's the trouble?'

'Ma chest, son. Awfy bad.' His voice seemed to have got much feebler since his first cheery 'That's me.' He was a man who looked about sixty and might actually have been anything from fifty to seventy. His hair was mixed silver and dark, curly but tidy, and his eyes rheumy and deep brown. He sported a moustache, a straggly Old Bill forever moist with snot and beer, and he had no teeth. By his own modest standards he did not look unwell, or even ill-kempt. He was fairly clean and had shaved within the week. The string round his coat was fresh, and a large, neat bundle of canes stood against the wall behind his head.

'What's bad about it?'

'Terrible cough, son.'

'Any spit?'

'Terrible, son. Havnae seen spit like it since one o' my mates died in the model.'

'What colour is it?'

'Green?' he said, looking up to see if Campbell were impressed.

137

'And whiles it's yellow. Years since it's been white. And of course there's the odd wee spot of blood. Nothing much. But it put me in mind o' yon fellow in the model.'

Campbell had heard that a section of the B list clientele kept a close track on staff turnover in the department, and arrived to take advantage of neophytes in the first days or weeks of their tenure. Having been almost two months in the job he did not feel specially vulnerable, but there was something in the man's manner that suggested he would welcome admission to a hospital bed which ensured comfort, warmth and three square meals a day.

'How much?'

'How much whit?'

'How much spit?'

'Oh, an awfy lot. Gallons. Well . . . no' gallons, but pints anyway. I dinnae collect it, mind, so I cannae tell ye right tae the nearest ounce. But honest, son, it's an awfy lot.'

'Breathless?'

'Oh, aye. Hardly got up the brae comin' up here. A wee laddie cairried my wee bundle o' sticks. Nice wee laddie he was. I gied him a wee tip.'

'Is that only with exercise?'

'Whit?'

'Are you breathless lying still, or breathless at night?'

'No' bad the noo, but wi' the slightest bit o' effort, I'm done, son, I'm jist done.'

'Can you sleep flat?'

'Whit?'

'Can you sleep lying flat without getting breathless?'

'I don't sleep very well, son. I don't think anybody would in yon place without a dram in them, or a couple of pints. It's aye fu' o' noisy drunks.'

'Do you get any pain in your chest?'

The old man paused, like a shifty witness considering where that and subsequent questions might lead. 'Not much now. I had a bad attack o' pain wi' breathin', at the beginning o' the week.'

'Where?'

'In ma back. On the left. It's went away, by God's mercy. But He's left me wi' a terrible spit. Wid ye like tae see some?'

'If you can. And I'd like to listen to your chest.'

'Help me up, son.'

'Staff.'

The staff nurse appeared from nowhere, and they sat the old man

138

up, and stripped his top half. He was pale but well muscled and there was an elaborate tattoo, in the form of a regimental crest, on his right upper arm. 'Where did you get that?'

'In the ermy, son. Doin' ma bit. Ye wouldnae think it tae look at me now, but a was a sodger in ma time. And I went because it was ma duty, no' jist tae get away frae the wife, like some. And I got that in Cairo, like many a daft laddie. But they'll aye ken I wiz a Gordon. Nice, isn't it? I wiz going' tae get a piper as weel, but the wee bugger wanted forty woodbine . . . I wisht whiles I'd got it done, though . . . about here.'

Campbell was quite interested, but the staff nurse was getting restive. He set to work and percussed the old man's chest in the approved manner, and then listened with his stethoscope to the variety of horrible rattles and squeaks inside.

'Cough.'

The man obliged with a great convulsion and a noise like a ton of coal going down a chute all at once. At the end of it his mouth was full and he gestured silently for something to empty it into. The staff nurse produced a waxed paper carton. The sputum was evil: yellowish green and liberally steaked with blood.

'What's his temp, staff?'

'Thirty-seven five.'

'Thanks. When did you last have a chest X-ray?'

'Oh, maybe two years.' If he were a B list regular it was likely he'd had one a lot more recently than that.

'You sure?'

'Oh, aye. Honest, son. And I wish I'd had another two or three since.'

'Why's that?'

'Oh, they're a grand thing. I aye feel rare for a good two or three weeks afterwards.' He smiled engagingly and Campbell began to feel that all this *faux-naif* winsomeness was getting out of hand, and perhaps indirectly reflecting on what he thought of as his tough casualty image.

'Ever had TB?'

The man's face went suddenly sad, and his eyes filled with tears. 'Is that whit it is, son? And it took my mither and my puir wee sister, and her only twelve year old.'

'We can do an awful lot about TB nowadays,' said Campbell firmly.

'Ye didnae save me puir wee sister.' He sobbed and his nose ran unchecked to fill his moustache. The staff nurse was nodding.

'D'you know him, staff.'

She mouthed 'Old TB' and Campbell murmured his thanks for the information. The blood was a little alarming but by no means as portentous an event as it might have been for a contemporary of Keats or the librettist of 'La Traviata'. Lots of old men with chronic bronchitis and cured TB coughed up blood, and usually because of the former rather than because of a recurrence of the latter. The routine was to see a chest X-ray and take it from there.

'It's time you had an X-ray again.'

'Thanks, son . . . I'll jist put mysel' entirely in your hands.'

'They usually X-ray him and it always looks terrible,' said the staff nurse.

'Thanks, staff,' said Campbell.

'D'you want mair spit?' said the patient, trying to be helpful or perhaps heading off the staff nurse's counter-offensive.

'No thanks,' said Campbell, 'but the more you can get up the better. Now I just want a quick look at the rest of you . . .'

'I'm sorry I'm no' very clean . . . I havenae really been fit enough tae look after mysel, the way I did when I wiz in the ermy . . .'

'That's all right. Just lie down again . . . Let me see your hands.'

Apart from his temperature and the awful noises in his chest, there was nothing to find on the man. His hands were normal, there were no enlarged glands in his neck and his abdomen was unremarkable, with only a moderate degree of liver enlargement, quite compatible with his observed and admitted habits. The most likely thing was an exacerbation of chronic bronchitis, with the blood in the spit accounted for by long-standing damage to his airways rather than by active TB. Campbell scribbled his notes on the case sheet and wrote out an X-ray card, filling the space marked 'clinical information' with 'Pyrexia, cough and haemoptysis. ? Exacerbation of chronic bronchitis?? Reactivation of old TB.' He gave it to the staff nurse to pass on to the X-ray girl. She read it and said, 'That's what they always put.'

The staff nurse left, and Campbell went quickly over the other patients from Bones' handover. There was an old man with fractured kneecap, waiting to be seen by the orthopods, a man with a perforated duodenal ulcer who had been assessed by the general surgeons and would go to their wards as soon as a porter became available to take him there, and an old lady with nothing in particular wrong with her, who had simply fainted at a bus stop, but whose subsequent misfortune in being brought up to Casualty meant that she would be very lucky to get off with less than a week's assorted investigations as an in-patient in the medical wards.

With trolleys tidied up, Campbell had no excuse for not getting on with the sundry ghastliness of a Friday night in Minor Trauma. A little later he found himself, clipboard in hand, facing the agitated youth with pink hair. On closer inspection, it proved that the colour of his hair was only one of a number of eccentricities. He also wore a peculiarly livid and glossy lipstick, eye make-up, a Regency beauty spot on his left cheek and something on his teeth that made them sparkle like cut glass. He had a purple shirt with lace cuffs, a mushroom coloured velvet jacket and a round enamelled badge on his right lapel inquiring 'How dare you presume I'm heterosexual?'

He smiled shyly up at Campbell, who took refuge in searching for the man's name in the notes on the clipboard.

'What's the trouble, Mr Abercromby?'

'I've had a spot of bother . . .'

'Bother?'

'Yes. Bother. With my nipples.'

'What sort of bother?'

The man looked round, in a hunted sort of way, pursed his lips and then blurted out 'Pain, actually. They've been most awfully sore.'

'Since when?'

'Since they were done.'

'Since what was done?'

The man was by now quite red, and visibly distressed. 'I'd been saving up and finally had them done . . . A couple of days ago. By a friend . . . who does that sort of thing.'

'What sort of thing?'

'You know, doctor.' He looked smoulderingly up at Campbell, as though that might help him to guess. 'I had them pierced,' he said abruptly.

'When was that?'

'Just a couple of days ago . . . I was ever so pleased at first. Gold sleepers. Slender but very lovely. And quite expensive. Then they began to hurt.'

'Swelling?'

'Oh, not a bosom or anything. But definitely a bit on the swollen side. And they oozed.'

'I'd better have a look,' said Campbell, drawing the curtains and wondering about getting a nurse.

'I'm not embarrassing you, am I? After all we're just like everybody else. We can't be expected to run our own hospitals and everything, can we now? And we all pay our stamp things.'

'Quite.'

'Would you like to see them, then, doctor?'

'Yes, please. I mean yes.'

'Oh, doctor, don't be shy. Nobody's a hundred per cent anything, these days, are they?' The man removed his jacket with a flourish, then his shirt, more carefully. His aftershave, if that was what it was, quenched the customary Minor Trauma odours of disinfectant, sweaty feet, drink and vomit. Campbell began to wish he had got a nurse. 'See, doctor. The left one's worse off, poor thing. Look, that could almost be pus . . . I'm ever so ashamed at having to come up here and bother you busy doctors. But I thought something dreadful might happen if I didn't. D'you think it still might, doctor? D'you want to feel them, doctor?'

'Evening all.'

Campbell turned round to find Hadden looking over the top of the curtain. The patient burst out giggling. 'Mr Hadden,' said Campbell, 'could you ask a nurse . . .' Hadden nodded gravely and went off. The patient continued to giggle and Campbell became embarrassed, and was eventually joined by a nurse who in turn became embarrassed too.

Through each nipple the man had had little rings of a yellowish metal, turning green where it was in contact with skin. The nipples and surrounding areolae were red and inflamed, and there were tender lumps in both armpits. Campbell asked the nurse to take the patient's temperature.

'I don't think they'll get better until the rings are removed.'

'Are you sure, doctor? You've no idea how much it cost.'

'Sorry,' said Campbell. It's a sort of foreign body reaction. The inflammation won't get better until the rings are removed. But with that, and a course of antibiotics, it'll clear up in no time.'

The man looked thoughtful then said 'This never happened with my earrings . . . Doctor . . .' Suspicion clouded his brow. 'Doctor . . .' He pursed his glossy lips again. 'Doctor, d'you think they might not be gold?'

Campbell knew very little about nipples and even less about precious metals. 'I really don't know. They're sort of turning green next to your skin.'

'The beast . . . And he left it until he was just going till he did me. The pig. Swore the gold alone was worth fifteen pounds . . . Doctor, d'you think . . .'

'No idea. Except they've got to come out. I'll do it for you as soon as I can . . . You could have them valued, I suppose.'

'Wouldn't lower myself . . . The beast. Him and his virgin gold.'

In the next curtained booth was a housewife who had splashed hot chip fat on her forearm an hour before, then sprinkled it, for some reason, with flour and wrapped it in a tea towel before coming up to the department for treatment. The burn was patchy and pink. Most of the doughy mess had been removed. Campbell made a note, and a sketch of the burn, and wrote her up for something for the pain, then sent her along to one of the treatment rooms to have it dressed again, using more conventionally medical dressing materials.

The next patient was a girl who said she thought she was pregnant. Detailed enquiries revealed that she had no grounds whatsoever for thinking so, but no explanation to that effect would satisfy her. Campbell gave in, and asked the nurse to arrange for a urine specimen to be sent for testing. When he had done that she confessed that she had really come up to get a prescription for what she called the Birth Pill. Campbell expressed his regrets and she left angrily.

The next patient after that was a man with tiny red marks between his fingers which he claimed were an industrial dermatitis that would not only enable him to claim large sums of money by way of compensation, but would also entitle him to a certificate, to be issued there and then by Campbell, stating that he was unfit to join a night shift which had started an hour previously. The marks between his fingers were little irregular red lines just beneath the skin. Campbell asked if they itched. They did. He then asked the man if he itched anywhere else. The man looked at Campbell as if he were being unnecessarily awkward.

'Bought a new pair of underpants a fortnight ago, come to think of it. Haven't been right since.'

'Itch?'

'Terrible. But that was before this industrial dermatitis affected my hands.'

'Can I see?'

'What?'

'The itch from your underpants.'

'That's not stopping me from going to work.'

'No, but it might just turn out to be something to do with the things on your hands.'

The man stood up and loosened his belt. Campbell hastened to close the curtains. There were scratch marks and lumpy red spots on and around the patient's genitals. A half-forgotten item of dermatological expertise, from a drowsy undergraduate tutorial at least three years before, slithered elusively around in the back of Campbell's mind. Until it surfaced he marked time with a few questions. Some itches were worse at night.

'Is the itch worse at night?'

'No.'

'Oh.'

'In fact it's better. It's much worse when I'm in bed.'

'What?'

'Like I said, I'm on night shift. It's much worse through the day, when I'm in bed.'

'Oh . . . Have you found anything that helps it?'

'Helps what?'

'The itch.'

'I tried some sort of eau de cologne stuff, to cool it down. But it hurt like hell. Thought I'd skinned my bollocks for good . . . Sorry doc. No. Nothing helps it.'

The penny dropped. 'Have you been in close contact with anyone with an itch . . . in the last few weeks?'

'No. I don't think so. There's just this stuff that's giving me the industrial dermatitis. A kind of paint spray at work.'

'No. I meant someone . . . not something. Anyone you know got an itch . . .?'

The man went suddenly pink and thoughtful. 'Yes . . . There's a sort of . . . girlfriend. Works in the paint shop. Mentioned something about going to her doctor because of eczema.'

'Is she all right now?'

'She got pills. But she's still got that industrial dermatitis too. Like just about everybody else in that paint shop. Can I pull my trousers up, doc?'

'Sorry. Of course. She's got industrial dermatitis? On her hands?'

'Much the same as mine. Much the same as everybody else's.'

'I see.' The subject of the soporific, half-recalled tutorial had been scabies. Scabies was passed on by what the dermatologist had called 'Warm body contact, the nature of which may sometimes be inferred from the distribution of the first lesions complained of, the genitals and, in the female, the breasts, being commonly affected.' From outside the cubicle came the noise of someone singing, and of someone else vomiting. The man was fastening his belt again. 'I don't think it's industrial dermatitis,' said Campbell thoughtfully.

'Oh. What is it then?'

'Oh. Something that's sort of . . . going round. Sounds rather as if it's going round the paint shop. But it's not from paint spraying. Anyway, it's quite easy to treat.'

Campbell left the man with his thoughts, and went off for an EC 10 pad, and wrote out a prescription for a tube of Lorexane. He returned and explained how to use it. 'Thoroughly. All over. Except your face. After a bath. And change your clothes. The itch takes a day or two to settle down after you've used the stuff.'

'Thanks, doc . . . Oh . . . by the way, doc, will this be enough for . . . one or two of us?'

'What?'

'Will there be enough ointment for everybody?'

'No. I don't think so. Two at the most maybe. But everybody who's got an itch should see their own doctor.'

'What is it anyway?'

'Oh. Well, it's a sort of contagious thing you get . . . usually by close physical contact with someone who's got it already.'

'What's it called?'

Campbell lowered his voice. 'Scabies, actually.'

'So we won't get compensation for industrial injury.'

'Shouldn't think so.'

'Thanks anyway, doc. Cheers.' The man left, looking thoughtful.

The next patient was a man with a big bandage over one eye, which made him look like an extra from a war film. He was drunk, but not too drunk to give an account of how he sustained his injury. 'A sort of wee accident in a pub. Just a wee friendly accident in a pub. A wee broken glass moved. If ye wouldnae mind havin' a look, doc. See the eye's all right, and that.'

The staff nurse undid the bandage. There was a jagged cut running along the man's eyebrow, and another over his cheekbone. The space between was filled with clot. Campbell removed this very carefully, using a gauze swab, and fearing the worst. The blob of clot slithered into a waiting steel dish and the man's eyelids were revealed, intact. They wrinkled together then opened to disclose an undamaged eyeball.

'Ah well . . . There we are.' said the man. 'No problem.'

'You've got a couple of cuts there that'll need stitching.'

'When'll you do that, doc? You don't mind me calling you doc, do you?'

'Soon as I can,' said Campbell, reflecting on the excellent design of the human skull, with the eyeball set far back between bony prominences, so that while injuries around the eye were common, injuries to the eyeball itself were rare. As he scribbled the rubric for all lacerations of any importance (wound toilet and suture, anti-tetanus toxoid and Triplopen) the staff nurse from trolleys interrupted him.

'A crash box call, Dr Campbell. An RTA. Three injured, they said. Two seriously.'

'How long?'

'Ten minutes.'

Campbell glanced into the remaining occupied cubicles in the row. There was nothing that couldn't wait for twenty minutes anyway. In the clean turret Hadden was stitching a rather complicated laceration on a forehead that might have been in contact with, or even through, a windscreen. Campbell passed the message on.

'Crash call. RTA. Two seriously injured. Ten minutes.'

'Thanks, lad. I'll finish this off and join you. How's trolleys?'

'Just going to check.'

In trolleys Mr Houghton's chest X-ray was ready for inspection. Without his old X-rays for comparison, it was difficult to assess the clinical significance of the various abnormalities, but as the staff nurse had warned, it looked terrible. The shadows of the diaphragms were low and flat, and the lungs had the threadbare, blotchy appearance of chronic chest disease. At the top, on both sides, were the dense, streaky shadows of old, inactive tubercle, or something that Campbell was fairly certain was old, inactive tubercle. But on the left there was a suspicion of a cavity, again possibly old, and the edge of the streaky shadow was softer and more blurred than on the right.

Campbell was of a generation of doctors for whom open TB was a rarity if not an anachronism. He had seen pictures of relevant chest X-rays in textbooks, and had handled 'typical' plates from collections, but he had never been given to look at a chest X-ray from a patient over whom hung the question 'Is this or is this not active tubercle?' It was a bit awkward. There had been a pipe-smoking, wide-flannelled cadre of post war medical graduates who had known all about this, and had earned their daily bread throughout the tuberculous fifties by making such decisions, but they were now dispersed, and their clientele for the most part either dead or cured. Campbell felt as unhappy as he would have been if asked to take the road in Dr Finlay's Austin Seven. The staff nurse watched him. He wondered how best to off-load this unwelcome responsibility.

The arrival outside of an ambulance in a hurry, brakes squealing and aerial rattling under the canopy at the main door, cut short his embarrassment. With the staff nurse, he went across to the resuscitation room and stood waiting. A policeman came in, running, and pulled up awkwardly, discomfited by the clinical calm of nurse and doctor waiting in the brightly lit and impressively equipped space. 'Two of them are really bad,' he said. 'Thought the boy was away when we got him.'

'What happened?'

'Drunk. And failing to stop when signalled. Stolen car. Got up to

146

eighty with us on their tail, then missed a bend. We nearly followed them.' The policeman was pale and shaken.

'They all conscious?'

'The boy's sort of semi. You know. Mumbly. Here he is.'

An ambulance man and a porter wheeled in a young man. He lay on the shiny red ambulance service stretcher, with its carrying poles still in place, on top of one of the department's trolleys. A light blanket covered him. His eyes were closed. He was breathing. He was pink. The staff nurse removed the blanket. The most obvious clinical abnormality was that the youth was in a high state of sexual arousal, readily visible beneath lightweight cotton trousers. Rather noticeably, the staff nurse noticed it, but did not comment. The ambulance man muttered 'Been like that since we got him' as though to exonerate his service from any imputation of impropriety in transit. The policeman stared. The nurse put the blanket to one side and started to count the man's pulse at the wrist.

Campbell went to the top of the trolley and said 'Hello'. The patient opened his eyes.

'Where's this?'

'The Institute. Edinburgh. You've been in an accident.'

'I know.'

'How d'you feel?'

'Hellish.'

'Any pain?'

'In my back . . . And a bit in my head.'

'Anywhere else?'

'No. But I can't feel my feet. Or my legs.'

'Where's the pain in your back?'

The youth reached round with his free hand to point in his back, low down, at about the level of his umbilicus. 'There. And there's a sort of lump in my back. And I can't feel my feet.'

'His pulse is seventy, Dr Campbell.'

'Thanks, nurse.'

'Can I take the stretcher, doc?'

'Could you hang on?'

'I'd rather not, doc. But if you say so, I can radio in to control and tell them you're holding it.'

'Please do.'

'Think his back's away, doc?'

'Might be,' said Campbell quietly. 'I certainly don't want to move him until we've seen X-rays.' The ambulance man took the hint and went away. Campbell turned his attention to the patient again. 'I'm going to examine you and then get some X-rays.'

From the door of the resuscitation room came the sound of a girl crying. 'Mind your backs,' said a porter manoeuvring a trolley into the second space. 'Make way for a sad one . . . I think she's broken her back.'

Campbell said 'Excuse me' to his patient. The nurse had already indicated to the newly arrived porter that he should say no more and go. On the second trolley lay a girl about seventeen years old. She was sobbing and saying over and over again 'I can't feel myself . . . I can't feel myself . . . What's happened?' A staff nurse was trying to comfort her and take her pulse all at once. Campbell turned back to the pale nurse and said, 'Get Mr Hadden on the intercom, please. Ask him to come through. He's in the clean turret.'

The girl on the trolley was pale and blonde, a badly dyed blonde with mousey hair growing in. Her face was dirty and her eyes red from crying.

'Mr Hadden, Mr Hadden,' said the staff nurse into the intercom. 'The two crash box cases have arrived. Could you come please.'

'What happened?' said Campbell.

'We were in a car . . .' Her breath smelled of stale drink. 'And the next thing I knew was waking up in a field. Will my baby be all right?'

'What?'

She started sobbing again. 'I'm six months pregnant.'

'Any pain? Any bleeding?'

'I don't know,' she sobbed. 'I don't know . . . I can't feel myself. Not anything from beneath about my shoulders.' She shuddered and sobbed again. Once more the staff nurse comforted her, holding her head, and smoothing back her hair. There were crumbly bits of soil on the pillow. Campbell went across to the intercom and pressed the button marked 'Neurosurgical Registrar'. The sound of a blaring television came back at him.

'Hello . . . Hello . . . Casualty SHO here. We've got two spinal injuries in the resuscitation room.'

'Thanks. I'll be right down,' said a voice, over the television noise.

On the evidence so far, a car had been stolen by three drunk young people, one of whom was a girl who was six months pregnant. The police attempted to stop them and there had been a chase ending in an accident, of which there were three victims. Both victims examined so far appeared to have catastrophic injuries, perhaps the worst that could befall young adults. The youth had back pain, loss of sensation from the waist down and had noted a bony irregularity in his lumbar spine.

148

It added up to a broken back, with an acute transection of the spinal cord. He faced a wheelchair life, dead below the waist.

The girl's state was less certain but perhaps no less serious. She had a higher level of loss of sensation, but she had not so far complained of back pain. It was still just possible that she had a temporary loss which might recover spontaneously, a so-called spinal concussion. The routine for sorting it out was the old familiar one of listening, asking questions, looking, laying hands on to find if things felt wrong, of organising special investigations and calling in the right sort of expert opinion. Campbell buzzed reception on the intercom and asked the girl there to send the X-ray girl along right away.

Hadden came in. He and Campbell had a quiet conference near the door.

'Nasties?'

'Looks like it. He's a definite spinal fracture. About first lumbar, I think. She's higher.'

'Where have you started?'

'He came in first.'

'I'll see her.'

'The neurosurgical registrar's coming down.'

'X-rays?'

'She's on her way. And . . . that girl. She says she's pregnant.'

'Sheeyit.'

'And she was unconscious for a while.'

'Bloody hell. Thanks.'

Campbell went back to the youth on the trolley. The staff nurse was standing with a stethoscope hanging from her ears.

'His BP's OK. One fifty over eighty.'

'Thanks, staff.'

The patient's face was drawn with pain now. Campbell wondered about giving him something to make him feel more comfortable but didn't know enough about spinal injuries just to get on with it. The neurosurgeon, who would know more, would be down shortly.

'Can we get him stripped, staff? It might be better to cut his clothes off. So as not to move him.'

'You sure, Dr Campbell?'

'Yes, please.'

A special pair of scissors, large and blunt-pointed, was kept in the resuscitation room for such eventualities. The staff nurse went across for them, and Campbell explained to the patient what was going to happen, then asked about the accident. The patient countered with a question of his own.

149

'Where's Roxanne?'

'Who?'

'My girlfriend.'

'What's she like?'

'Blonde.'

'Was she in the car?'

'Yes.'

'Was there anyone else in the car?'

'Yes. Andy. Her brother.'

'She's here.'

'How is she?'

'Another doctor's just seeing her now.'

'Is she all right?'

'I don't know.'

'Did I hear somebody say her back's broken?'

Campbell thought angrily of the porter who had brought her in. 'She's just being examined now.'

'We're getting married,' said the youth.

'How did it happen? Were you trapped in the car?'

'Must have been thrown out. Woke up in a field with a cop shining his torch in my face.'

'What happened?'

'We were in a car . . . Andy was driving. A nice car . . . A sort of sports car. Open.'

'What time was that?'

'I don't know. Maybe half an hour ago. What time is it now?'

'Eleven o'clock. Tell me about the pain in your back.'

'It's going sort of . . . numb now. But the feeling in my legs hasnae come back.'

'Can I feel your back? The patient made as though to turn over. Campbell discouraged him. 'I'll just slide a hand under.'

'D'you want him stripped now, Dr Campbell?'

'Thanks, staff.'

Rather cautiously, the staff nurse began to slit up the side of the man's trousers, from ankle to waist. She did one side then started on the other. When she had finished she pulled gently on the remains of the trouser legs, so that the divided garment slid out, to leave the man lying in his underpants. His erection was more obvious than ever. She opened his light windcheater and his shirt, and slit open the sleeves and again pulled the remains gently from under him. He was almost naked. 'There we are,' she said soothingly, putting the blanket over him to restore his modesty.

Campbell turned the blanket to one side and slid a hand under the man's torso at waist level. Just as he had described, there was a step-like bony irregularity in the ridge of the spine. As Campbell palpated it, trying to determine which vertebra was involved, and hence what level of spinal cord injury had been sustained, the man groaned.

'Sorry . . . Now I want to test the feeling in your skin.' He removed the blanket entirely, and ran a finger from the patient's collar-bone down across his chest. 'D'you feel that? Is it normal?'

'Yes.'

'Tell me when it changes.' Campbell's finger tracked lightly down over the man's chest, past his nipple and beyond the edge of his rib-cage. 'Tell me if the feeling changes.'

'It doesn't change . . . It's just disappeared . . . Where you were just now.'

'Tell me when it comes back.'

Campbell checked the level by running his finger back from the man's hip bone over his abdomen towards his chest.

'There.'

At a point a few inches below the navel, normal sensation re-emerged. 'And what about the other side.' Campbell repeated the exercise.

'There.'

'Have you tried moving your legs?'

'I can't feel them.'

'Try moving them.'

Nothing happened. There was a pause.

'Doctor . . .'

'What?'

'Is my back broken?'

The youth had a thin face and a few straggling hairs on his upper lip. His teeth were not clean. He looked up at Campbell. His lip trembled.

'Is my back broken?' He stressed 'my', as though he had already accepted the fact that his girlfriend's back was broken. Campbell hesitated.

'We're getting X-rays done. And a specialist's coming.'

'Doctor . . .' Tears filled the man's eyes. 'Is my back broken?'

The girl on the adjoining trolley started to have hysterics. She shrieked uncontrollably. Even the gasps of indrawn breath between her shrieks were terrible to hear. She shrieked and struck blindly out at Hadden and the staff nurse and threw her head from side to side. The youth on the trolley wept silently, and tears ran back from the corner

151

of his eye to fill the hollow of his ear, then overflowed it and ran on to the dark shiny surface of the washable pillow.

Hadden and the nurse tried to immobilise the girl to minimise further damage to her cord. They did not try to silence her, but slowly her shrieks subsided to frantic sobbing, then a low, interrupted moan.

'Who d'you want pictures of first?' A radiographer with an armful of unexposed X-ray plates stood waiting.

'Him, please.'

'I'd better get a screen between them.'

'You better. She's pregnant.'

The X-ray girl's face registered sudden shock. 'And you think they've both . . .'

'Yes.'

'How many months?'

'About six. So she says.'

'That's not so bad as earlier.'

'For the X-ray thing?'

'No. Which bit of him d'you want pictures of first?'

'Lumbar spine. And lower thoracic if you can.'

'Get them both on one. And I'll put them straight through then do anything else you want afterwards.' She slid the plate into its slot under the trolley, directly underneath the site of the injury Campbell had felt. She too glanced at the still turgid penis, now only partly concealed by the patient's underpants. Then she manoeuvred her overhead camera, while Campbell pulled a lead lined screen between the patients. Everyone retreated behind it, leaving the male patient lying alone on his trolley, still weeping quietly.

The X-ray buzzer sounded, and the warning light went off. The radiographer moved in and retrieved the plate from the slot in the trolley. She went off to develop it. Another white-coated figure had joined the huddle behind the lead screen.

'Christ. They're only kids.' Campbell turned round. The stranger was a short man with an unidentified colonial accent.

'Neurosurgical registrar?'

'Yeah. How'd they do it?'

'Drunk. Stolen car.'

'Christ. What age?'

'Not sure. Teens, I think.'

'What level?'

'He's high lumbar. Or maybe lower thoracic. She sounds like a high thoracic. And she's pregnant.'

'Jesus Christ. Pictures through yet?'

152

'Just coming. His anyway.'

'Knocked out?'

'Probably both of them.'

'Bellies and long bones OK?'

'Couldn't be sure yet.'

'Better be, before we shift them. Jeeze. He's got a fair old stand. That's tough.'

'Why?'

'Makes it a near cert for a transection. Total spinal write-off.'

'Really?'

'Yeah. Like hanging.'

'Oh?'

'My old boss used to call it Custer's sign.'

'That's a bit sick.'

'He was. Real bastard . . . They married or anything?'

'They were going to . . . She's pregnant.'

'So you said. Anything to feel in his back?'

'A step at the first lumbar. He'd noticed it himself.'

'What about her?'

'Don't know. Mr Hadden's seeing her.'

'Foetus OK?'

'Don't know.'

'I'll start with the bloke.'

'Thanks.'

With a casualty registrar and a registrar in surgical neurology looking after the two patients in the resuscitation room, Campbell felt suddenly superfluous. He remembered the little queue of people from Minor Trauma waiting to be stitched, and the old basket-maker in trolleys, who still hadn't been sorted out. And meanwhile, in quarter of an hour at about the busiest time on the busiest night of the week, any amount of new trade might have rolled in off the street. He went back to trolleys.

Mr Houghton's chest X-ray was still displayed on the illuminated viewing box, a pointed reminder of Campbell's indecision. He remembered that he had half made up his mind to off-load the problem to the medical registrar. Before doing so he parted the curtains where the old man lay on his trolley, to check him over before finally referring him. He looked better.

'Hello, son. All right?'

'Fine. How are you?'

'No' sae bad, son. It's fine and warm in here. Any chance o' stayin'? It might dae my chest good.'

'Well, we'll see. I'm going to ask another doctor to come down and have a look at you. We'll see what he thinks, Mr Houghton.'

'Thanks, son. God bless you.'

'Did you get much spit up?'

'No' much, son. But there's blood in it yet.'

Campbell went round the back to bleep the duty medical registrar and tell him about the case. The exchange put out a call for him, and after a few minutes' wait the extension rang. Campbell picked up the phone.

'Hello. Two five seven one.'

'Hello.' It was a girl's voice, light and pleasant.

'I'm trying to get the medical registrar. Casualty here.'

'Oh . . . Yes. I'm answering his bleep for him. Can I take a message?'

'Oh. Can I speak to him?'

'He's asked me to take any message.'

'Who's on as medical registrar tonight, please?'

'It's Dr Ratho tonight. He's asked me to answer his bleep for him. Who's speaking please?'

Campbell, who had expected the doctor concerned to get directly in touch with him immediately, was not impressed. It was a sign of something bad if the duty medical registrar in the Institute stooped to the GP tactic of employing a professional obstructionist to deal with his telephone calls. 'I'd like to speak to Dr Ratho, please. It's Dr Campbell in Casualty.'

'Oh, hello,' said the girl in a more friendly tone. Perhaps she knew Campbell, though he could not have said that he knew her. The voice said 'I'll get him for you right away, David.'

'Thank you.'

'He's been terribly busy.' Campbell had worked with Ratho, and knew roughly what that implied. There was a dull irritating clunk as the girl laid down the receiver, then the sound of giggling laughter, then Fraser Ratho came on to the line.

'Hello, David. Holding the fort tonight? That's good. Ah, yes.' He was doing his ho-ho jolly-pleased-to-hear-from-you thing, familiar from of old, and signifying nothing. 'What can we do for you?'

'We?' Would he bring his receptionist/secretary/amanuensis down to Casualty with him to add a little lustre to his management of a consumptive tramp?

'I've got a patient with an acute on chronic chest. Terrible X-ray.'

'Oh? Sounds interesting.'

'Might be TB.'

'Really? Jolly interesting.'

'A down-and-out from the Grassmarket.'

'Oh.'

'He's in trolleys.'

'What's his name?'

'Houghton. John Houghton . . . You might know him . . . He's the one who . . .'

'I doubt it, David. But I'll come down and see him when I can . . . Probably fairly soon, but can't promise. I'm awfully busy.'

'Thanks.'

With Hadden still in the resuscitation room, Campbell was responsible for the rest of the department. He went back to trolleys because that was where, with any luck, the illest patients would be. The next in clinical priority were patients as yet unassessed in Minor Trauma. Last came the sad little queue of people who had been seen in Minor Trauma and still awaited definitive treatment, a group whose number currently included the man with the cut eye and the youth with pink hair and brass rings in his nipples. It was regrettable, but they had to wait. Sometimes, on a Friday or Saturday night, such patients might wait up to two hours for a few stitches or a procedure taking less than a minute, but the routine was defensible in terms of safety. The known were safer than the unknown. Cuts could wait, unassessed patients could not.

Campbell checked the curtained spaces one by one. There were a handful of direct referrals to the receiving physicians and surgeons. Mr Houghton lay contentedly on his trolley awaiting, did he but know it, the ministrations of the suave Dr Ratho. The various patients mentioned by Bones seemed to have been spirited off to their respective destinations. There were only three cases whose curtains bore the blue label signifying that they were the responsibility of the Casualty Officer.

The first was a young soldier with a very ordinary appendicitis, which he thought might have been getting better as a result of his having drunk eight pints of beer. The second was a man who had had a coronary while watching the slow action replay of a winning goal on a TV sports programme. The third was an old lady who had been knocked down by a car, whose driver had promptly bundled her into the back and brought her up to the Department. She was so loud in her praises for the latter action that she seemed to have overlooked the fact

155

that he had knocked her down in the first place. She had a compound fracture at the right ankle.

None of these patients presented any problems of diagnosis or disposal. Campbell dealt with them quickly but without haste, earmarking them respectively for the general surgeons, the intensive care unit and the orthopaedic surgeons, and dictating the notes direct to the night typist, who sat in a smoke-filled cubicle opposite the porters' box.

When he had finished with the notes, he went round the back again to make the appropriate phone calls. Hadden was pouring himself a cup of coffee. He made one for Campbell too.

'Been through triviatrics. Nothing there that won't wait for the space of one well-earned cup of coffee. Your nipple man's getting restive, so I told him you'd be along soon. And both those kids have gone up to surgical neurology.'

'What happened about the third one?'

'I saw him. Silly young bugger with a sheepish grin and a bruised forehead. Pissed as a handcart. Rang the bell on the breathalyzer. The crystals turned tartan and the sergeant murmured ''Bravo, M'sieur''. He's helping the police with their enquiries.'

'What did the X-rays show?'

'The chap you saw is neurological wreckage. Sliced in half at T.12. She might just be lucky. No bony displacement. And she had some tingling in her feet just before she went up to SN. So she might just get away with a spinal concussion.'

'What about the foetus?'

'I had a listen. Sounds OK. Who was that wee neurosurgeon? Antipodean?'

'Never seen him before.'

'He seemed all right. How's trolleys?'

'A few referrals. This and that. Nothing difficult.'

'Ah, well. Back to triviatrics, I suppose. If it settles down, I might poke off about midnight. No point in depriving you young chaps of scarce clinical experience, as old Fordyce used to say, leaving me three breasts, a gallbag and a couple of hernias to hack out while he went off to do some private varry veins.'

'Are there any doctors there?' said the intercom. Hadden muttered 'Two. I've just counted them.'

'Yes,' said Campbell.

'The man with pink hair wants to see someone. Says he's waited long enough. Thinks he's being discriminated against.'

'All yours, sweetie,' said Hadden, perhaps quietly enough not to be picked up by the listening intercom.

'I'm on my way,' said Campbell, more loudly. 'Five minutes.'

At half past twelve Campbell took another break, and made himself some coffee to keep awake. Hadden wandered in. 'It stinks and I am ready to depart,' he remarked, taking off his white coat. His shirt tail was hanging out. He stuffed it impatiently back into place. 'Have your sandwiches come?'

'Not yet. I've just asked staff to send someone down for them.'

'Staff Nurse Mittelschmerz?'

'Who?'

'The pale one with dysmenorrhea.'

'Yes. The one doing nights in trolleys this week.'

'Yes. That's the one. She's beginning to get through to me. Has the odd rush of O-levels to the head and goes doctoring. Did an ECG on a coronary, and then phoned the intensive care bod before I'd seen him. And she'd given him morphine. You know the sort of thing. "Would you mind writing up that morphine we've just given, Mr Hadden?" Florence wouldn't like it.'

'She's done that a couple of times with me.'

Hadden rummaged in his locker, and produced two cans of beer. 'You better have a can, young Campbell, for sandwiches rendered. Did you ask her to give that paraplegic chap morphine?'

'No. Thought about it, but left it to the neurosurgeon.'

'She's done it again. I had to sign for it.'

The door opened and an auxiliary came in with a parcel of sandwiches. She put them down on the table, exactly midway between the two cans of beer, and smiled as she left.

'Thank you, ma'am,' said Hadden, reaching forward. 'Mm. Chicken. Ah, yes . . . Nurse Mittelschmerz. Competent but well worth keeping an eye on. They get like that in Casualty, you know, because we come and go every six months, and they just go marching on and on and on, like old McCraw, learning nothing, forgetting nothing and thinking they know it all. It's a syndrome. Like ingrown toenails. Cheers, lad. Keep taking the red cans.'

'Thanks. Cheers.'

The department had quietened down. The onslaught of drunks had been duly processed through Minor Trauma. The vast majority had by now repaired to home and hangover, a few had been removed to custody for the ritual tumble down the steps at the police station, and a rump of half a dozen, who by reason of extreme drunkenness or the suspicion of a head injury required overnight observation, snored

157

obscenely on trolleys parked at the back of Minor Trauma, in an area referred to by Hadden as the vomitorium.

The resuscitation room was empty, and indeed had not been in use since the two spinal injuries from the road traffic accident had required its facilities. In trolleys all was quiet. Those thought fit for discharge had gone home, and the rest had all been carted away to the various wards and departments. The curtains had been slung up over the rails, and a cleaning lady had set to work with a lustral mop and bucket. Order reigned in the Casualty Department.

Round the back, Campbell drank a can of beer while Hadden drank two, and they shared the sandwiches. For Campbell, the prospect was a sleepless night, as late revellers drifted in, sufficiently fortified by alcohol to bother an unknown doctor with unimportant complaints, and the tardier victims of Friday night violence found their way to help. After that came a day to rest and sleep, followed by the same again or worse on Saturday night. Hadden, on call from home for the rest of the night, was not actually on duty again until Sunday morning. He was in no hurry to leave, but sat eating and drinking and talking until almost one o'clock, when he departed, leaving Campbell in sole charge till morning.

A bed was provided for the duty SHO, in a little room at the back of the department between the kitchen and the cleaning cupboard. Some casualty officers never used it, preferring to turn night into day for one week in three, and sleep through the day at home. Others, Bones included, went to bed at every possible opportunity, and suffered the frequent inconvenience of being called out, with greater or lesser goodwill. It was Campbell's routine to stay up all night on the busy nights at the beginning of the spell of duty (Friday, Saturday and Sunday) then ease the transition back to normality by using the SHO's bedroom on the later and usually quieter nights. For the wakeful weekend nights he usually brought in an improving book.

On this occasion his book was an allegedly popular account of the life of Thomas Carlyle, which transpired to be too improving to be readable. Campbell decided to go back to the unfinished *Flesh of Life*, which he eventually located under three *BMJ*s and a *Reveille* on a shelf marked 'Current Journals'. It proved to be just as irritatingly precious and nugatory as it had first seemed in daylight, and he abandoned it in favour of the *Reveille*.

At half past one a third year student nurse came round to tell Campbell that the staff nurse was not looking well. He confirmed that the girl in question was the one from trolleys, who had never looked well at any time in their six weeks working acquaintanceship. With the department now quiet, there seemed no reason for her to endure her premenstrual martyrdom, or whatever it was, on duty. Nurses usually sorted these things out for themselves and Campbell felt no wish to become involved. 'Is the other staff nurse still around?'

'She's off at lunch,' said the student nurse, quite unaware of the temporary confusion created in the non-nursing minds by the nomenclature of night nurses' meal-breaks. 'Then she's going up to thirteen. They're busy and we're not . . . Dr Campbell, I think you should see her.'

Campbell used the *Reveille* as a bookmark in Carlyle, rather than the other way about, which would have been more honest, and got up.

'She looks quite ill. I'm sure it's not just the curse.'

'Oh.'

The student nurse was tall and thin and quite pretty. Walking along the corridor behind her, Campbell noticed that, under her tights, her legs were remarkably hairy.

'She's in here.'

The staff nurse was sitting on a chair in a little room near the dirty turret which was reserved for the disinfestation of lousy patients and the laying out of the dead. She was slumped forward with her elbows on her knees. Her face was not visible. Campbell could not remember her name, if indeed he had ever known it. It was not Mittelschmerz.

'She's called nurse Balint,' said the tall girl. 'Her pulse is sixty and I haven't taken her blood pressure.'

'Nurse Balint.' There was no immediate response. 'Nurse Balint.'

Slowly the nurse lifted her face from her cupped hands. She looked very tired. Sometimes night nurses lived on coffee and never went to bed for days on end. That, with her known gynaecological history, might account for everything. Then Campbell remembered one or two other things about this particular nurse.

'D'you want her on the trolley?'

'In here?'

'Might as well, Dr Campbell. Quieter. And she's staff. You know. Works here.'

'All right.' Campbell and the student nurse helped the staff nurse on to the trolley usually reserved for the infested and the dead. The nurse went off for a sphygmomanometer and Campbell asked the girl on the trolley how she felt. Her eyes opened slowly. 'Tired,' she said, in a small, distant voice. 'Leave me alone.' Her eyes closed again. Just as they did so an important abnormality registered.

'Open your eyes.'

The girl lay quietly with her eyes closed.

159

'Open your eyes.'

The tall nurse returned with a sphygmomanometer and wrapped the cuff round her colleague's arm. Campbell leaned over the supine girl's face and rolled back one of her eyelids. There was little of the resistance and blinking that action would usually elicit.

'Eighty over fifty,' said the student nurse, looking up from the sphygmomanometer, her face close to Campbell's.

'Look,' he said. His finger and thumb parted the lids of the staff nurse's left eye. Blank and blue, it looked up at them. The pupil was tiny. 'Like you said, it's not just the curse. Have we got any . . .?'

'Nallorphine,' said the student nurse promptly.

'That's the stuff. The morphine antagonist.'

'I can look. She's got the keys.'

The departmental key ring was an impressive affair, suggesting by its weight and complexity perhaps top security files if not high-risk prisoners. The student nurse frisked her colleague on the trolley, until her left breast appeared to clink and rattle, and the keys were revealed attached to a safety pin on the inside of her apron. 'Won't be a minute.'

While the student nurse went off for the drug, Campbell wondered what to do about this distressing turn of events. The simplest thing, he decided, would be to treat her meantime as a patient, i.e. not as a colleague on the one hand, or a criminal on the other. He would get on with trying to make her better, and depending on how successful that was, the next step would be to refer her to a physician (and even Ratho, in these unusual circumstances, could probably be relied upon to be both prompt and discreet) or, less preferably, to throw her on the tender mercies of the nursing hierarchy. The latter would have the distasteful aura of turning her in, and moreover the nursing hierarchy was represented that night by a lady whose fierceness and stupidity was conspicuous even among her fellow nursing officers.

Whatever happened in the short term, the whole horrible machinery of investigation and prosecution would eventually take over. Campbell aimed only to fend it off for a few hours, for the girl's sake and his own. On reflection, he did not feel particularly clever about his diagnosis. Confronted with a nurse, now suffering from acute morphine poisoning, who had to his knowledge broken the rules about handling the drug at least three times in the last few days, he had managed to put two and two together. This was the nurse who always wanted people's pain treated, who preferred not to be watched while giving injections, who asked doctors to sign for drugs already given and had looked vaguely ill for as long as he had known her.

160

It was now so obvious as to be embarrassing, yet Campbell wondered if anyone could or would have done much on the evidence preceeding the crisis. No-one wanted to be the first to put the finger on an erring colleague. (The agreeably distant example of Mr McGrogan came to mind.) And now that it had happened, he would prefer to remain as a doctor for as long as possible, and stave off the prosecution witness role as long as he could.

In the event, the option was lost. The student nurse returned with a syringe of the morphine antagonist, which Campbell injected. The recovery of Nurse Balint was at first miraculous, then terrifying. Her pupils widened, her breathing, having been dangerously shallow, became normal, and her colour improved. Then a series of events, recognisable as acute withdrawal, hit the unfortunate staff nurse, who might have been on her illicit morphine for some time. She quaked and sweated, and lay staring at a room which must have been to her both familiar and frightening in its associations. Her teeth chattered. She was pale and clammy and her whole body shivered. She gibbered deliriously and had just become coherent enough to yell for more morphine when the nursing hierarchy, in the person of the fierce and stupid Miss Tyrrell, walked in.

Afterwards, Campbell wished he had been more immediately assertive in preserving the unfortunate nurse's status as a patient. In the event, the student nurse had performed rather better than he had himself. The nursing officer, standing just inside the door of the little room, had drawn a huge breath and gathered herself into a posture of dreadful threat, rather in the style of an all-in wrestler about to liven up a dull, fixed bout. Campbell had felt confused and uneasy. The student nurse had simply smiled politely and having acknowledged the presence of her superior, even though in this case the intruder was the nocturnal representative of the entire nursing hierarchy, got on with the task of looking after the patient, who had sensed just enough of the occasion to refrain from further shouting, and from the use of such provocative terms as 'morphine'.

Miss Tyrrell did not go on to stamp her feet, grimace, roar and wave clenched fists above her head, as she had seemed likely to do. Prompted by the student nurse's conduct Campbell had continued to examine the patient, and the angel of vengeance, the harridan of dreadful visitation, had been transformed into a superfluous, indeed an unseemly, spectator on a clinical encounter. The deep drawn breath that might have emerged as a shout or a scorching tirade was held for a moment of uncertainty, that exhaled audibly but slowly, leaving her three sizes smaller.

The student nurse spoke again. 'Nurse Balint is sick.' Her voice was sweet and rational, soft, gentle and low, everything that had not been expected of Miss Tyrrell's. 'Nurse Massie is upstairs,' she continued, 'helping out in ward thirteen.' In the circumstances to state the obvious quietly showed a touch of style not far short of genius. The diminished harridan took her cue. 'Thank you, Nurse McCorquodale, I'll see that she comes back down down shortly.' She turned and left, looking even smaller from the back.

'Thanks,' said Campbell. 'I thought she was going to shout "Off with her head".' The student nurse laughed. She had nice white teeth. Campbell laughed too. On the trolley Nurse Balint began to shake again, and clutched at Campbell with cold, sweaty hand. He made a decision.

'I'll ring Dr Ratho, the medical registrar. She'll have to go somewhere quiet on the medical side. They're bound to have a single room somewhere . . .'

'I'll watch her meantime.'

'Thanks.'

Campbell went round the back and phoned the duty medical registrar's bedroom. Ratho answered sleepily, and Campbell remembered something Jean had once told him about Ratho's pyjamas, which she had viewed in circumstances above suspicion, when he had been on duty in Intensive Care.

'Hello. David Campbell. Casualty.'

'Hello, David.'

'A tricky one, Fraser. Have you got somewhere quiet to put a staff nurse from the department?'

'What's the problem, David?'

'Drugs.'

'Oh dear.'

'DDA things. It's going to be a nasty, but she's really ill just now.'

'I think we can take her.'

'Thanks. Will you come down here or will I just send her across?'

'Send her over to two. I'll see her there. Given her anything?'

'Nallorphine. She hated it.'

'Best thing, I'm afraid . . .'

'Thanks, Fraser.'

'Glad to be able to help. Very distressing business, particularly of course with trained staff . . .'

Campbell listened politely until he was finished, then put the phone down and went back to the room beside the dirty turret. Student nurse McCorquodale smiled as he returned. Nurse Balint, pale on her trolley, still looked ghastly. She was not making any noise.

'How is she?'

'Her skin really does feel like cold turkey.'

'Does it? Ugh.'

'But she's more settled.'

'Settled' was a nursing word for which Campbell knew no exact English equivalent. It covered a range of clinical states from 'Less troublesome' to 'Still alive' and on occasion might even include 'Haven't a clue'. But Nurse Balint was certainly less agitated.

'Two are going to take her. Dr Ratho says he'll see her over there. Who's on in two?'

'Nursing?'

'Yes.'

'A sensible girl in my year. I'll ring her.'

'Thanks very much.'

A few minutes later the trolley left the department, escorted by Nurse Massie, who had come back from ward thirteen. Miss Tyrrell had not returned. A full dress enquiry would doubtless follow. Meantime a kind of humane decorum had been maintained.

Not that Campbell had much time in the course of the rest of the night to contemplate the mysteries of nursing discipline. A town councillor, gloriously drunk, had been rescued from a stalled car in the middle of an ornamental pond by two firm but understanding policemen, and brought into the department. He required a full clinical examination as he claimed to be suffering from loss of memory following a dizzy spell during dinner. He was a dapper, podgy little man, embarrassed by his dishevelled clothing and wet feet, who improved a little with knowing, and became greatly distressed as a realisation of his predicament dawned. He was a man of substance, he claimed, a solicitor, a JP, and a member of the board of governors of a school he named and which Campbell had always held in some suspicion. By the time he left the department he was abject and weepy, a pitiable figure who reminded Campbell quite compellingly of Mr Toad. Would he go on to escape from the High Street cells next day, disguised as a washerwoman? From the demeanour of the policemen, it seemed unlikely.

At three a man came in with his face covered in blood. Campbell took a history and translated it into Casualty notes. 'Victim of alleged assault by three unknown assailants. Blunt injury (bottle) to forehead. Bottle intact. Conscious throughout. Local pain and tenderness only. No significant symptoms of head injury.' For eight weeks Campbell had written that, or something very like it, at least a dozen times a week. The laceration was irregular and its edges were contused. The man had clearly never had much cause for personal vanity, and came perhaps from a sub-culture where facial scars were not held in disesteem. Nonetheless Campbell did his best to minimise the disfigurement, and the man was drunk enough to co-operate magnificently.

In the clean turret, with proper lighting, green drapes, gloves, a mask and such other adjuncts of decent surgery as were necessary and available, Campbell set about it, infiltrating local anaesthetic around the wound, trimming its bruised edges neat and straight, and drawing them together with the finest gauge of suture material, dabbing away blood and clot, so that the final line was clean and closed and lay easily within the natural creases of the man's brow. Five days later the stitches would come out. Perhaps as many months later, the swollen pink of the fresh scar would have shrunk and faded, leaving, with luck, hardly any trace of Campbell's handiwork, or that of the three unknown assailants.

By four Campbell began to feel tired, but a series of problems, minor and major, presented themselves and demanded his attention. A patient who had had three teeth out the previous afternoon came in apologetically expressing the view that he might bleed to death if he delayed seeking help until morning. One of his sockets was oozing steadily. Campbell made him bite on a folded swab for quarter of an hour, and this proved to be a perfectly satisfactory haemostat. The man went home with a handful of spare swabs just in case. A night shift worker with a sprained ankle came in because he had been quite properly informed by his shop steward that industrial injuries should be seen and assessed right away. He received the ritual X-ray and supportive bandage. A man was brought in from cells by the police. His scalp laceration was sutured and he returned whence he came. An old lady in a black coat who had forgotten her address and been found wandering in the centre of the city by an ambulance crew, remembered it after a nice cup of tea, and, after a telephone call to her distracted daughter, went home in a taxi. A haggard and bedraggled man, a known drug addict whose particular poison was a barbiturate, was wheeled in stunned by the usual for perhaps the twentieth time in his carreer, and sent off to the medical wards after a particularly troublesome and malodorous stomach washout in the dirty turret. A poor crazed youth whose wrists were already a mass of scars came in having attempted to cut them yet again. As Campbell stitched him up he chatted drowsily, having identified Campbell quite wrongly as a fellow competitor in the final of the all-Edinburgh under-twelve eighty yard dash some ten years previously. At about six the department went quiet again.

Campbell was resting round the back, and had almost fallen asleep in his chair, when the student nurse came in.

'Hello. The rolls have come. Want one?'

'Oh. Thanks. I'll make some coffee.'

'You look shattered. I'll do it.'

'I'm not. But thanks.'

She still looked fresh and pretty. She had changed her apron at half time, as Casualty nurses often had to, and was carrying a tassled leather saddlebag thing instead of the usual Little Red Riding Hood nursey basket. The rolls smelled good.

'Want marmalade on yours?'

'Yes please.' Campbell got up and stretched his legs. Outside, it was just beginning to get light. The worst of the first night was over. He would be in bed in just over three hours and meantime a nice girl was making his coffee and buttering him a roll. He watched her hands at work. They were slender and efficient. He began to think of Jean.

'Sugar?'

'No thanks.'

'Milk?'

'Yes please. But I don't think . . .'

'I brought some.' She delved into her saddlebag thing and produced a cheerful red and white half pint carton and tweaked it open, splashing some on her fingers. Immediately she licked them. It seemed an odd, obvious, nice thing to do. Campbell watched and smiled and she smiled back at him. He went across and picked up his coffee. She smelled faintly of soap but not at all of perfume. Campbell thought about that and decided it went with hairy legs. He wondered if she were extremely religious, since among female medical students of his acquaintance perhaps five years previously, hairiness had been next to godliness. He remembered her name was McCorquodale even without checking her name badge, and then went on to wonder what her first name was.

She took her coffee and her roll and sat down and Campbell did the same. His Carlyle book lay between them on the table.

'You reading that?'

'Sort of.'

'Any good?'

'Don't know yet . . . I've been kind of busy.'

She smiled. 'I know. Quite brisk, wasn't it?'

Outside the sky lightened slowly, from grey to pink. Campbell sat comfortably, almost too tired to reach for his coffee, wondering how much more would happen in the remaining three hours, and whether, workload permitting, he would be able to sit here for a while and find out a little more about the intriguing student nurse McCorquodale. She finished her roll in a very businesslike fashion, took a sip of her coffee and reached once again into her bag. Campbell made a little bet with himself. Knitting.

He lost. She pulled out a large paperback with a bright red cover and a clenched fist on the front. She opened it at a bookmark. Campbell was somewhat taken aback by this, and more so by the title, when he had managed to read it. The book was bulky and perhaps American. It was called *Unburnt Bras: the Negative Option. A study of 2137 unliberated women.* Nurse McCorquodale settled in her armchair. The bookmark indicated she was half way through it, and her air of extreme and exclusive seriousness suggested that an attempt at light chat on Campbell's part was not going to hold her back. By way of reprisal, he reached for Carlyle.

'Dr Campbell . . . Dr Campbell.'

Campbell woke and Carlyle fell from his knees.

'Dr Campbell, sorry to wake you . . . There's an ambulance outside.' The tall student nurse was standing close over him. She picked up his book and smiled. 'It didn't look very interesting.'

'What's the problem?'

'Someone in an ambulance.'

'Oh. BID?'

'Yes. 'fraid so. The ambulance men thought . . .' She paused and looked serious.

'I'll go now.' Campbell got up and felt momentarily dizzy after his snooze. A BID was 'Brought In Dead', and the routine was to make a brief inspection and confirm the death immediately, to permit another routine to proceed. The corpse, once officially so designated, then went off to the city morgue to await a decision as to how far the manner of its dying should be investigated. The business of BIDs was one of the less pleasant aspects of Casualty work: while a fatal coronary left a clean seemly and composed corpse, victims of fire, violence and accident were sometimes more memorable to view.

Outside it was full daylight. An ambulance driver stood by the open rear door of his vehicle, silent and unsmiling like an undertaker's man. The steps were down and Campbell went in. The corpse lay on the left, with a blanket over its head. Campbell unclipped his pen torch from his top pocket and turned down the blanket.

It was John Houghton, white in death. His eyes were half open and the cornea already dull and glazed. His hair and moustache looked darker against his pallor. A glistening blob of clear snot lay in one nostril. His expression was calm, with something of the veiled hauteur of a well turned out serviceman awaiting inspection. Campbell remembered his saying earlier that he had been a soldier in his time.

'He was probably just away when we got him. Poor old bugger.' The driver had followed Campbell into the ambulance and stood watching as he shone his torch in each eye. The pupils were wide and dark and fixed. Campbell smoothed the lids shut, and glanced at his watch then asked the driver where the corpse had been picked up.

'In the West Bow. Half way down.'

If indeed Mr Houghton was 'just away', and the temperature of the corpse supported that, then it was likely that he was half way up the West Bow rather than half way down. After his encounter with Ratho, who had presumably discharged him, he must have gone down to his night shelter, and later decided to seek help again, and not made it up the hill. Campbell opened the old man's shirt and laid his stethoscope against a silent chest, listening for a half a minute.

'Poor old bugger,' said the ambulance man again, respectfully. 'I'll take him away.'

Campbell left the corpse and went back inside. The receptionist had emerged from her nocturnal retreat opposite the porters' box and sat at the desk by the front door.

'BID, Dr Campbell?' she enquired with morning cheer.

'Yes.'

'Houghton or Howie or Doig?'

'Yes.'

Her fingers flickered over the long files of index cards. She fished one out and drew two firm parallel lines diagonally across it, and put it in an empty chocolate box on her right.

'Nice morning.'

'Not too bad.'

'Would you like to check your notes before they go out?'

'Thanks.'

She handed him a sheaf of notes, the top copies of transcript from his tape-recorded summaries of the proceedings of the night. There were perhaps twenty or thirty of the pale blue sheets. Campbell flicked through them on his way round the back. 'Shallow abrasions, right knee. Savlon wash and dry dressing. ATT. Triplopen. Review by GP in three days.' 'Forced inversion injury left ankle. Tender swelling . . . Clinically no bone injury. X-ray. NBI.' 'Contused laceration left eyebrow. Would toilet and suture. ATT. Triplopen. Remove stitches in five days.' 'Cord transection at L.1. Admit Neurosurgery Unit.' 'Acute appendicitis. General Surgeon please see . . .' '. . . Brass rings removed with wirecutters. Ampicillin 500 mgs qds for five days. Discharged.'

Campbell read them through in detail over a cup of coffee and gave them back to the receptionist, who would despatch them in the mail to the various general practitioners who in theory still retained overall clinical responsibility for each patient, and were therefore entitled to know what had been done on their behalf. Mr Houghton's summary, addressed to a GP who had been dead for at least fifteen years, included, after Campbell's 'Medical Registrar please see', a contribution from Fraser Ratho. 'Exacerbation of chronic bronchitis. Recurrent attender. Healed TB on X-ray. Ampicillin. Discharged home.' It was not the custom to scribble a PS explaining what had happened later. A separate note following his second attendance would be despatched into the void, to inform the dead practitioner of the demise of his patient.

The last hour of night duty passed slowly. Campbell sat in the back room, from which he was summoned once or twice to cases in Minor Trauma. Cleaning ladies, their floor polishing machines making noises compatible with large scale Warsaw Pact manoeuvres, ground through the department deafeningly and ineffectually. Nurse McCorquodale had gone off without ceremony at half past seven, leaving the department in the temporary care of Nurse McCraw until Sister came on later. At nine Hadden and Hakeem would take over and Campbell would be free to go.

By a quarter to, Campbell was exasperated, sticky and exhausted. A bath and six hours' sleep, perhaps only half an hour away, assumed the tantalising allure of a desert mirage. He hoped only that nothing complicated would arrive in the last quarter of an hour, and consoled himself with the thought that Friday night, the first of seven on duty, was over, and the first night was often the worst.

Hadden came in five to nine, taciturn and grumpy at first, but warming to the day's work as he donned his white coat and blearily savoured the first coffee of the morning. By ten past nine Hakeem had still not arrived, and Hadden said that Campbell should simply go, and leave him to it. Campbell waited, not so much to help Hadden with the work, of which there was as yet very little, but because he wanted to find out how his colleague from the new commonwealth had fared in the exam. He sat around until half past nine and then began to wonder why that most punctilious of doctors was so late for duty in a department where, in his own words, he was doing his best to carry out an honest day's work.

At twenty to ten Campbell found Hakeem's off-duty phone number and rang it. There was no reply. With morning and the day asserting itself all around, Campbell felt less tired, but had enough experience of coming off night duty to know the frailty of that illusion. He sat for a few minutes, and then Hadden came round the back again. Campbell told him about the attempted phone call.

'He's probably slept in after a hard night's export, and is on his way over now. Push off, lad, and get your head down. I'll let you know tonight how he got on in the wee test, and if he doesn't turn up I'll ring J.G. and let him take it from there.'

'I wonder if he's just pushed off.'

'What?'

'Failed. And pushed off without saying anything.'

'I doubt it. But maybe.'

'Where does he live?'

'Not sure . . . Marchmont, I think.'

'Might be best if I dropped in on the way home.'

'You could. But he didn't answer the phone. Anyway his address'll be in the staff file on J.G.'s desk.'

'Thanks.'

Campbell got the key to J.G.'s office from the receptionist's keyboard, and found to his surprise that Hakeem's address was just along the street from his own. He tidied up the last of his notes, chucked the Carlyle book in his locker, hung up his white coat and put on his jacket. On the way out he handed his last tape to the day receptionist for typing. As he walked across the park to Marchmont the day was clear and bright.

There was a blue and white police car, parked and empty, opposite the number he was looking for in Marchmont Terrace. The main door at the foot of the stair stood open. Campbell realised that he did not know which flat in the stair Hakeem occupied, and hoped that there would be something in the way of a nameplate on the door to help him. The air in the street level passage was stagnant and offensive.

As Campbell climbed the common stair the smell grew much stronger. He glanced at the doors as he went up, looking for Hakeem's name. On the third floor landing a policeman was standing holding a pale blue handkerchief over his mouth and nose. A door stood open, and hideous stench came from the dark hallway.

The policeman was vaguely recognisable as a young constable who was sometimes seen in the Casualty department in line of duty. He recognised Campbell with more assurance. 'Doctor?' His voice was muffled by his handkerchief. 'You're from the Institute aren't you?'

'Yes. Doctor Campbell. Casualty.'

'The sergeant's in there. With one of your chaps.'

'What happened?'

'Did it himself, most likely. Pills we think.'

From the hallway the sergeant emerged into the light of the landing. He was coughing. He too had a handkerchief held to his face. He recognised Campbell.

'It's your man. He's in a terrible state. But if you wouldn't mind seeing him . . . Makes it simpler for us.'

'All right.'

Campbell followed the sergeant into the flat. The hallway was dark, bare and old-fashioned. The sergeant pushed open a door and Campbell found himself looking into a bedroom at the back of the house. He took out his handkerchief and pressed it to his nose and mouth.

The room was lit by brilliant sunshine. Even through a handkerchief, the stench was appalling, a thick and nauseating carrion reek that made Campbell cough and retch. A bloated cadaver lay on a single bed under the window, fully dressed in a dark suit and wearing highly polished black shoes. Putrefaction had expanded its girth to the limits the jacket would permit and even the sleeves seemed stiffly inflated. The corpse's face was discoloured and engorged but still recognisable as that of Dr Hakeem Subhadar. His neck, engorged and yellow, had burst the top button of a neat white shirt. He was wearing the tie of a Fellow of the Royal College of Surgeons of Edinburgh.

Campbell looked round to the sergeant, who was standing by the door. A wave of nausea rose and ebbed without irreversible effect, but only just. Campbell retreated.

'You've identified him and would certify he's dead.'

'Yes.' said Campbell, making with quickening pace for the door at the other end of the hallway. He leaned on the bannister, breathing deeply. By comparison, the air on the common stair was now fresh and sweet.

The sergeant came out and pulled the door shut behind him. Campbell noticed that the wood around the lock was splintered. He looked enquiringly at the policemen. 'We broke in,' said the sergeant. 'After a telephone message from a neighbour complaining about the smell.'

'No wonder, said Campbell.

'I switched off his electric blanket,' said the sergeant. 'A bit late though.' They walked downstairs together, the air clearing as they descended.

'Would he have had any particular reason for doing that?' the

170

sergeant asked when they had reached the cool sane world of the street.

'He'd had . . . one or two personal difficulties,' said Campbell, not to dishonour his dead colleague.

'Can I have your name and address, please, doctor?'

Ten minutes later, in the back room of the Casualty Department, Campbell told Hadden why Hakeem had not reported for work that morning. Hadden listened without obvious emotion. 'Poor bugger,' he said when Campbell had finished. It was the second time that morning that Campbell had heard the phrase used as an obituary. 'Somebody had better tell J.G. And think about getting a message to his next of kin. Does he not have a wife?'

'Yes. But won't the police do that, from letters and things?'

'I suppose so . . . I'll ring J.G. now. You better sit down. You look hellish.' Hadden went over to the phone. 'Must have been nasty, cooking up on an electric blanket. . . . Oh. There's a message here for you. From that bird in Endocrinology. She must want her glands seen to again.' He handed Campbell a little note which had been sellotaped to the phone. It was in Sister's handwriting. It said 'Please ring Dr Moray (Endocrinology Dept) when convenient.' Campbell crumpled it up and switched on the kettle. It boiled almost immediately. He made himself a cup of coffee. There was no milk.